Lizzie,
Thank you for being a great friend, and always being there for me!
Love you girl!
Kellis xx

Depths Of
DECEIT
A DARK ROMANCE

KJ ELLIS

Acknowledgments

First and foremost, I need to thank my family for getting me quiet time and letting me get this one finished. I hit an all time low mid-way through writing this and I never thought I'd finish it, but you all had my back and gave me the determination I needed to complete it. I love you all massively.

My editor, Karen Sanders, you came into my writing career when I needed you most. You teach me something new with each book I write. It's because of you that I no longer dread the moment edits come back. Your encouraging comments are so in depth, I can easy work my way through them. I treasure you and our friendship dearly.

Thank you to the fabulous Sienna Grant @VR Formatting for making my book look so amazing. I really appreciate you and love our friendship that we've had for a few years now. And you really are the best. Love you!

To my beta team, jeez there's so many of you now it would take a full page to name you all, but you know who you are. I value each and every one of you for taking the time to read through my work and picking up on all the typos that may have been missed and more importantly giving me such amazing reviews. It means the world to me that you enjoy my stories still.

Thank you so much to Francessca Wingfield for creating the discreet cover, it really is a masterpiece and I love it so much.

Emma Lloyd, you know what you mean to me. I'm officially running out of words to say, but just know I love you for sticking with me but more importantly letting our friendship grow and grow to what it is today.

Lastly, to my readers. Without you all, I wouldn't be able to do what I love. Every single review, share, comment and like is seen and very much appreciated.

I hope I don't let you down with this one, and stick with me for what I hope is many more years.

Thank you xx

PROLOGUE

TILLIE

My day starts like any other. Boring as fuck. Being the daughter of a mafia boss has its perks, but it also comes with plenty of downsides.

It's been drilled into me from a young age to be aware of my surroundings at all times and always think before I act. With my father high up in the mob chain, I'm a target. The fact I'm female makes me the easier target of the family and, believe me, the people who have visited my father in the past would have no remorse for hurting a woman to gain an advantage.

That's how I've lived my life for the past seventeen years. I found it extremely hard to make friends, wondering if they befriended me because of who I am, if they were seeking information on my father, or if they wanted to get closer to my brother, who was next in line to inherit the 'throne'. I'm glad he was born first. It means I don't have to worry about the weight that would be on my shoulders. Keanu would never admit it, especially to me, but I see the strain this knowledge has on him. Taking orders, regardless of what they are, proving himself worthy to run the Knox empire.

He'd needn't worry; he'll succeed. It's what he's been training for since the day he could walk. He's good at what he does, and my father could see that from the get-go.

One day, when the time is right, Keanu will make an excellent leader, ruthless and firm, earning him the respect and loyalty of the men who once served my father. That's his nature.

Mine? Well, that's to defy my father's orders. The worst one being tonight. I've never acted out to the point of putting myself in danger, only occasionally staying late at a friend's house, or not informing my father or brother of my plans, but this is really stepping out of line. Somehow, my friends, including my best friend, Kacy, convinced me to tag along to a new club that had opened up just outside of town——not on my father's turf. Apparently, it was the place to be on a Saturday night.

I'd got sick and tired of always missing out, listening to them all talk about their amazing nights without me. This time, I put my foot down. To hell with it. I'll deal with the aftermath from my father or brother when it comes… if it comes. I'm hoping they never find out.

"What's to say you'll get caught?" Kacy's words from the other day play on repeat in my head.

That's what convinced me it would be a good idea.

What's the worst that could happen?

How wrong had I been? I was naive and purposely put myself in harm's way when I was told numerous times of the dangers, and the only person I can blame is myself.

But this isn't my story, it's my brother's—Keanu Knox. The notorious mafia boss of London and Knox Estate.

CHAPTER 1

KEANU
Sixteen months later

"Someone better have answers for me," I bellow, full of rage and frustration. It's been sixteen months since my little sister went missing, and I'm no closer to finding out why. I fucking told her one of these days something was going to happen if she continued to defy orders. Why didn't she listen to me? Our father and I may have been hard on her, but it was for a reason, and always with good intentions of keeping her safe, but she chose to act out and fight us on everything.

I'm all she has left now. Our mother died whilst giving birth to her, and I swore to my father when he was having the heart attack that killed him that I would do everything in my power to find Tillie and bring her home as he was unable to do that himself. All the stress this caused him brought on the heart attack. It had to be. He was in perfect health before Tillie disappeared.

From the moment we found out she was missing, it was all hands on deck, especially my father.

A distasteful shudder runs through me as I recall the moment I found out Tillie was gone. I'd just finished a job with Lincoln, my right-hand man and best friend, that my father had ordered us to do. I was just leaving my father's office after a debriefing when my phone rang.

I STOP IN MY TRACKS AND STARE DOWN AT MY PHONE, CONFUSED AS TO WHY Kacy, my sister's best friend, is ringing me. It's almost midnight. I lift my head, nodding at Lincoln to carry on. "I'll catch you up."

My phone cuts off as I'm about to answer, but the ringing immediately starts again.

I answer swiftly. "Kacy?"

"Keanu." I sense fear in her voice.

"Kacy? What's wrong?"

"It's Tillie. She's... missing." She breaks down in tears.

"That's impossible." I'm already storming through the estate, heading for Tillie's room. "She's in her room sleeping if she knows what's good for her."

"No, Keanu... she isn't."

I swing the door open, expecting to see my sister lying in her bed, fast asleep, but I don't. Her room is empty. "What the fuck?" I say, more to myself than Kacy.

"I'm sorry, Keanu. She snuck out... and... and we..."

I start to lose my restraint. "Fucking spit it out, Kacy!"

"We went to a club. She only went to the bathroom, but she was gone for ages, so I went to check on her. I... I couldn't find her. I've looked everywhere for her. That's when I found her purse and phone. It was in the back alley, smashed to pieces. I... I..." She breaks down again. "I'm so sorry. I should have gone with her."

Tillie never leaves her phone. It's always attached to her hand, and apart from a few scratches, her phone was in one piece.

I ignore her pleas for forgiveness; I don't have time to fix her bruised feelings. I need to find out what the fuck is going on.

"Kacy, I need you to pull yourself together. Can you do that?" I shout over her cries.

"O... okay."

"Tell me what club you're at?"

"Erm, it's the new club that opened in Camden Town a few months back. About thirty minutes from us in Chelsea." I know exactly which one she's referring to. My chest expands as I breathe in hard to control my anger.

Why the fuck would she go there? I know why. Because it's out of the

Depths of Deceit

Knox area, and our father would have received word if she stayed closer to home. She should have known better. She would have if she was brought into the loop of the shit that's going down around us, but our father kept her sheltered from most of it. I remember asking him once why Tillie didn't know everything about the business dealings and the dangers that were involved for her just being a part of the family. She deserved to know, but all I got from him was that our mother wouldn't have wanted that.

It was okay for me, but Tillie was a different story. At first, I hated it. Because I was a boy and the first born, I already felt the weight on my shoulders of following in my father's footsteps. Now I've lived this life, I wouldn't want that for Tillie. She wouldn't have handed it too well. I'm glad it was me and not her. I've seen horrific stuff, done unspeakable things for the sake of this family. I wouldn't wish that for her. It would break her. If our mother was still alive, I know she would have made the same choice as our father did, and now I'm older, I hold no grudge.

I know I've been hard on her lately, but that's only because she was acting out and being a little bitch. My job's hard enough as it is, without worrying about her. I suspect my father doesn't know half the shit Tillie has been up to.

I shake my head, ridding my thoughts of what Tillie's behaviour has been like and concentrate on the matter at hand.

"How long ago was it?" I question.

"How long ago what?"

"When did she go to the bathroom? How long ago was that?" I ask harshly, but every minute counts, especially if what I'm thinking is true.

"Twenty minutes or so. I swear I've looked everywhere for her, Keanu. I..."

"Was she with anyone?"

"Just me and a couple of other friends."

"Anyone spoken to her that she didn't know?"

"Erm, no. At least, I don't think so."

"I know it's hard, but I need you to think. It'll help, I promise. No matter how small the detail, I need to know, Kacy. Think... please." I march from Tillie's room back towards my father's office, ready to deliver him the news I know he's been dreading all his life.

"At the bar... she was talking to someone."

"Did you see who it was?"

"I only saw the back of his head." She gasps. "Oh, God. You don't think…"

"We don't know anything yet, Kacy. I need you to do me one last thing."

"Anything. Name it."

"Are you still at the club?"

"Yes."

"Great. I need you to collect Tillie's purse and phone from the alley you said you found them at. Are they still there?"

"I already picked them up. I have them in my hands now."

"Great. I'll Send Lincoln to collect you. He'll bring you here, just to be safe." I enter my father's office, his head lifting at the sound of the door opening. The moment he sees it's me, his smile falls.

I cover the bottom of my phone with my hand. "Call Linc back, now," I mouth to him. He gets on his phone straight away. The whole time, his eyes never waver from mine.

"Stay in the open and with someone you trust. Lincoln will be there soon." She quickly agrees and apologises again, but I end the call and pocket my phone. A couple of minutes after, Lincoln knocks at the door.

"What's going on?" my father asks, standing abruptly from behind his desk.

I let Lincoln in the office, taking a moment to compose myself before the nightmare starts.

The second I lift my head and look at him, he knows.

"It's Tillie, isn't it?"

I don't bother sugar-coating it; I was brought up not to. "I think she's been taken."

"What, from her damn bed?" I was expecting this reaction.

"She wasn't in her bed. She snuck out."

"That girl never listens. What do you know?" He gets straight to the point.

That's the thing about our world. You have to push your feelings aside to get the job done. Doesn't matter if it's personal or not. If you don't, it could get you killed.

"Not much. Lincoln, you know that new club that's just opened in Camden?"

His eyes narrow. "I know it."

Depths of Deceit

"I need you to head there and collect Kacy. She's waiting for you."

"On it." He turns and leaves.

My father slumps back in his chair now it's just the two of us. "What was she playing at? First, she lied, and now she's put herself in danger. What if..."

"Don't you fucking dare finish that sentence," I shout, halting my father's words. "If you think that now, then she's got no fucking hope, has she? She's a Knox. She's strong, and we'll find her."

He gives me a stern nod, his moment of weakness now in the past. "What do we have to work with?"

I filled him in on what Kacy told me over the phone, which wasn't a lot, but that's never stopped us before.

"What I want to know is how she managed to slip past the fucking guards. There are half a dozen grown-ass men guarding the grounds on this place and she got past them all." He's furious, and rightly so. I was too busy trying to get information from Kacy that the thought never crossed my mind.

"We'll deal with the guards later. Right now, we need to get our shit in order. Once Lincoln comes back with Kacy, we can work out where to go from there. It's almost one in the morning and, if I remember correctly, the club closes at two. I'll call Linc and get him to make sure they don't shut the fucking place until get there so I can scan the CCTV footage."

My father nods. I return it with one of my own and turn to leave, but he stops me. "Keanu, we will find her."

"Damn right we will."

"Boss?" Lincoln's deep voice filters through my thoughts.

"What?" I didn't hear a single word he said.

"You good? You looked like you weren't even in the room for a second there."

If only he knew.

I'm exactly where I was back then. The only difference is, it's me sitting behind my father's desk now. It doesn't matter how much time has passed, it still takes some getting used to. The day my father died was the day I took over. My father taught me everything and prepared me for it. I trained to become him. Be better than him. So far, I've succeeded. I became ruthless, brutal, and earned the respect of all the men who served under my father and the new guys I've taken on. It takes a strong-willed person and an even stronger stomach to do what I do—what all my men do. There ain't no sunflowers or rainbows in my world. Only darkness, blood, and death.

"I'm here. You got new intel?" So far, in all the time Tillie's been missing, all the information we had was useless. We took prints from her phone, hoping that the person who took her may have left a partial print, but besides Tillie's and Kacy's, there weren't any others. The CCTV was no help. The manager of the place was reluctant to show us at first, but after some persuasion, he relented. Of all the cameras in the club, not one of them captured Tillie's movements——which I thought was strange, and I still do. The only camera that was broken was the one in the alley where Kacy found her belongings. I've told a couple of my men to keep an eye on the owners of the club, as I have a gut feeling they played a part in her abduction. Something just seems off.

"Actually, yeah, I do." He seems pleased with himself, so it must be good.

"Care to share?"

"There's a present waiting for you in the basement."

I'm out of my chair and through the door quicker than a bullet being fired from a gun.

Normally, I don't like surprises, but this one sounds like it'll be the best one I've had in a long time.

CHAPTER 2

HARPER

"Harper, I'm away on business for a couple of days. Can I trust you'll behave yourself while I'm gone?" my father calls from down the hallway of my room before he sticks his head and protruding belly around the door.

"I'm sure I can try," I tell him sarcastically.

It isn't unusual for my father to spend days away from home. It's all part of the job, or so he says. I know my father's into some dodgy shit, but I imagine I don't know the full extent.

I kinda like it that way. What I don't know can't hurt me, right?

Wrong.

I get into all manner of trouble, regardless of not knowing what he actually does. If I ask the wrong question or mention something he doesn't like, I get his wrath. It's not as if I'm a kid anymore, which he seems to forget, but only when it suits him.

When he's home, on rare occasions he can be nice. We can have a conversation without it turning into a screaming match. That doesn't mean he's a loving, doting father like you'd expect.

Most of the time, he shouts at me, telling me to shut up, and if I backchat him or try to argue my point, then he makes sure to shut me up with a thick lip.

The safest place for me is out in public. That's when my father is loving and devoted. He's so fake; it's laughable. He acts as though I'm his little princess and would go to the ends of the Earth for me. The truth is, I doubt it very much. It's more likely he'd drive me to the end of the Earth and leave me there.

He's the biggest pretender I've known, and I've seen a fair few enter our home. He says he's all about trust and respect, but he's yet to earn that from me. He might have fooled many people, but not me. I see the man behind the mask, and he's vile. I'm just the unfortunate one who has to call him Father and bow to his every command.

I've been on the receiving end of his backhanders more than I care to admit, earning my first one at eight years old. It continued from there and only got worse.

One particular day, a new member of my father's staff was caught talking to me. I was flirting with him because he was hot. I was fifteen and starting to like boys. My father saw the interaction and didn't like it. He frog-marched me to his office where he beat me for acting poorly just because I'd realised my body was starting to change. I developed breasts. Bigger than any of my friends' were. I had shapely hips, taking me from my child-like frame to a curvaceous one. I was reaching womanhood. I didn't know how to deal with it all, and from my father's reaction, neither did he.

Come to think of it, I never saw the lad again.

"No daughter of mine will act like a hussy, especially with my men. I suggest you go clean up and get changed. That outfit shows way too much and you look like a slut. Show a bit of class, for Christ's sake."

He went back to his business without a backward glance at me crying in a heap on the floor.

I've taken a few more of his beatings since then when I refused to fall in line with what he wanted, or if I pushed his buttons a little too far. I was a teenager. What did he expect?

I wasn't like every other teenage girl. I grew up in a world where mistakes were deadly. They could easily break a person, or worse... get them killed.

On the other hand, I'm an adult now. When he goes off on his business trips, leaving me to my own devices for days on end, I'm at my happiest. I get to live life as much as I can, even though he never left me without at least one of his men. But I'd take it rather than hide who I am for fear my father won't like it.

I lift my head from the book I'm reading. I'm just getting into it. I notice my father is still standing in my doorway.

"Was there anything else?" I didn't mean for it to sound rude, but it did.

"Don't get smart with me, young lady." He strides towards me, full of pent-up frustration. "Do I need to smack that mouth again for you to learn some damn manners?" I curl into a ball to protect myself. He reaches the bottom of my bed, a few steps away from me, hand in the air, ready to strike. I close my eyes, waiting for the pain, but he's interrupted.

"Sir, the car's waiting." My eyes fly open to witness the displeasure on my father's face. He enjoys my pain.

What father gets a kick from being the reason his daughter is hurting?

If he can treat me this way, what is he like with our enemies?

I dread to think.

He smirks at me. "Today must be your lucky day, princess." His tone is sadistic. He turns and sneers at Evan before he brushes past him and leaves my room without another word. Evan doesn't even flinch at my father's rudeness. He waits until my dad has turned the corner before he winks at me. I let out the breath I was holding as they leave.

Not everyone working for my father agrees with his ways——not that they'd go against him. Some of the men who are left to watch over me let me get on with my day. Some of them like to talk to me and are more like friends than bodyguards. It's silly when I think about it, but I spend more time with the burly men than I do with real friends.

Then you get the hardcore Geoffrey Benson arse lickers. They're strict, mean, and snitch on me if I so much as walk past a man who gives me the eye, even if I did nothing wrong.

I think most of them treat me that way because they see the job of babysitting me as punishment. Makes me wonder if Evan will be staying behind now after he interrupted him.

"That was a close call," I mutter to myself now I'm alone again.

Only when I hear the rumble of the engine does my body relax, and the tension begins to leave my bones.

I often wonder why I don't have the loving father that every other woman seems to have. Many times, I've walked down the street and seen girls holding their father's hand and looking happy.

I silently begin to weep for the child in me that missed out on all that because her father doesn't give a shit about her.

I sometimes let my mind wander to what I want my life to look like. I fantasise about the characters in the books I read coming to rescue me and taking me away from here.

They'd love me like they do the heroines in the stories. They cherish them and treat them right. They don't lay a hand on their wives. Well, not in the way I'm used to, anyway. They have a love that isn't perfect, but for them it is. A love that will last forever.

A love I doubt I'll ever have.

CHAPTER 3

KEANU

Rushing to the basement, I get a tingling in my spine the closer I get. Every step is full of purpose. It's the same sensation I get when I know I'm close to something good or something is about to go down.

I knew the second Lincoln told me there was something in the basement waiting for me it was a person of use. This could be it, the person to give me the information my father and I have been seeking. This could be the day I finally get a step closer to finding my sister and bringing her home.

I hear Lincoln laughing behind me, telling me to calm the fuck down, but without thought or slowing my pace, I barge my way through the basement door to find a man tied to a metal chair with his head slumped down.

I make my way over to the limp body to see who I'm dealing with. His face is so beaten he's barely recognisable. "You sure he needed that much persuasion?" I ask Lincoln as he smirks and shuts the door behind him.

"Fuck off. He put up a fight, so I floored him. Don't worry, he can still talk… for now." He's cocky, and if he wasn't my second in command and, more importantly, my best friend, then I would have laid him out myself for his smart-arse comment.

"Are you going to tell me who he is, or am I meant to be guessing?" I ask over my shoulder.

"You remember Kacy saying she saw someone talking to Tillie at the bar?" I nod. "That's the guy. Don't ask me how I found him, but it's definitely him."

I don't need to ask. Lincoln is my tracker and a fucking good one. He's never let me down yet, and I trust him with my life.

"Has he given you anything?" I ask.

"Nothing but moaning and a few grunts." Lincoln shrugs.

"I'll give him something to fucking groan at." I stroll to the corner of the room where a stool is stationed, dragging it back with force. The metal scrapes against the concrete. It's ear-piercing, and the man bound to the seat takes notice. He lifts his head. His right eye has started to swell, but that's okay. He'll soon see who I am and what I'm capable of.

I drag the stool to a stop in front of him, sit down, and lean towards him so we're eye to eye.

"Where's the girl?" I ask calmly. He ignores me. I ask again, only this time, it's harsh. "Where the fuck is the girl?"

The guy has the audacity to laugh right in my face. He's either brave or stupid. I swing my fist back and launch it forward, sparking him across the jaw. His head whips to the side and he loses a tooth. We both watch as it dances along the floor, stopping a short distance away.

"Don't make me ask again." I sit back down on the stool and wait for him to turn his head towards me. When he does, he spits blood on the ground, only just missing my shoe. I stare at the red splatter, counting to five to simmer the demon that wants to take over and end this guy just for having something to do with Tillie being taken, but I'm smarter than that.

I need answers first, and I will fucking get them.

He starts laughing again, so carefree. Not at all how a person tied up and beaten to a pulp should be.

"Which one?" He chuckles again.

I school my features, giving nothing away.

Was he meant to tell us that, or was it a slip in his cockiness?

Depths of Deceit

Lincoln circles me, standing behind the guy in the seat. He gives me a look. One that tells me he's thinking the same as me.

"You know exactly which one. I'm not in the mood for games." I cross my arms over my chest, the muscles sitting tight against my shirt.

"I can do this all day. You don't know shit." He smiles, showing me his blood-soaked teeth and toothless gap.

It's time to step it up a notch. I've waited long enough to find some decent intel on where the fuck my sister is. I still have hope she's alive. If she wasn't... I'd feel it deep in my gut. The only thing throwing me is that no one came forward for ransom money or gloated about getting their hands on a top dog mafia daughter.

There's a reason she's been taken. A purpose, and I still don't have the answers.

My anger flares. I'm done pissing about. I roll up the sleeves of my shirt and reach down into my boot, grabbing my trusted switchblade from its holder. I flip it up, wasting no time. I stand abruptly, and in one swift movement, I jab my knife straight into his collarbone. I watch in pure satisfaction as his eyes widen in shock, and he yelps out in pain. I twist the knife, causing more damage, he whimpers and it's music to my fucking ears.

"Fuck," he roars, gasping to draw breath. He's panting like a damn dog. I release the knife, wiping it clean on the sleeve of his jacket.

"Now that I've got your attention, let's try this again."

Lincoln has moved and is now leaning on the wall on the far side of the basement, observing the situation. I slowly circle the chair and stare down at the rear view of our hostage's head.

"You were speaking to a girl at a bar in Camden Town sixteen months ago. Why?" I don't need to give him the specifics. If he's the right guy like Lincoln said he was, then he'll know.

"You're questioning me about something that happened over a year ago? I don't remember what I did last weekend," he scoffs. "You must be desperate."

His laugh drives me crazy, and I lose my shit. I grab a fist full of his hair and yank his head back, putting strain on his neck muscles. I hover my switchblade across his throat. Not enough to cause serious damage, but enough to draw blood. He swallows hard, the movement making the knife pinch the tight skin. I bend so I'm close to his ear as I utter my next words with menace.

"Either you tell me what I want to know, or I'll make you suffer for longer." I wiggle the blade. "This is nothing compared to what I can do."

"I don't know what you're talking about. I don't recall talking to a girl."

"Bullshit." I release his hair from my gasp at the sound of Lincoln's voice in the distance. If I'm honest, I'm pissed that he interrupted me, but I want to see where he's going with this.

"You see, Mark... I can call you that, right? I mean, it is your name after all." Lincoln strolls over to the table on the opposite side of the room from where he was standing and picks up a file.

How did I not notice that when we walked in?

"I had a feeling you would deny any involvement. So I did some digging. For someone who works at a burger joint on minimum wage, you sure like living above your means. Then I checked your bank account. You had a hefty twenty grand transferred to you the day after the girl in question went missing. You want to explain that?" I come to stand in front of the weasel, crossing my arms over my chest and smirking down at him. His chest rises and falls as his heart rate gallops in panic.

"How... how did you get my information?" he stutters.

"Did you even know who the girl was? I doubt it. Otherwise, you wouldn't have agreed to it." I study Mark's face as sheer dread replaces cockiness.

He doesn't have a fucking clue, and everything is starting to click into place.

"Have you never heard of the Knox family?" I ask him casually.

He nods and gulps.

"Well, the girl you spoke to was the daughter of that family and, let me tell you, they weren't too happy to find out she had been taken. But you know who's more pissed off?"

His whole body begins to shake, just like his head is.

"Me, Mark. You played a part in Tillie Knox's disappearance, and that got my attention because Tillie is *my* fucking sister." I roar the last bit, my voice echoing off the walls. "I'm the head of the Knox family."

His eyes widen, and the pathetic prick pisses himself. I watch as the liquid soaks his trousers and appears at his feet, making a disgusting pool on my floor.

This guy is a nobody. Just someone's pawn to do the dirty work, right at the bottom of the chain of command. But that doesn't mean he can't be useful to us.

"I... I... swear, I didn't know," he stutters.

"Well. now you do. You'd better start talking, or pissing yourself will be the least of your issues."

"I don't know anything. I swear. Some guy offered me a job in exchange for some quick cash. I didn't know she was your sister, honestly. I just really needed the money. They didn't give me any details, just a couple of steps to follow."

"Which were?" I probe.

"They handed me a picture of a girl, told me to keep a look out for her. I spotted her at the club. I couldn't believe my luck." I sneered at his poor choice of words but let him continue. This is good information. More than we've had since she went missing. "I was told to call a number when I saw her. Someone met me at the club not long after and handed me a little bottle, a liquid of some kind. I had to get the liquid in her drink without her noticing. That's why I was at the bar with her. I saw my opportunity and I took it. So, I waited for the drug to kick in. She told her friends she was going to the bathroom, and that's when I grabbed her. I had to get her out the back through the fire escape, and a van pulled up and dragged her inside. That's all. I don't know who they were or what their intentions were, and I've heard nothing since. I swear on my life that's all I know."

"So you drugged my sister?" I'm murderous. She wouldn't have been able to defend herself. She never stood a chance.

"Ye... yes."

I charge towards him, closing the small distance between us. I stick my finger into the hole I put in his collarbone and push with force. He curses and screams at the pain, but I don't let up on the pressure.

"How did they contact you? Was it a burner phone?"

"Yes. Yes. They took it off me the moment they arrived with the van," he pants.

I remove my finger and spin around. "Fuck," I roar at the ceiling.

"Hang on a minute. So you're telling us that you were picked at random?" Lincoln interjects.

I grab a cloth from the table and begin cleaning the blood off my hand.

Mark nods, his eyes shifting back and forth between me and him.

"Whoever it was couldn't have just picked you up from off the streets. They picked you for a reason. Why?" I ask, knowing where Lincoln is heading with his questions.

"I don't know. I was at a restaurant. I go there every other Saturday. That's... that's where they collared me."

"What restaurant?" Linc and I ask in unison.

"Cheetos."

"The little Mexican restaurant down on Fourth Street?" I question, raising my eyebrow. It's not a coincidence that this restaurant is smack bang in the middle of here in Chelsea and the club in Camden.

"Yeah."

I throw Lincoln a quizzical look, and he just shrugs. We both turn at the same time and head towards the door we barrelled through.

"Wait... are you going to leave me here?"

I spin around to face Mark. His hopefulness is laughable. "Yes. I'm not finished with you yet. I don't know if what you've told us is true. Until then, you can sit tight." I smirk, turn my back to him, and slam the door, closing him in the cold, dark basement. He'll soon pass out from the pain his shoulder is causing him.

If what he's told us doesn't check out, then he's really going to feel my wrath. If he thinks a blade to the shoulder was bad, that was only a smidgeon of what I'm truly capable of.

"What are you thinking, boss?" Lincoln asks the second the door is locked from the outside.

"Recon. I don't want these fuckers to know I'm looking for them. Not yet anyway." I glance at my watch to see what time it is. The dial reads nine-thirty p.m. "You fancy some Mexican food?"

Depths of Deceit

"I thought you'd never ask." The mischievous glint in Lincoln's eyes only fuels my adrenaline.

This is the only solid lead we've had regarding my sister's kidnapping, and I'll do everything I can to make sure I follow it through.

"Cheetos it is, then." I pat Lincoln on the back as I walk past him and head for the car.

I'm not wasting another second.

CHAPTER 4

HARPER

"For the love of God, Harper. I swear you were born purely to test my patience. You'll do as I've asked without the attitude. We're going to dinner together whether you like it or not. Even if I have to drag you there myself," my father bellows.

He got back from his business trip this morning and, like he always does, he came back like nothing ever happened. Like he didn't intend to take another swing at me the day he left.

He demanded that I dress up appropriately and that we have dinner reservations at Cheetos, his favourite Mexican restaurant. I'm not sure of the reason for this visit, but it normally coincides with business. When it comes to business talk, I get sent to hang out with the owner's daughter, Anita. We got pushed upon each other the first time I was dragged there, when I was not to be privy to what my father and his business associates were talking about. She'd always be sitting at a table with her head in a book. We became friends of convenience, and it was nice to have someone there to talk to.

"Harper, are you fucking listening to me?" my father barks. I fidget, but then remember the pain he's caused me, and I don't want him to know how much he affects me.

Digging my heels in a little bit more, I stay rooted to the spot and smooth out the invisible creases in my navy satin dress. It's one of my favourites to wear, with the soft material gliding across my skin. It's

Depths of Deceit

sexy with its spaghetti straps, doing nothing to hide the fact I'm not wearing a bra. A 'fuck you' to my father. The neckline is draped in the middle, allowing just a snippet of cleavage to peep out. It's conservative in length, coming to just below the knee with a small slit at the back of the skirt.

"For fuck's sake, Harper. Stop being a brat." My father grabs my wrist tightly, pulling me towards the car.

"Ow. You're hurting me." I try in earnest to retrieve my hand from his grip, but his fingers dig into my wrist. I continue to fight against his strength, twisting my limb to no avail. The friction burn where my skin is stretching threatens to bring tears to my eyes.

I've had to endure worse than this. *Come on, girl. Hold it together.*

"Why won't you do as I ask, just once in your life?" he spits and tugs me with frustration, knocking me off balance. Seeing the opportunity while I'm not able to pull back from him, he swings me around in the direction of the open car door and rams me into the back seat. He only lets me go once I'm sprawled out in the car.

Seeing no way out, I sit up and clutch my wrist to my chest, hissing in pain as the sting to my skin short-circuits my mind for a second. I look down at my forearm, sighing deeply. The bruises in the shape of my father's fingers begin to form, an eyesore in contrast to my pale skin.

There's no mistaking what the cause of its appearance is. There's no hiding it, though I doubt my father would even give a shit. It's not like anyone would dare to question it.

The journey to the restaurant is quick and quiet. I have no reason to make conversation with the despicable man I call my father. I would rather gouge my own eyes out with a blunt knife than speak to him.

The car door opens on my father's side and, after he shuffles his way out, my door opens next. I won't fight him this time. If I cause a scene, he'll only punish me more when we get home. So, I climb out myself and follow him through the entrance of the restaurant.

"Mr Benson, so good to see you again. Your usual table is waiting for you. Your guests have arrived and are already seated." The waiter picks up some menus and guides us to the table. I don't know why. I could find it with my eyes closed.

Apprehension takes up residence in my body. The slight quiver is undetectable to anyone else unless they were to touch me. I want nothing more than to go home to the relative safety of my room.

The two gentlemen already sitting at our table stand as we arrive. I've never seen either of them before. The one to my left pulls the chair out for me like a true gent, but I'm not fooled. If he knows my father then he is bound to be as dodgy and dangerous. I smile politely, just to keep the peace.

The waiter leaves us while we peruse the menus. I zone out to all the small talk going across the table under the guise of choosing what to eat, not that it would make a difference, if I'm around they always speak in code so I never know what has been discussed anyway.

I suddenly start to feel uncomfortable, as if being watched. I peek over the top of the menu, all three men deep in conversation with one another. I look over to the spot where Anita always sits, but tonight, she isn't there. I must have imagined the uneasy feeling.

I return my gaze to the menu. I don't know why I bothered. I know I want tacos, but there's no way my father would allow it in a public setting. *'A lady never eats such foods when in company. Show some class.'* He's since given up. Now he simply chooses a more elegant meal for me, and I have no choice but to eat it.

The hairs on the back of my neck stand to attention. I glance around the restaurant and spot the culprit. All the air quickly leaves my lungs as I lower my eyes so Daddy dearest doesn't see what or who caught my attention. I quickly disguise it and clear my throat, reaching for the water that had already been poured for me from the pitcher in the centre of the table.

Once I regain my equilibrium, I look up through my lashes to see the most beautiful yet dangerous-looking man I've ever seen. He's staring right at me, peering into my soul. His eyes are like lasers, and they're focused on me.

I quickly glance over my shoulder, wondering if he's actually looking at something behind me, but there's no one there. He's definitely gawking at me, his narrow eyes assessing me.

The waiter returning to take our order breaks my trance. As predicted, my father orders for me.

Depths of Deceit

The whiskey the men ordered is placed on the table, but no alcohol was ordered for me. He insists I don't drink when he wants me to be on my best behaviour. I had already shown on the way here that I'm not playing his game tonight, so I'm being punished.

I can still feel the sexy stranger's eyes on me. I can no longer bear it. My pulse has quickened and I can feel a slight flush burning up my chest and neck. I have to remove myself from the situation before my father picks up on it. We all know what happens when a man shows me any unwanted attention.

I stand with grace and, with a small smile, excuse myself to the little chicas' room.

As soon as I'm out of sight and in the privacy of a cubicle, I stumble and slouch against the door. All thoughts go straight back to the brooding stranger.

Who is he?

I've never seen him around here before. I would remember a guy like him.

One glance and I'm already fully invested in knowing who he is.

The sound of the bathroom door opening and closing, followed by shuffling feet getting closer, brings me back to the here and now. I flush the toilet and leave the cubicle, face-planting into a hard-as-steel chest.

Fucking hell. Are they wearing plated armour?

For some reason, I know without looking up who the chest belongs to. I crane my neck back to look up. I feel the moisture of my arousal soak my underwear, and my legs squeeze together. Holy shit, his scent is intoxicating and heady. I don't know what aftershave he uses, but it suits him. His gaze is that of a predator waiting to pounce, but I'm far from afraid.

"This is the ladies' room," I state.

"I don't care." His husky voice sends shivers down my spine. "Why are you here?" he adds, moving closer to me.

"Erm, I'm using the toilet," I sarcastically reply. I shuffle from one foot to the other as he looks over me with a steely gaze.

"Who are you?" he asks with a little less forcefulness to his tone.

What's with all the questions?

I end up giving him what he wants without a second thought.

"Harper. And you are?" I throw his question back at him, but I get nothing. The moment is strange, and I realise I've been gone for a while. "Look, my father will be coming to look for me if I don't get back out there soon." I move to step past him again, and thankfully, he lets me.

I quickly rinse my hands, watching his reflection in the mirror. He turns, watching my every move but makes no effort to speak again. I leave him standing in the ladies' bathroom as I return to my seat, wondering what the hell that was all about.

"What took you so long?" my father hisses in my ear. I'm just about to answer when I feel a presence behind me. I look up to see the man from the bathroom. My heart plummets to my stomach in panic.

No, no, no. Please just leave me alone. What's he playing at? He's going to get me into serious trouble.

I lift my gaze and notice his focus pinned to my wrist and the purple bruise that has formed there. I quickly tuck it away under the table. But then I see fury flash in his eyes at the sight of me being a marked woman.

I switch my gaze from his to my father's as he speaks. "Knox. It's not like you to be in my neck of the woods. What do I owe the pleasure?" I frown at the name. It rings a bell. Where have I heard that name before? I recall overhearing my father talking about a John Knox——one of Father's many enemies. Surely, not this Knox. The way my father described him made him sound much older, given that they had known one another for many years.

I'm so confused.

"Don't worry, Benson. I was just leaving. I'm sure our paths will cross again very soon." He smirks my way.

What the fuck does that mean? I don't have time to dissect the comment as Knox shoots me a wink and turns to leave. I manage to keep my face impassive as I try to read my father's reaction. Judging from the redness, I'd say my father wasn't pleased to see him here.

My mind is in overdrive as I try to figure out what the man's intentions were in the toilets, let alone with my father.

I feel a storm coming.

CHAPTER 5

KEANU

I never expected to see the blonde beauty sitting with Geoffrey Benson.

Who was she?

Was she the daughter of one of the men sitting around the table? Fuck, was she Benson's daughter? I wasn't aware he had one, I'd never seen him with one before, but that doesn't mean he's childless.

She blindsided me. Her beauty was intoxicating. I couldn't help but stare at her, and from the way she was looking around, she felt something too.

I knew Lincoln was talking beside me, but I didn't hear a word he said. I was preoccupied with her presence. From her body language, I could tell she didn't want to be there. She was shifting in her seat, clearly uncomfortable, yet she was there anyway.

Why come if she didn't want to?

I had so many questions I wanted to ask her, who she was for starters, and when she excused herself, I made quick work of following her without drawing attention. The moment I was close to her, all thoughts left me. She made me forget everything… almost. I didn't let my guard down completely. I still have a job to do and I was led here for a reason. She wasn't it.

That didn't mean I couldn't have some fun, though.

Harper cut the conversation off before it had even begun, but the way she seemed so fragile and panicked about her father coming to look for her had her jittery and full of nerves. She was fearful of him.

So, I let her go.

I'd have a chance to talk to her again. I'd make it my mission to. I was intrigued by her, and when I'm invested in something, I do everything in my power to get what I want.

I waited a minute or two before I followed her back out the way we came. She was just sitting down when I approached their table. Her eyes widened at seeing me there, but what caught my attention more than her scared features was the angry flesh mark on her wrist. She hid it instantly, but it didn't matter. I'd already seen it and I didn't like it. The fact someone had hurt her didn't sit right with me. I couldn't explain why I felt so protective towards her. I'd only just met her, for fuck's sake.

I hid my disgust well and addressed Geoffrey. He didn't hide his feelings at seeing me there. He was furious at my walking on his turf without being notified.

That's the difference between us. I know what's going on over on my side of London. Nothing gets past me. Since Tillie went missing, everything changed. More so when I took over from my father.

I kept the conversation short, leaving him confused about why I was really there, but not before throwing Harper my panty-dropping wink that always gets me what I want.

Lincoln silently followed me out of the restaurant, walking alongside me as we headed the short distance to the car.

Only when we're in the car driving back to the estate does he speak.

"You wanna tell me what the hell that was all about? Talking to Benson was never part of the plan. I thought we were just checking shit out." He throws a look my way. I glance from the windscreen over to him. He arches his brow.

"*She* was never part of the plan, Linc. Our objective was to do some recon on the restaurant. I never expected... her," I state like it explains everything.

"Again, care to elaborate?"

Depths of Deceit

"I wish I could, but I can't. Fuck. I never anticipated her." I rub my fingers across my forehead in frustration.

"You keep saying her, but I have no clue who you're talking about."

"Harper. I think she's Benson's fucking daughter."

"Are you fucking kidding me? You diverted from the plan for a woman?" His anger fills the small space in the vehicle.

"I know, I know. It was a stupid idea. I——"

He cuts me off. "You could have gotten us killed. We had no backup, and for all you know, Benson could have had more men lurking around!"

"Careful, Lincoln. You might be my most trusted advisor and friend, but remember who you're talking to. I already knew Benson only brought one guard with him. He was sitting in the far corner. The fact he was looking at everything and everyone bar the menu was a clear giveaway." His anger starts to dwindle. "I may have gone off plan, but never question my capability."

"Noted. What now? Did you get anything useful?"

"Possibly." I tell him about the mark on Harper's wrist and how she acted in the presence of her father. "I think it was him who hurt her. If I'm correct, we can use her to our advantage." I don't tell him that I have other ideas where she's concerned.

"I see where you're going with this. You think by getting close to her, she'll slip up and tell you all of her father's secrets."

I quickly look back over to him. He's smirking.

"Something like that." I shrug.

"I'm on board." There's a silence between us. "Her own father hurts her? That must be a shit life," Lincoln ponders.

My earlier anger rises again. From the way she acted when I stood by the table, she was scared I'd say something in front of her father and unintentionally get her into trouble. I have a feeling that wasn't the first time he's hurt her, and most definitely won't be the last. My grip on the steering wheel tightens, turning my knuckles white. The thought of him hurting her again makes me murderous. I know I've hurt people, broken them down to the point of no return, but never have I laid a finger on a woman. It goes against the Knox code.

There are other ways to get what you need from a woman without using violence, and my way never fails.

By the time I pull up at the Knox Estate, all I see is red. Red like the burning marks on Harper's wrist, and I need to take my pent-up frustration out on something or someone. And I know just the person to help me with that.

I ram the handbrake up on the car and wait for Lincoln to get out before getting out myself. I'm already headed inside, flicking the fob on my keys to lock the car.

Lincoln jogs to catch up with me. "Where are you off to in a hurry?"

Only one word is needed. "Basement."

Lincoln follows without saying another word. I nod at one of my men, Sam, who's standing guard outside the basement door just as a precaution. You can never be too careful, especially in my line of work.

Sam unlocks the door as I approach. I burst through it, the motion sensor lights basking the room bright white, blinding Mark, who's squinting in my direction.

The smell of iron lingering in the air hits my nostrils, but it doesn't faze me, it only fuels me.

I storm towards his slouched body, getting straight to business. "Do you know who Geoffrey Benson is?" His body stiffens at my words. The little fucker knows more than he's letting on. "I'll take that as a yes. How do you know him?" His eyes are downcast. "Look at me, you fucking pussy." He lifts his head but doesn't utter a word. "Answer me!"

He finally opens his mouth. "Yes, I know him, but not like you think."

"Start talking."

"I can't. If I talk, they'll kill me."

I laugh sadistically. "If you don't talk, I'll kill you."

Lincoln is in his usual corner, silently watching. That's what he does if he's not the one interrogating. It's how he spots loopholes in the captive's story. If something seems off and I'm too busy causing pain, he clocks on to it.

"You don't understand. It's bigger than your sister," he shouts at

Depths of Deceit

my retreating back. The tools lining the table catch my eye. I pick up the blowtorch, holding it high above my head so Mark can see what my intentions are. I pretend to take an interest in it, but then change my mind and pick up a pair of pliers.

I turn and smirk, showing him what I have in my hand. I angle my head and look at his hands. His arms are tied to the chair, giving me perfect access to get to work on breaking him. His eyes widen when it clicks with him what I have planned.

I slowly close the distance between us, circling him a couple of times.

"Wh... what are you doing?" he stutters.

"I'm trying to decide what finger I like the look of most."

Lincoln chuckles at my play.

"Please, you don't need to do this," he says, but it's useless. I'm past the point of playing nice.

I swing my body around so I'm standing directly in front of him and randomly choose a finger. I show him the size of the pliers and hover them over the index finger on his right hand. "Are you by any chance right-handed?" I smile at my sarcasm.

"Yes, why?" He tries to retreat in his seat, the ties around his wrists pinching his skin in his efforts to pull free. It's a pointless exercise.

"No reason." I clamp the pliers down on the tip of his fingernail and begin pulling. His nail slowly begins to lift from the nail bed. The more I pull, the louder his screams get. With one last tug and squeeze of the pliers, I rip the last bit of skin from the nail. I hold the fingernail up so he can see my handiwork. Tears run down his face, his skin is clammy, his shirt is covered in sweat, and his chest is rising and falling as his breathing comes short and sharp.

"One down, nine to go." I flick the pliers, releasing his nail. It drops to the floor somewhere, but I'm already selecting the next finger.

"Please, stop." Mark's voice is small and tired. "Just stop."

"I can't stop now. I've only just started." I start tugging on the nail of my choosing; same finger, but on his left hand. It takes a little more force, but eventually, I succeed. "Two down, eight——"

"Enough, please. I can't take it anymore." I watch in pure satisfaction as his body gets weaker, loss of blood and lack of energy enabling him to stay awake.

I slap him across the face. "Now isn't the time to sleep, Mark. I want answers, and I'll continue to extract your fingernails until you tell me what I want to know." I'm preparing to remove my third nail when he starts thrashing about.

"Okay, okay. Please, don't. I'll tell you everything I know." His body sags with relief when I move the pliers away.

"Well… I'm waiting."

"Yes, I know Benson. He's frequently at Cheetos. That's where I first met him. It's where he has meetings to discuss certain parts of his business."

I arch my brow and fold my arms across my chest. "Why hold meetings there and not at home? Wouldn't that be safer?" My question is aimed at Lincoln, but I don't care who replies.

"He has one meeting there. With the different people. Only now, it's the same people every time. It's been like that for the past eight months."

"What are the meetings for?" I enquire.

"Jeez, come on. It's not like I'm invited to them." I lean forward with the pliers again. "No, no, wait. I overheard something." I pause and stare at him, waiting for him to continue. "It wasn't much. Something about it's all in motion and girls and a price."

I swing my gaze over to Lincoln as he pushes himself from the wall, stepping out from the shadows.

"Is that why they used you?" That was my next question, but Lincoln beat me to it.

"What do you——"

Lincoln marches towards Mark, grabbing him around the neck, and begins to squeeze.

"Don't play fucking dumb." Mark's face turns red and he's gasping for air. "You've done this more than once, haven't you? Tillie wasn't the first girl you drugged and sent off to God knows where in the back of a van. You knew exactly what they wanted you to do. Admit it, you fucking lowlife piece of shit." Lincoln's menacing voice fills the room.

I roll my eyes. "Linc, loosen your grip. How do you expect him to

Depths of Deceit

talk when you're choking him to death?" He eventually loosens his hold, but not before he snarls through his teeth. "This is your last chance, Mark. If I were you, I'd tell me what your role for Benson really is, or I'll have no choice but to end you," I tell him calmly.

"Doesn't matter if I tell you not, you'll kill me anyway," he says between gasping some much-needed air into his lungs.

"True, but it's that or you go back a snitch. Do you really want to be known for that? From the look of things, you're so far down the food chain, they wouldn't miss you, and when they find out I had my claws in you, they'll kill you. I'll show you some mercy, whereas they won't. Either way, you're a dead man."

His eyes wander from mine to Lincoln. He's at breaking point. He's weak. I've hardly touched the guy and he's giving me more intel than we've gathered since Tillie went missing.

"Fine. I was the guy that would collect the girls. They did research on which girls wouldn't be missed. You know, homeless girls, hookers, no family. That kind of thing. My job was to talk to them, drug them, and deliver them to the man with the van." His shoulders drop in defeat. "They got word that some mafia princess visited the club once or twice before and wanted her too. I didn't know nothing about her before that. They don't normally go for high-end targets, so she must have been special for them to risk it." He slumps further in the seat. "That's all I know, I swear to you."

I hate the way my sister has been dragged into this just because of who she is, but the way he's speaking tells me he was shocked by this request. "I believe you." And I do. There's no way a guy as weak and pathetic as him would make up any of this. But the guys who hired him for this job clearly thought that giving him this snippet of information wouldn't have done any harm. They're wrong. Mark might have been nothing but a pawn, but they still told him more than they should have and now I have new information. It's nothing that leads me to the top of the chain, but it's a step closer. But I'm almost certain that Benson and the two guys are involved.

"You do?" He's surprised.

"Yes." I nod firmly. "Untie him."

"What?" Lincoln asks in shock. "But.."

I raise my voice slightly. "I said untie him. We have no use for him anymore."

Lincoln gawks at me like I've lost my damn mind but starts to remove the rope around his ankles before the ones around his wrist.

"You're... you're letting me go?" Mark's voice is hoarse.

"Yes. I suggest you leave now before I change my mind. You know where the door is." I nod my head to the exit, closely watching as Mark contemplates what to do. I know exactly what he'll do.

He slowly pushes himself up from the seat he's been strapped to for more than twenty-four hours. He cradles his shoulder with his hand and pretty much drags his sorry arse toward the exit——his escape.

Lincoln comes to stand at my side. "Surely, you're not going to let him walk out of here?" he whispers.

"What do you take me for, a fool?" I smirk.

"Then what are you—" I hold my hand up, cutting him short.

Mark's almost at the door when I reach behind my back. My hand wraps around my trusted Glock. I pull it free, raise it, aim, and shoot. A single bullet pierces the back of his head, and his body falls flat on the ground. Lifeless.

He played a part in Tillie's disappearance. It doesn't matter how small it was. For that, he paid the price. No one messes with me or my family and gets away with it.

My gun gets tucked back into the waistband of my trousers. "Call the cleaners. I want his body disposed of and this place bleached clean. We need to scope out Cheetos some more and find out who the two guys Benson was meeting with were." With a stern nod, Lincoln is on his phone, following through with my orders.

CHAPTER 6

HARPER

I arrive at my and Chelsea's favourite little cafe in Chelsea's town centre. Convenient, right? Of course, I have one of my dad's goons with me as usual, but I thank my lucky stars that he's one of the good guys. He stays out of my way but makes sure I'm always in his view. It gives me some privacy to speak freely with my best friend. I need to tell her about the guy from yesterday at the restaurant. He's all I can think about. His strong presence and masculinity were like nothing I'd felt before.

I'm first to arrive, but Chelsea sent me a text saying she's on her way and to order her usual builder's mug of tea.

I flick through my social media, but nothing grabs my attention, so I change course and look at the entertainment sites to see what scandal celebs are creating this week.

The young girl behind the counter brings over the drinks just as Chelsea arrives, looking flustered. I can't help but chuckle at her state of dishevelment.

"Hey, you okay?" I ask.

She throws her hands up in the air. "Oh my God, you will not believe who I spent last night with," she tells me as she settles in her seat and takes a sip of her tea.

"Are you going to tell me, or am I to guess for the next hour?" I love my friend more than anyone in the world, but fuck, she can be so dramatic sometimes.

"Do you remember the hot guy that we met at the bar the other night but he had to leave early because he got called into work?" I nod enthusiastically, letting her know I remember the sex on legs, built like a brick shithouse man. "Well, I was in the kebab shop last night, and he came in while I was waiting for my order. He asked if I was free and we went to his place with our food. It turns out, he's a fireman and he was on call the night he was at the bar."

"Does that mean you'll be seeing him again?"

"He's picking me up once I'm done here and we're spending the rest of the day together," she says with the biggest grin on her face. I'm happy for her, I really am, but a part of me is jealous. She can date who she wants, when she wants, with no consequences whatsoever. Whereas, I don't have that luxury. My father doesn't let me out much to even meet a guy, never mind date one. Don't get me wrong, there have been guys in my life, but no one worth my time. They were either scared of my father or so far up his arse that they practically became a version of him. I'd rather be single for the rest of my life than date someone like that.

Chelsea's sweet voice drifts through my ears. "So, what's going on with you? Your message this morning was vague to say the least." I had sent her a text asking her to meet me here, and that I needed to talk and not on my father's estate.

My slight jealousy towards Chelsea fades, and hope and desire take its place.

"Last night, my father dragged me off to dinner again." Her eyes leave mine and home in on the bruise she knows she'll find peeping out from under my sleeve.

"Son of a bitch." It's not the first time she's seen marks on me at the hands of my sperm donor.

"Never mind that." I wave off her concern. After all, she's seen it many times and that's nothing compared to what I've endured before. "When we got there, I had this weird feeling I was being watched. I looked around to find the most alluring male specimen I've ever seen. He took my breath away, Chels. His eyes bore into my skin, setting me on fire. I excused myself to the ladies' in the end just to try and replenish the air back into my lungs." I sigh, leaning back in my chair, remembering every single detail of him. His scent, the size of his broad shoulders and how tight his tailored jacket hugged his muscles, his husky voice that had my underwear soaking wet, to the way his domineering nature had me obeying his every command. I could tell he was dangerous. There was a look about him that screamed 'stay away', but for some reason, I found that part to be most intriguing.

"It sounds like he got under your skin. What happened?"

"He followed me into the toilets." I tell her about the weird exchange we had. "He smelt so good and... manly. I nearly came there and then." I whisper the last part. Chelsea stifles her laugh at my expense. I sound like a crazy person. "It was... odd. He asked me who I am, but he wouldn't tell me anything, so I left the bathroom and went back to my table, but he came over, and from my father's reaction, he knew who he was and wasn't best pleased. Someone named Knox, apparently."

Chelsea almost drops her mug, and by the look on her face, she knows something I don't. That's not unusual. It's not like I get out much.

"Fuck, Harper. As in *the* Mr. Knox?"

I shrug, "I mean, possibly. My father did say Knox."

She pulls her phone out and types out something. "Was this the guy?" She pushes her phone in my face. Staring back at me is a picture of the man in question in a body-hugging black suit.

Jeez, this man is mighty fine.

"Yeah, that's him. I've seen him before. Do you know him?"

"Shit, Harper. That's Keanu Knox. From what I hear, he's mafia. His father was top dog before he died. I'm guessing from what little I've been able to read up about him, he's taken over the estate, which would make him the head of the mafia now. At least on his side of London, anyway."

Where did she find all that information? I've scanned the internet and come up empty. My mood takes a nosedive. I don't fucking believe it. The first guy to give me fanny flutters and keep me up all night thinking of him is another bad guy, and not just any bad guy, but the head of a fucking mafia family.

Like my life isn't shit enough.

"But..." Whatever I was going to say dies on my lips.

How can something so wrong seem so... right?

"Whatever you're thinking Harper, don't. Your dad will go fucking mental if he finds out you're mooning over this guy. I mean it. This will only end badly for you. If you know what's best for you, you'll leave him well alone."

I know she's right, but I don't have to like it. I release a deep sigh. Once again, my father inadvertently stands between me and a potential suitor. I inwardly laugh at myself. Yeah, right. Like I could be well-suited for a man like Knox.

"Why would you say that? Now I want him even more."

The fact I know it'll piss my father off makes it sweeter.

"Sorry, sweet. I know I can't stop you from making your own decisions, but I'm your friend and only looking out for you." She places her hand in mine, rubbing her finger over my palm.

"I know. Thank you."

We eat our lunch, choosing to talk about anything that isn't related to my father or Keanu Knox. Not that it stops my mind from drifting back to him. I know I shouldn't go down this route, but I need to find out more about him.

Chelsea's new man comes to collect her from the café, and I leave with lead in my heart as it copes with the conflicting feelings between my head and my lady bits.

My name is shouted the second I walk back through the door from lunch with Chelsea. I release a silent moan before I head towards my father's office, my bodyguard three steps behind me.

I paint on a false smile and knock. I only enter when I've been granted permission.

"Did you enjoy your lunch with Chelsea?"

That was random. He never asks how my day went.

Depths of Deceit

"Yes." I answer without delay, even though I'm full of doubt.

"Did she behave?" This question is aimed at someone behind me.

"Nothing to report," the guy who shadowed me answers.

"Good. That will be all." He waves me off with his hand.

I turn and leave quickly. Something seemed off with my father. There were no follow-up questions, or him wanting to know everything. It was rather vague. Does he want something from me?

Maybe he's had an epiphany, realising that the way he treats me is appalling.

"Yeah, right," I scoff.

"What's that now?"

My whole body stiffens, but I soon relax when I see it's Evan. "Evan. Didn't see you there." I chuckle awkwardly.

"I gathered." He smiles. "You were talking to yourself again."

I play dumb. "Was I?"

He nods, scanning our surroundings before gently taking my forearm and guiding us into a corner out of view. I'm baffled by the sudden movement.

"You need to be careful, darling. Your father's acting strange," he whispers, his face full of concern.

"I... I don't understand. Why are you telling me this?"

Is this a test? Has my father put him up to this? I wouldn't put it past him.

"Because I made your mother a promise before she died," he states.

I gasp at the mention of my mother. It's forbidden in this house.

"A promise? What promise?" I ask.

"To protect you both."

"Protect us? Why do I need protecting, and from who? It's not like my own father would ki——"

The sympathetic look he gives tells me otherwise.

"Your father is capable of many things, Harper. I know more than most. Your father is the kind of man who only looks after himself and this." His hands gesture around the estate. "He'll do anything to keep what he has, even if that means sacrificing his... daughter." He looks in pain at the thought of me being the daughter of a man like Benson. The tears I'd been trying to hold back begin to fall. Evan gently wipes them away. "Your mother knew this. When she was pregnant with you, she thought he would change. But then they found out they were having a girl. Your father wasn't exactly pleased. Deep down, your mother knew he wanted a boy. Someone to take over and keep the estate and name going long after he was gone. From the moment you were born, your mother never left your side. Not even once. She knew she had to protect you. And she did, until her dying breath."

My emotions are all over the place. "Why are you telling me this now?"

"I promised your mother I would help her. She never wanted this life for you, and she was trying to find a safe way out. But with Benson alive, it was never an option. She never succeeded. But one day, I promise you'll be free from your father's abuse and cruelty, even if it kills me. I will not break the other half of my promise I made to your mother. I may have failed her, but I won't fail you."

I wipe the remains of my tears away roughly, noticing how sad talking about my mother is for him.

Was there more going on between them?

Now isn't the time to ask, so I put that question to the back of my mind, at least for now.

"Trust no one, Harper. I don't know why there's a sudden change in your father or if anything's happened, but I'll find out." Evan seems rattled, and that's unlike him.

His determination is applaudable, and I believe him. More importantly, I know I can trust him. My mother once did, so that's enough for me. From a very young age, I forged a bond with Evan. He was always around my mother, caring for her and driving us places when my father was too busy. Evan's eyes were always caring. For a tall well-built man, I want to say in his mid-fifties, he's in extremely good shape, someone to be feared, yet I never felt scared around him. He makes me feel safe, something my father never does. In some ways, Evan was more of a father figure in my life than my real one.

"Does this have something to do with the meeting he had last night?" I ask.

That gains his interest. "Could be. Was that meeting any different from the others?"

Depths of Deceit

"Well, he met up with two guys I've never seen before, but what rattled him more was the unwanted guest." I act like I don't know anything about him.

He grips my arm, not enough to hurt me, but it still catches me off guard. "Who, Harper?" His tone changes to one of desperation.

I narrow my eyes, doubt creeping in on me. "How do I know I can really trust you?"

"Would I be telling you this if you couldn't? I'm trusting you with my life here. You need to do the same."

He's right. I could easily go to my father and tell him what Evan just told me, but I won't. It could get him killed like he's just pointed out, and Evan has been nothing but kind to me.

I'm swayed towards trusting him again. "Someone called Knox," I say like it's no one of importance, but from the way Evan's eyes almost fall from his head, I'd say Keanu Knox is very important, and not in a good way.

"That explains a lot."

"For you maybe, but not for me."

"I don't have time to explain everything right now, but I will, I promise. I'm still trying to piece some things together myself. I get the feeling your father isn't being straight with me about certain parts of the business, but don't worry about that. Just try to keep your head down." He looks around the wall. "It's clear. Go." He urges me out from hiding with a gentle push on my back. I walk the way I intended before he stopped me, only to be stopped again when he whispers my name. "Harper, this conversation never happened."

I give him a firm nod and briskly walk to my room.

If Evan thinks something is off, then it most definitely is. Something weird must be going on and I want to know what. But it's not like I can just walk up to my father and demand answers.

If my suspicions are correct, then there's only one person who can give them to me and, one way or another, I'll find out.

CHAPTER 7

KEANU

I'm in the office, struggling to find what I'm looking for. I know it's here somewhere. I've turned the whole office upside down trying to find it, and I'm starting to lose my patience, but I can't give up. It's important.

There's a knock on the door. "Yeah?" I yell, not bothering to look up.

"You having a midlife crisis?" Lincoln asks.

I pop my head up over the desk and look at him with a raised eyebrow. "I'm thirty, Linc. So, no. What's up?" I continue with my search.

"Nothing much. I have guys watching Cheetos around the clock, and Yates has managed to hack into the club's security system. He's on constant surveillance duty."

That grabs my attention.

Yates is the newest member of my team. He's a computer wiz, and a great one, but he's young and inexperienced. He's only twenty-two, but Lincoln says he's up for the task. I haven't asked Lincoln where he found the lad, but I don't need to. Lincoln's never failed me before. He knows if shit hits the fan where Yates is concerned, he'll take the fall. That was the deal I made with him and it still stands. This is the time for Yates to prove his worth to me. I guess time will tell.

Depths of Deceit

"Seriously, Keanu. What're you doing? It looks like a fucking bomb went off in here," Lincoln says, taking in the mess I've created.

"I'm looking for something, so don't just stand there. Help me look."

"And what am I looking for?"

"How the hell am I meant to know? Just something. You'll know when you see it."

"At least give me a clue." He steps over a pile of folders and loose paper.

"My father kept notes on every enemy he made. I know he's got one on Geoffrey, but I can't find it. It wasn't with the rest of the files." I point to the pile he's just stepped over.

"That's odd." Lincoln begins shifting through some stuff on the desk. I take a break and throw myself in the chair that sits behind the desk.

"I don't need you to tell me what I already know. I need you to help me figure out why and where it could be." I know I'm taking my anger out on him, and the fact he doesn't bite back tells me he gets it.

"Is there anything that looks out of place?"

I hold my hands up, circling the mess around us. "Erm, I'd say yes."

"I meant before you went on a paper-throwing bender." He rolls his eyes.

"No. Everything was how my father left it. I was busy trying to keep the estate going and finding Tillie. I haven't got around to redecorating the office."

"Have you checked everywhere?"

"Yeah, unless he's got a hidden wall I don't know about," I joke, but Lincoln doesn't laugh with me. "You think he has a hidden wall?"

"Your father was ruthless at keeping anything personal from his enemies. It wouldn't surprise me."

I nod, filled with a new purpose. I jump out of the recliner and begin scanning the room, searching for anything that seems unusual. Nothing jumps out at me.

"Since when did your father like fishing?" Lincoln asks from behind me. I spin around and find him at my father's cabinet where the good liquor is held.

"He didn't," I tell him as I spot the same thing Lincoln did.

On the middle shelf is a photo of my father with a man I don't know. They're holding fishing rods in one hand and both pointing off to the right. I screw my face up, confused about why he'd have this in his office.

"You know the guy in the photo?" Lincoln questions.

"No. And I've never seen that picture before. My father must have put it there before he died. How did I miss that?" I pick the frame up and look closer. There's got to be a reason this particular photo was placed there.

"Anything clicking with you yet?"

I wave my hand at him. "Quiet. I'm thinking."

He silently backs away, letting me do what I do best. Figure shit out.

I'm drawn to the way they're standing. If it was just one of them pointing at something, it would be normal, but the fact that both of them are pointing in the same direction... it's got to mean something.

I place the frame back down, in the exact position it was in before, and stand back. It takes me a moment, but I think I've finally figured it out.

"Got something," I announce. I follow the direction of where my father is pointing and come to the wall above the door. To anyone else it would be a dead end, but not for me. Above the door is a small vent.

"Linc, grab me a chair," I instruct.

He grabs the overturned chair, pushing it towards me. "What's the chair for?"

I don't reply. Instead, I place the chair by the door and climb. The vent is held on by tiny screws, but when I touch one, it moves. It mustn't have been screwed back in properly the last time it was opened. I pull the vent off and hand it to Lincoln, who's now at my side. I peer inside and send a thank you to Father.

I know there's a reason he never told me about the vent. I get it. The less I knew, the better. I couldn't reveal to our enemies what I didn't know. However, I need to know now.

Depths of Deceit

"Bingo." I grab everything out of the vent and close it back up loosely.

I hand Lincoln a thick binder whilst I jump down.

"Fucking hell. I've never seen a folder this big before. What the fuck is all this?" He looks from the file to me like I know the answer already.

"If you give me a chance, I'll open it and find out." I take the folder from his hands with a shake of my head.

I swipe the desk clean, not caring about the other stuff as it drops and scatters on the floor. Lincoln follows me around the desk and peers down over my shoulder as I get comfortable and flip the file open.

"Jackpot." The name Geoffrey Benson beams up at me like a beacon. I begin to read the lines of my father's handwriting.

SON,

IF YOU'RE READING THIS, MY TIME HAS RUN OUT AND I'M NO LONGER *with you.*

THIS FOLDER HAS EVERYTHING I HAVE ON GEOFFREY BENSON.

He's wanted my turf and estate from as far back as I can remember. When I was Tillie's age, your grandfather told me all about Benson Senior, and believe me, it was nothing good.

From then on, my suspicions about Geoffrey Benson only heightened, so I continued to follow up on my instincts. That was when your sister went missing.

This man is into some dirty, fucked-up shit, and I have proof that he's involved in Tillie's disappearance and so much more.

Evan Porter is Benson's right-hand man. He can be trusted to a degree. He's keeping secrets from Benson, I just don't know what or why.

Benson also has a daughter, but I don't know how much she

knows. She's only ever appeared in public with her father on rare occasions.

Find out what she or Evan may know and you'll soon be on the right trail.

It's up to you now, Keanu. Take care of business like a true Knox and find my daughter. I know if anyone can do it, it's you.

Finish what I started.

I know I never told you this, but I'm proud of you, and I know your mother would be too.

Dad.

I slide the note my father left me to one side and start flipping through the documents my father has found on him. Details of his whereabouts. There must be months if not years of surveillance here. There are pictures of Benson with his men at different locations, including Cheetos.

We were on the right track after all.

"Fuck me, your father was thorough. Now I know where you get it from."

I smile on the inside. "This whole file needs going through with a fine tooth comb. Nothing is to be missed out. Everything needs to be looked at and looked at again. I want this son of a bitch, Lincoln." My voice rises with my words.

"You got it, boss." I hand over some pages and proceed to the back half, wondering what else my father found out.

That's where I find pictures of Harper Benson. My father was watching her too. Maybe he thought she would come in useful, just as I did. Jesus, we really are alike. I scan through the photos quickly to go undetected by Lincoln. The last thing I need is for him to rant at me about the dangers of finding this woman captivating. The fact it's now confirmed she is Benson's daughter will only add fuel to the fire. But I can't deny it to myself. She's the most beautiful woman I've ever laid eyes on. She's innocent, so pure, and when you live in a world full of darkness, it's a rare sight. But fuck... I want to explore that road.

I push the photos back together and stand abruptly. "There's something I need to do."

"You need me?"

"Not for this, no. You keep flipping through that. Call in Yates if you need to. Find me a lead we can use."

"Boss." He nods, and I head out of the office.

I know what I'm about to do is stupid, but that doesn't stop me from getting in my car.

What are the chances she'll be there?

CHAPTER 8

HARPER

I can't cope in this house any longer. The way my father is acting has everyone on edge, myself included. I need some air.

The last thing I want is for my father to come looking for me to take his frustration out on. I haven't slept all night, overthinking everything Evan told me. I slept with a kitchen knife underneath my pillow in my own home, for God's sake. I don't feel safe here anymore, not even in my room. If it wasn't for the fact that I don't have access to enough money, or the fearlessness I need I run from my father, I would have left by now. But in the back of my mind, thinking about what he'd do to me after hearing what Evan said, has me shuddering about what would happen if he caught me again.

Could my father really be capable of killing his own daughter?

I wouldn't put anything past that man. I may be his flesh and blood, but that's nothing to a man like him. Evan was right. My father cares more about his money and his empire falling apart than the one person he played a part in creating.

I gather some much-needed courage and seek him out in his office, praying he's in a better mood than he was early this morning.

I knock twice and wait for permission to enter.

"What!" my father bellows. I gulp.

There's no turning back now I've knocked. I peer around the door slowly,

Depths of Deceit

"I don't have all fucking-day," he adds.

"Sorry to both…"

"What do you want, Harper? Can't you tell I'm busy?" He gestures around the room. What I'm meant to be seeing, I don't know. He's lazily sitting behind his desk and drinking from a crystal tumbler. Nothing busy about that.

I notice Evan sitting quietly on the lounge seat off to the side of the room.

"I'm just going to head out for some fresh air." I might be twenty-five, but I still have to ask his permission on pretty much everything I do. I hate it, but it beats feeling his wrath. I live a very sheltered life for someone my age, with very limited freedom, but when pleasing your father is a day-to-day obligation just so you don't receive backhanders or blows to the body, I pretend my intellectual level is that of a sixteen-year-old. Don't get me wrong, there are things I've done that thankfully my father has never found out, but I'm a girl with needs and it's normal for a woman my age to find a man sexy and want to have sex with him. I'm not a nun. I've had boyfriends, but once they meet my dad it's pretty much over before it begins.

It's not like I have a choice. It's all about survival for me. He's my father and there's nowhere I can go where he wouldn't track me down. If that were the case, I'd be better off dead than dragged back after pulling a stunt like that. I shudder inwardly, horrified by the thought of what my life would become if I ever did find the courage to run away.

"And where might that be?" he asks, sipping his drink.

"The cafe I go to with Chelsea." It's not far from the estate and a place my father knows I go to a lot.

"Will Chelsea be there with you?"

"Erm, no. I think she's at work today." She's from a normal family and is allowed to do that. I wanted to say that out loud, but I know better.

"So, you want to go out, by yourself?" He arches his brow at me.

"Yes, if that's okay." He's looking at me like what I've said isn't a mundane thing to do.

"Your life sounds very… lonely and boring."

I only just stop myself from huffing and laughing in his face. I open my mouth before my brain can register what's happening. "If I didn't have a fa…"

Evan stands abruptly, halting me from finishing my sentence. One I'm glad I didn't get to finish. "I can take point today, Geoffrey. I'll get one of the guys to assist you with the matter at hand while I'm gone."

I watch as my father contemplates the idea. "Very well. You have an hour. I expect you back for dinner." With that said, he waves us off and continues sipping the brown liquid in his glass.

I feel Evan's hand on my back, pushing me out the door with urgency.

Once the door is sealed shut and we're a few feet away, Evan says, "Are you trying to piss your father off on purpose?"

"I wasn't thinking straight. I'm sorry." I'm telling the truth. I wasn't thinking clearly, because all I could think about whilst staring at my father was how he's capable of ending my life without a second thought. He's meant to love me, but he doesn't. I hate the person he's become, and more so for the person he's made me.

I looked into his eyes and not once did I see an ounce of love towards me. When I truly think about it, I don't feel my father ever loved me. I'm nothing but a burden to him.

Evan tapping my head with his finger brings my mind back to focus. "You need to use this more."

He's right. I need to use my brain. I'm smarter than my father thinks, and I should use that to my advantage.

"Don't give him a reason to hurt you any more than he already has."

"You're right. Sorry."

"Let's go before he changes his mind." I follow Evan through the front door and hop into his car as he unlocks the door. "Where to?" he asks when he starts the engine.

"The café," I told him.

"Double-checking. I thought you might have said that to your father as a cover for where you really want to go." He narrows his eyes at me.

Depths of Deceit

"And where would that be?"

"You tell me, Harper."

"Do you know something I don't?" I ask, getting straight to the point.

"That depends on you. Should I be worried about anything?"

He's playing games. He wants me to admit to something he doesn't know.

We head through the electric gates. "Other than my father potentially killing me one day, no," I say sarcastically.

"That is nothing to joke about, Harper. But I won't let that happen. I've told you. I made a promise and I'll keep it."

"Sorry. I don't want to make this harder for you. I can only imagine how this is for you. Lying to my father and going behind his back can't be an easy task."

"Stop apologising. And you let me worry about that."

For the remaining car ride, I keep my lips tightly shut. Evan is the only person in my life I feel like I trust apart from Chelsea, and I don't want that to change. He's all the hope I have left.

Ten minutes later, we're pulling up outside the little cafe I like. I wish I'd messaged Chelsea now, in the hope she wasn't working. But it's too late. I'll just have a coffee and a muffin and head back. At least I've managed to escape my father, even if it's only for an hour.

Evan follows me into the cafe wordlessly. When I find a table, he continues to walk past me and sits a couple of tables away, so I climb into the booth he chose instead.

"You can sit in your usual place, Harper. I can see you from here," he says, pointing to the seats Chelsea and I always sit in.

"That's okay. I'll sit with you." I smile awkwardly at him.

"I know your game, missy." He smirks. "But it's not happening."

"What game is that?" I ask, not giving anything away.

"You want to play twenty questions." He looks over my shoulder, and his smirk soon vanishes.

"Evan... are you..." I don't get to finish my sentence, because all of a sudden, I get a whiff of men's aftershave, and not just anyone's. It's the same delicious scent I smelt the other day.

I turn in my seat and spot the man in question. He's casually resting his arm across the back of the booth and he's staring right at me.

"Wow, if looks could kill." He doesn't take his eyes off me, but I look away. I quickly glance at Evan, who's about to blow a gasket. That's who his words are aimed at.

"What the fuck are you doing here, Keanu?" Evan grits through his teeth. I hear the disturbing sound of a gun being cocked. I glance under the table and notice Evan has his gun pointed at Keanu Knox.

"That's not important. What is… is Benson," he states before sliding into the booth beside me. "You can put that away, Evan. It's not needed," he adds, not at all fazed at having a gun aimed at him.

Evan pauses, studying Keanu before he pops the safety back on the gun, placing it in the holster inside his jacket.

"How did you know we'd be here?" Evan demands.

That is a very good question, and one I'm glad he's asking.

"I have my ways. You should know that better than anyone. You've been in the game long enough." Keanu chooses that moment to brush his huge thigh against mine.

I gasp silently. My eyes widen, but I quickly compose myself. When I glance at Keanu, he smirks at me.

He made that move on purpose. He wanted to see what my reaction would be.

But why?

He turns his attention back to Evan when he speaks.

"Too long, but longer than you. Showing up on Benson's side of town twice in one week. You got a death wish, boy?"

"As you can see, I'm not a boy anymore. I'm all man, and one you don't want to mess with."

I watch in satisfaction as they eye one another up. I can't take my eyes off Keanu.

Dammit, why am I finding him so attractive when he could be a danger to us?

"And why's that?" Evan crosses his arms over his chest, leaning back in his seat.

Depths of Deceit

"Because I can help you."

I swipe my gaze at Evan, his eyes are filled with something I've not seen for a while... hope.

Colour me intrigued.

CHAPTER 9

KEANU

I hung around outside the location I saw in the pictures, almost ready to give up, but then I spotted her. She's wearing a long white dress. She's... angelic. Her long brown hair is dancing in the wind as she walks with purpose inside the cafe. She's being escorted by a suit, but I can't quite make out who from here. He takes one last look around before entering with her. That's when I notice it's Evan. Benson's right-hand man. He's aged since the last time I saw him.

I'd waited in a car long enough. I was expecting to see Harper on her own, but to my dismay, she wasn't, but that doesn't stop me from heading inside, not fully thinking about my actions. Don't get me wrong, I'm packing and can handle myself. That's not what has me contemplating this idea. It's the brunette. Geoffrey kept her well hidden when she was growing up. I don't think I ever saw her when she was younger.

Evan's gaze lands on me and his defences go up, but that doesn't stop my stride, and I slide up to the booth like I've known them for years. It's less conspicuous that way, and I'll blend in. The smell of Harper's shampoo drifts over me and I ball my hands into fists under the table to stop myself from grabbing her and bending her over the table. That would fuck up my plans. I make small talk with Evan. He was shocked at seeing me. Good. I need Benson to know

Depths of Deceit

I'm sniffing around. To rattle him and have him making stupid mistakes.

I vaguely remember my father talking about Evan. It wasn't much, but I recall my father saying he was a good man, just like the letter did. I'm taking a massive gamble telling Evan I can help him. It's a stab in the dark, but it might be worth it in the end.

"You? Help me?" He laughs. "I highly doubt that. You have nothing I want or need."

I study him for a few seconds. He's shifting in his seat. Yeah, he's definitely worth looking into.

I came here hoping to talk to Harper one-on-one and gather any intel she could give me. I know she doesn't have the best relationship with her father, but is it enough to have her cross him? I still don't know, but I also wanted to get my daily fix of her, which I have, but seeing Evan here with her is like my father sending me a helping hand. The letter I found earlier mentioned him by name.

"I beg to differ. Anyway, I have business I need to attend to. I'll see you soon, Evan." I slide from the booth and take Harper's hand. I bring it to my lips and kiss it, like a gentleman.

I'm not a gentleman, but she doesn't need to know that. "It was a pleasure seeing you again, Harper." I throw her a wink and walk away without looking back.

I GET BACK TO THE ESTATE, HEADING STRAIGHT FOR MY OFFICE, AND IT looks like all hell has broken loose.

Yates is storming out of my office in a hurry, almost colliding with me. He manages to swing past me with no contact and throws an apology over his shoulder. I enter my office and Lincoln is leaning over my desk with the contents of the file splayed out in front of him; his hair is dishevelled. Clearly, he's been at this since I left him.

"What the fuck is going on?" I yell in frustration at the lack of respect from Yates and the fact Lincoln has made my office look worse than I did.

"Boss! I've been trying to call you. I think I've figured out what

Benson is up to." That piques my interest, and Yates and Lincoln are both forgiven.

"My phone died. What you got?" I round my desk and try to puzzle together what Lincoln might have already done.

"The two guys we saw with Benson at Cheetos… they're known for trafficking. Guns, drugs, people. The list is endless." He starts flipping through photos of the two guys. "These two are shady fuckers. So I kept digging, or should I say Yates did the digging. He's been on his laptop for hours pulling up any dirt he can on those two."

"And? What did you find?" I stand up straight.

"Boss, you're not going to like it."

"Give it to me straight, Lincoln."

"Yates backtracked the digital footprint bouncing from cell towers. It leads back to the club."

My jaw tightens and my nostrils flare. "Are you trying to tell me that those fuckers had something to do with Tillie going missing?"

"Possibly. We don't know for certain if Benson is orchestrating it. As far as we can tell, the two guys are broke, so they have to be getting funding from somewhere. I think it's Benson. We just need proof."

"There's no way Tillie was taken at random. She was a target all along. I just don't know why they would Keep her for so long." I don't address the elephant in the room. Tillie is not dead. She's still alive and will stay that way until I find her or her skeleton.

Lincoln nods. "I agree. I've just sent Yates back to study these two more and keep track of their movements."

I pat his shoulder. "Great work, Linc. And Yates too. Seems he's fitting right in."

"I wouldn't have got this far without him. He did all the legwork."

"Still, it's good intel." I perch in my chair, leaning back and rubbing my finger over the two days' worth of stubble.

I'm getting closer than I've ever been to finding out what happened to Tillie. It's been sixteen long months, but I'm hoping it's not sixteen months too late.

CHAPTER 10

HARPER

"We're leaving now," Evan announces as soon as Keanu Knox is gone. He's out of his seat and ushering me out of mine.

"I don't understand. What... what's going on?" My voice is jumpy. That might be because I'm still reeling from the after-effects of being so close to Keanu again.

"We need to get you back home."

"Why the rush? If it's because of Keanu, he's gone now."

"Harper, please just do as I'm asking and get in the car. You don't know Keanu Knox. He's dangerous. Potentially more dangerous than your father."

That has me pausing.

Could there be someone more dangerous than my father?

Geoffrey Benson is an evil man, so what does that make Keanu?

The devil?

I shudder at being in such close proximity to someone who's worse than my father, and his presence has rattled Evan.

"But my father... he'll know what to do, right? He can't be that menacing."

"Trust me. He's dangerous, that's all you need to know."

"Why?" I push.

"Why? Because he's a man on a fucking mission. He's out for

revenge, and when he gets it... he'll be more deadly than any man we've ever encountered."

There are so many questions I want to ask.

What's he seeking revenge for?

Does it have something to do with my father? If so, what?

I'm shaking just thinking about what he could be on our side of London for.

I'm tugged forward by my arm, ridding my mind of all thoughts before I'm practically thrown into the back of the car and Evan pulls out into oncoming traffic.

There's an urgency about this whole situation that I wasn't getting beforehand.

Seeing Keanu has put Evan on edge, and there aren't many people who can do that. Therefore, I'm starting to panic about the reality of what might come our way.

I peer up at Evan, who's eyeing me in the rear-view mirror. "Evan... you don't think my father is the reason for Keanu's sudden appearance, do you?" I gulp harshly, fearing what the answer might be.

"Honestly, I wouldn't know. But it's nothing for you to worry about. Let me tell your father what happened. You go straight to your room, do you hear me?" I stare, unblinking. "Harper, I said do you hear me?" Evan's voice echoes, causing me to jump in my seat.

"Yes, yes. Straight to my room."

Moments later, we're pulling up outside the gate. Evan enters the code, waiting for them to open. Once they do, we speed up the drive and park the car.

I go to open the door, but Evan stops me. "Remember what I said, Harper." His eyes show sadness. But at what? Is it aimed at me? Are things really that bad where Keanu is concerned?

I shudder at the thought of how my father will react. He wasn't best pleased when he saw him at Cheetos.

"I remember." I jump out of the car and follow closely behind Evan. That is until we come to my father's office. I have to pass by it to get to my room.

Evan pauses outside of the office door, giving me time to pass, which I'm grateful for. The last thing I want is my father taking his

Depths of Deceit

anger and frustration out on me. When I'm out of view, Evan knocks, and seconds later, he enters. I wait for what seems like a lifetime before the roaring sound of my father's voice strikes me, followed by a smashing noise. I'm guessing his tumbler of brandy was the thing that went flying. Whatever Evan told my father, it wasn't what he wanted to hear. It's not looking good, and immediately, my feet start moving.

Once I'm in the safety of my room, I breathe slowly and heavily, trying to calm my racing heart. It doesn't help my nerves because I start overthinking everything.

Why is my father so angry at the thought of Keanu Knox?

Does my father have something to do with Keanu seeking revenge?

It's the question that keeps coming back.

It's times like this that I really miss my mother. I'm scared of what my father will do next. She was my safety net. She'd keep me calm and tell me that everything would be okay.

She died when I was twelve, but it still feels like yesterday. Her death was unexpected and sudden. And to this day, I don't get why it had to be my mother. I often tried to ask my father what happened to her, but he shot me down every time, sometimes resorting to anger. Now, it's like she never existed. Once the funeral was over, all her stuff was removed from the house, and there's not a single photo of her in sight. I'm lucky I still have one. It's from my tenth birthday. We were standing outside the back of the compound when it was taken. The pair of us were smiling like we had all the time in the world together. Little did we know she'd be gone less than two years after that.

I have to hide the frame it's sitting in because I know if my father saw it, he'd blow a fuse and remove it. It's the only piece of her I have left, and I'll die before I let him take it from me. Many nights when I'm feeling low, afraid, or just want someone to talk to, I take it out of my drawer and speak to her. It's my little piece of solace.

The sound of my father's voice gets louder, followed by the thud of his feet along the floorboards. He's coming this way. I panic, not knowing what to do. I have less than thirty seconds to remove myself from the door and not give him a reason to be more pissed off. I sprint to my bed and grab my Kindle off the nightstand to act like I'm reading.

The door crashes open. I swing my head around when it rebounds off the wall, my gaze meeting my father's red face.

Why is he mad at me? I've done nothing wrong, but it doesn't stop me thinking, wondering if I've upset him but come up empty.

"I've got a job for you. One that isn't up for discussion." The hairs stand up on the back of my neck, and when I get a glimpse of Evan standing behind my father, looking over his shoulder at me with sorrow in his eyes, I know it's not good.

"What... what kind of job?" I stutter.

"One you'll do, no questions asked."

"Okay... but a job requires some details in order to fulfil it, right?"

My father marches over to me and backhands me across the face with so much force I fall off the side of the bed and hit the ground with a thud. My Kindle goes flying across the floor and I hope it's not broken. Pain slices up my cheek and the throbbing kicks in. I cradle my cheek.

"Less of the smart mouth. I've asked you to do something and you'll do it. I'm your father. What I say goes. Get up. You look weak down there. No Benson is weak. You're a fucking disgrace to this family and you don't deserve to have my name."

I stand on shaky legs, my knees knocking. I don't know what to do, so I just stand still, with my bed between us.

"Perhaps doing this job might earn you a little more respect from me," he sneers.

"Are you sure this plan will even work, Geoffrey?" Evan asks, gaining my father's attention

"Of course it'll work." He turns. "Why wouldn't it?"

"Well, Harper will be in unknown territory. Do you think she's ready for something like this?" Evan's words have me on edge.

Ready for what? What territory? What has my father planned for me?

"Then you'll teach her. Make her ready and make it fast." My father doesn't even glance back at me. Instead. he pushes past Evan and leaves the room.

I slump on the bed, deflated yet still shaking.

Depths of Deceit

The bed moves, and I jump in fright when Evan gently places his hand on my shoulder.

"I'm so sorry, Harper. I tried to make him see sense, but he was having none of it. He's planned a huge party and the guests... well, they aren't the sort of people you're used to interacting with, but for some reason he wants you to attend. I just don't understand why. I won't let anything happen to you, though. I promise."

I don't say a word. A few seconds later, Evan leaves my room, shutting the door as he goes.

Only when I'm alone do I let the tears fall.

What does my father want me to do?

CHAPTER 11

HARPER

I've spent the last four days learning the arts and crafts of seduction; at least, I think that's what Evan called it. I've changed into many sultry dresses, showing off parts of my body that would normally be covered. I've studied seduction using my voice to get me what I want and altered the way I walk and move to have a man falling to his knees.

I still don't know why I have to do all this, but Evan was under strict instructions from my father to have me ready in time.

I've been preparing for this evening all day. I've showered, dried, and curled my hair in loose waves, applied light makeup, and slipped into the dress Evan laid out for me.

I feel like a fraud. I don't look like myself at all.

Evan told me I need to play my part, be someone I'm not, and I'm definitely not this person. I don't like how it makes me feel. I've asked Evan what the point of all this is multiple times and I still haven't had a straight answer. Whenever I mention it, he looks away and changes the subject.

I'm still as much in the dark as I was when my father forced me to do this.

The day my father slapped me across the face was the last time I'd spoken to him or even seen him; not that I'm bothered by that. Evan

Depths of Deceit

has kept me busy and away from him as long as he could, and that's the one positive thing I'm taking from this charade.

I stare at myself in the mirror above my dresser and take in my appearance. I should feel beautiful, sexy, but I don't. I'm nothing but a puppet, and my father is the one pulling all the strings.

I don't know how much longer I can cope with being mistreated by him. I've put up with his behaviour for most of my life, taken his beatings, and not once have I fought back. I've never dared. It would only mean a bigger and harsher punishment, so what would have been the point?

There's a knock at the door, startling me. I take one last look at myself in the full-length mirror and turn.

"Come in." I know it's not my father or one of his most trusted goons as they never knock. I'm certain it's Evan.

The door opens, and as I expected, Evan enters. "Wow. You look just like your mother. Beautiful and radiating such elegance." I blush at his compliment. It's something I'm not used to. "I have something for you." He produces a black box from behind his back and walks towards me. "May I?" He points to my neck.

I nod. I turn towards the mirror again and he rounds my back. I hear the snap of the box before a gold chain is placed around my neck and an oval-shaped diamond glistens back at me.

"It was your mother's," he adds, fastening the clasp.

A small gasp leaves my lips. "I thought all my mother's belongings were removed from the house."

"They were. Everything except this. It was a gift from me, and I'm certain she would've wanted you to have it." He turns me around to face him.

I take another glance at the piece around my neck before looking up at him.

"How? Does my father even know about this necklace?" I start panicking, afraid my father will rip it off me the moment he sees it. I'm about to voice my thoughts, but Evan places his hands on the side of my arms.

"Your father has never seen this piece of jewellery, as your mother never wore it around him. She kept it hidden." I see a flash of sorrow in his eyes.

"You loved her, didn't you?"

He doesn't speak at first, clearly trying to compose himself. "It was complicated," he finally says.

"Did you ever tell her?" His eyes turn downcast, and I get my answer.

"She knew she meant a great deal to me, but I never got to tell her that I loved her and would risk everything I have for her. If she knew, it would have put her in more danger." A single tear falls down my cheek.

"The night I was going to tell her was the night she died, Harper. She phoned in complete distress and I got the feeling something went down between her and your father. I gave her a location and told her to meet me there, but she told me there was something she needed to do first." His arms drop from my shoulders. "She never made it to me. At first, I thought she changed her mind as the risks were high, not only for her, but you. Just coming to meet me would have gotten you both killed if your dad found out. I drank so much that night, drowning in misery. I didn't hear about the crash until the next morning when I walked into your father's office. What made it worse was the fact that you were also banged up." I listen intently as that part of my life is still a blur. "When your father broke the news about you both, not once did he shed a tear. I doubt he even loved your mother; not like I did. I would have done anything for her… for either of you. I could have made her happy, Harper. I couldn't stand watching your father disrespect her, but she wouldn't let me do anything about it. She knew what he'd do if he was to ever find out. He would have made me suffer by killing you and your mother in front of me. So I've kept the secret all my life, and I'll continue to do that until I know you're safe."

I stare at the man in front of me as tears roll down my face at the pain and heartache he's been through.

"You should have left when my mother died. There was no reason for you to stay."

"I've already told you, Harper. I promised your mother I would protect her, and I failed. I'm not about to make the same mistake where you're concerned. Until you're safe from Benson, where he can't find or harm you again, I'm sticking around. Only then will I be able to move on."

I can't control my emotions any longer. I launch myself at him and wrap my arms around his neck, squeezing him tight. At first, I think he's in shock because he just stands there, but he soon reciprocates and hugs me back.

We stay like that for what feels like an age, but in reality, it's a few seconds.

"Right, lady. Time to apply that war paint and make daddy dearest proud," he tells me, brushing a strand of hair from my face.

"Evan, who am I seducing? Is he dangerous?" I ask once more, hoping this time he'll give me more information so I can prepare better.

"Oh, Harper. I'm so sorry. There was only so much I could do without causing suspicion. If there was any other way I could get you out of this situation, believe me, I would. I need you to be brave. Can you do that for me?"

I don't get to answer him as we hear movement just outside my bedroom door. Evan puts some distance between us.

"Ah, you're ready. Good. I don't like to keep our guests waiting." My father's irritated voice filters to my ears. "She knows what's expected of her tonight?"

His question is aimed at Evan, like I'm not even in the room.

"She is. She'll play her part… just as you asked," Evan answers. I get the hint of resentment in his voice, but my father doesn't seem to catch it.

"She'd better. I need this to work in my favour. Let's go." He turns without looking my way. Evan offers me a smile of encouragement before following, leaving me no other choice but to do the same.

Here goes nothing.

CHAPTER 12

KEANU

"Something isn't right, Lincoln," I announce in the silence of the car.

"I get that feeling too, but we're prepared for whatever happens tonight."

"Benson knows I've been sniffing around, so why invite me here?"

"Beats me, but we're here, so I guess we'll find out soon enough." He points out the window at the estate in view. My driver pulls up at the gates and pushes the button for the intercom. Seconds later, it opens, and we're driving through. There are rows of cars lining up alongside one another. Expensive rides too. What kind of party is it? This isn't something I would ever do. Inviting your enemies to gather in one place. That's just asking for trouble. Are these people more associates of Benson's? That would make more sense, but associates of what exactly?

I step out of the car, glancing around. I only recognise a handful of the people here, and what they're known for has the hairs on the back of my neck rising. That's not a good sign.

"There's definitely a stench in the air, Lincoln." My senses are on high alert, looking out for potential threats.

"I smell it too, but we're here now, so we might as well so what it's about."

I huff loudly but nod. I'm not stupid. I wouldn't turn up some-

Depths of Deceit

where not knowing the ins and outs without a few of my men. I trust each of my men with different jobs, but more importantly, I trust them with my life. Tonight, alongside me are Lincoln, Yates, Sam, and Dean. If shit goes down, I know I'm covered at all angles.

I quickly pull my gun from the waistband at the back of my trousers, checking the magazine before tucking it in again. My Glock goes everywhere with me, along with my trusted knife, tucked away safely around my ankle.

"Let's get this over with. Watch your backs." My men swiftly move as one, flanking me on all sides until we're indoors.

My eyes are everywhere as I glance around the place. It's nothing like the Knox estate, which has been modified to make it more modern. This place looks like it hasn't had new décor for decades. It's old-fashioned, boring, and it leaves me feeling cold.

"Keanu Knox." Scrap that. The reason I'm feeling cold is because of the prick blocking my way.

"Benson." Every time I say this man's name it tastes like acid on my tongue.

"Glad you could make it." He smiles, but it's sadistic and fake.

"I'm sure you are," I say lazily, showing him how bored I am. "Why did you invite me here?"

He nods at something over my shoulder, but I'm not falling for that. I don't take my eyes off him, not even for a second.

I wasn't expecting anything else, but the fruity, heady scent that filters up my nose has my heart beating wildly.

"You remember my daughter, Harper?" Benson pulls Harper's arm harshly. Clearly, she was taking too long to make an appearance.

"Vaguely." I'm not that easily fazed, but there's something about this woman that has my heart skipping a beat and I can't put my finger on why. I don't look in Harper's direction. I know that's what Benson wants. Why else would he ask her over here? "Why the sudden invite?" I ask Benson again, ignoring Harper's assessing eyes.

"Well, you've been seen in my part of town a lot lately, so I thought we could talk it out, like real men." He thinks he's being clever by knowing my whereabouts, but I've not exactly been hiding that fact. I wanted him to know I was sniffing around, but I never thought it would get me this close. He's doing me a favour.

"You thought wrong."

"Yet you showed up anyway." He smirks.

"You're 'invite' was vague. I like vague. Makes putting the pieces together more fun." I cast my eyes on Harper when I finish speaking. It's the first time I've looked at her, and when I do, the wind is knocked out of me. She looks breathtaking in a long, black simple ball gown with thin strips, showcasing her slender neckline. It has a low front and as she turns her body away from her father, I just about make out the low dipped back exposing her delicate skin. She's wearing makeup, and her hair is styled. She's more put together tonight than she has been the other times I've seen her.

Benson is definitely up to something, and I suspect it involves his daughter.

Is she even aware that her father is using her for his own gain?

I highly doubt it. If so, she has a damn good poker face.

"Harper, why don't you show Keanu where he and his men can get something to drink? Knox, I'll be over shortly to discuss 'business'. But first, I have guests I need to greet." With that said, he walks away and speaks to some other men in suits.

Harper awkwardly links her arm around my bicep. "This way."

"Stay close, but give me room to work," I whisper to Lincoln.

"Boss."

I follow Harper to the bar. She perches on one of the stools, crossing her legs one way, uncrossing them, and crossing them again, making the dress slide and exposing one of her slender legs. I never noticed the split up the side before, and I'm having a hard time controlling my instincts.

I get the feeling she's trying to seduce me, but to what end? I keep those thoughts to myself to see how she plays this.

Why does this woman play havoc with my senses? Why is she so different from any other?

"Penny for your thoughts?" she asks as I take a seat beside her.

"Trust me, you wouldn't want to hear what's in my head," I tell her openly.

Depths of Deceit

"I'm sure it can't be that bad." I look across at her. She offers me a smile. It's soft and sweet, which is everything I'm not. I'm as far away from that as you can get.

"Bad, no. Fucked up... yes."

"I'm used to hearing fucked-up things. I'm sure nothing you say would shock me."

A glimpse of doubt passes through her eyes, "I highly doubt that, princess."

"What makes you think I'm a princess?" She rests her arm on the bar and places her head against her knuckles.

She wants to play games. I'm down for that. But there will only be one winner. "Do I really need to answer that? Take a look around." I watch her reaction. She suddenly appears sad, which soon disappears and is replaced with fear. I follow her line of sight and find her father in the distance not paying us any attention, too busy mingling for now. Her father clearly has a hold on her. Was she forced to interact with me tonight?

A bartender heads in our direction and takes our order.

"From your reaction, I'd say you're not a big fan of your father."

"My father is into some shady shit, and the fact you share a dislike towards him doesn't come as a shock considering you're his biggest enemy."

"Biggest enemy." I smirk.

Her neck twitches as she gulps. Perhaps she's shared more than she meant to. She fidgets in her seat.

Our drinks are placed in front of us, and Harper is way too eager to pick hers up.

"Why am I here, Harper?" I whirl the amber liquid around in the tumbler, impatiently waiting for her to answer.

"We're at a bar having a drink. Why else would you be here?"

She's being smart, just like she was the first time I was close to her in the ladies' room at Cheetos.

"That's not what I meant and you know it. Try again, and this time, I want the truth. There's a reason your father invited me here, and I think you know why."

She stares at me for a beat. "I don't know what you're talking about," she eventually says. "I'm just being polite and having a conversation with you."

I study her movements, looking for any sign she's lying. "Do I scare you, Harper?"

"Should you?"

"Yes. If you know what's good for you, then you will run." I move towards her, closing the distance between us.

"What... what if I don't want to?" She's stumbling over her words, completely unsure of herself.

"Then you'll be making a grave mistake, princess."

CHAPTER 13

HARPER

I honestly don't know how I've held myself together so far. The moment my father ushered me over to him and five men in tailored suits, I knew it was time for me to play my part, no matter how unsure I was of the reasons why.

It wasn't until I was at my father's side that I noticed the man standing toe-to-toe with him was none other than Keanu Knox, only this time, his eyes were as black as night. I'd never seen him look so murderous, and it was all aimed at my father.

My legs almost gave way, and if it wasn't for the death grip my father had on my arm, I'm pretty sure I'd have crumbled to the floor.

Keanu hadn't looked at me the whole time he was having a conversation with my father; if you could call it that. The hatred came off them in waves.

I was grateful when my father dismissed us. It gave me room to breathe as all I'd been doing since I left my room was charm the pants off everyone here tonight. I may have told Keanu I didn't know anything, but that wasn't entirely true. I knew I needed to seduce him. I just didn't know the full extent of why, but I had a job to do, and if I failed, my father would most definitely punish me. I shuddered at the thought, hoping Keanu didn't see it as he followed me to the bar.

His men were close by, but we were alone. I started the conversation simply, but it soon turned up a notch.

I'm openly gawking at him, then remember what he said.

"I've many regrets, Mr Knox," I said. "Made a few mistakes, but running from you isn't an option for me."

Something passes in his eyes, and I stand abruptly. I'm walking a fine line with Keanu and telling him more than I should.

He grabs my wrist, stopping me. "I suggest you sit your arse back down unless you wish for Daddy to see you failing at the one thing he's asked you to do tonight. I'm not stupid. Your father asked you to seduce me, didn't he?" His words are distasteful but spot on.

He's smart as well as handsome.

"You've just made your first mistake with me. You lied to me. Do you know what I do to people who lie to me?" I stare straight ahead, fearing the look he'll be giving me, and instead find my father watching us with narrowed eyes from across the room. "I kill them."

I gasp. Would he kill me?

Would it be more dignified than how my father would end my life? It doesn't matter what I do. I'll feel the wrath of either of these men.

I plaster on a fake smile for my father, enough to remove the narrow brow he was giving me, and sit back down on the stool.

I gather some much-needed courage and swing my gaze to Keanu's. He's really staring at me, trying to get a read on me. I had been given some guidance from Evan about what was expected of me. Be class and interact with the guests. Be seductive, when necessary, but I never anticipated that one of the guests would be someone like Keanu. How naive was I?

"Are you playing me, Harper?" he asks far too calmly.

I gulp but mask my fears the best I can. "What makes you think that?"

He shrugs. "I'm good at reading people."

"And you think you can read me?" I laugh softly.

"I know I can."

"You don't know anything about me." I turn my gaze away and take a sip of champagne from the flute.

"Are you underestimating my capability?"

"I don't know enough about you to make that kind of assumption, Mr Knox."

Depths of Deceit

He regards me intently. "You're not the same person you were days ago. No one changes their personality that quickly... unless..." I can feel my heart hammering against my chest and I've lost the ability to think clearly. "Unless they're pretending to be someone else." Keanu arches his brow. "So, I'll ask again, did your father put you up to this?" I hear the venom in his voice as he speaks about my father.

I finally find my voice. "I... I don't know what you're getting at, but you're wrong."

"Am I? Your father is using you as a pawn to get information out of me. He thinks I'll fall for your charm, doesn't he?"

He starts laughing uncontrollably, gaining unwanted attention from people; my father included.

"What? No. That's not true. I didn't even know you were going to be here tonight." My words are rushed as I try to explain he's got this all wrong. "Please, I'm telling the truth."

"Your father is pathetic. Did he really think this would work?"

"It's not like that. I was ordered to charm all of the guests here. I just assumed I was meant to do the same with you," I admit in desperation.

"Wait, what? So, all that... he asked you to do it with every person in this room that speaks to you?" He gives me a quizzical look.

I'm confused, so I get why he is too. "Yes. I don't understand why, but he's my father, and... of I don't... he'll..."

"Hurt you?"

"Yes, or worse." I have no fight left in me. What's the point? Keanu knew I wasn't acting like myself the moment we sat down at the bar. Why prolong my embarrassment? We lock gazes. "Please... I'm begging you. Don't ..."

He holds his hand up, cutting me off. "What is it you're begging me for? Not to let your father know I'm on to him, or are you begging me for something else?" He moves closer to me. "Tell me, Harper."

His face is only inches from mine, and I lose my train of thought and do something that not only shocks Keanu but myself. I lean forward and press my lips against his. It was the briefest of touches before he pulled back.

His eyes are wide and full of something sinister. He grits his teeth and squeezes his eyes closed.

"I'm... I'm so sorry. I shouldn't have done that." I have no idea what came over me. Panic maybe. Desire for this man that I truly know nothing about. Thankfully, my father isn't anywhere to be seen. I go to stand, but his hand on my leg stops me.

"Then why did you?" He slowly opens his eyes again.

"I... don't know."

"You shouldn't have done that. That was your second mistake."

"Keanu... I—" The next thing I know, his mouth connects with mine, and he kisses me bruisingly. I should pull away, but I don't. I kiss him back. The feeling is something I've never felt before. It's all-consuming.

He pulls away, leaving me breathless and in a daze.

"I hope my daughter hasn't bored you." My father's voice makes the hairs on my arms stand on end and has me pulling away from Keanu quicker than lightning.

"Father... I was just—"

"Save it. I have a room full of people to entertain tonight. Ones you should be mingling with too."

Keanu turns his attention towards my father. "Why so tense, Benson?" My whole body stiffens. Will he tell my father I screwed up? "Are you annoyed because I touched her? You afraid I'll taint her?" Keanu smirks at him.

"Harper, go find Evan. Keanu and I need to have a little chat." I give Keanu one last look before leaving, hoping he doesn't tell my father that his plan failed.

I reach Evan on the opposite side of the room and watch the exchange between my father and Keanu closely. My father's back is facing me, so I don't know what mood he'll be in when he's eventually alone with me.

"Evan, I think I fucked up," I whisper, not taking my eyes off Keanu as he stands, looming over my father.

"How so?" he asks.

"Well, for starters, Keanu knew the play before I even sat down." I bow my head, waiting for his disappointment.

Depths of Deceit

"I doubt that even matters." Evan turns on his heels, facing me, so I do the same. "I've been watching you tonight. You did exactly what your father asked of you. He wanted you to interact with as many people as possible, and you did that. I just don't understand why yet." He frowns before shaking his head. "I also watched your every move with Keanu. I think he was fascinated with you before tonight."

My eyes widen in surprise. Evan must be wrong. There's no way a man like Keanu would find anything about me fascinating. I open my mouth to ask Evan more, but once again, my father halts me.

"Evan… it's time." I look from my father to Evan, clearly missing something. I've done my part. I might have failed. Hell, I might have succeeded if Evan's words are anything to go by, so what is it time for now?

Evan's face turns oddly resentful towards my father, but it disappears as quickly as it appeared.

What the hell is that all about?

I'm spinning in a full circle, looking for Keanu or one of his men, but they're nowhere to be seen.

Did my father ask him to leave?

Was Keanu done with my lies and the fact I was deceiving him?

I stand on the spot while my father ascends the staircase and Evan disappears through a set of doors. My father addresses the room, thanking them all for joining him and some other bullshit, but I block it out, continuing my search for Keanu. I put on a fake smile; in case my father still wants me to play my part.

That's when I hear my father's most disturbing words yet.

I can't believe what I'm hearing. But that's not the worst. What I'm seeing is heartbreaking and hard to watch. Evan and another of my father's men start escorting young girls into the room and line them up in between my father and the guests. The girls don't quite seem to be with it, like they've been highly dosed with something.

Are they even aware of what's happening to them?

I want to vomit so bad.

How can my father stoop this low?

It makes me sick to think all these people are here for the sole purpose of these girls, and my father had me engage with them and be sultry...

Is that why Keanu was here?

The noise around the room intensifies.

Why are these people interested in young girls?

My question soon gets answered.

"Come and claim your goods," my father shouts to the old man at the back of the room. He just sold a young girl off. She can't be more than sixteen.

I knew my father was into some shady stuff, but never in my life would I have said he was into human trafficking.

I have no clue what to do. I want to run away from the situation, but I can't. I have nowhere to go. I have to do what is expected of me, or who knows what will happen to me?

Evan catches my eye from his position next to my father. He gives me a slight head nod as he no doubt sees the look of fear on my face.

Stay strong, Harper.

I look around the room, taking in the excitement on all the men's faces. Some women's too. How can they be enjoying this? Don't they want to help those girls? Nothing makes any sense. To think I was chatting and charming these people at my father's request...

I gasp, covering my mouth quickly as the mystery finally becomes clear.

No... My father wouldn't, would he?

Everything turns silent as my eyes whip from one face to another. My heart is already racing from all these things I've just learnt my father is involved in, but now my lungs feel like they're constricting from lack of air. I need to get out of here.

My feet start moving of their own accord, but when I'm about to burst through the back door, my father's voice stops me.

"Harper, my dear. Where are you going? You're about to miss the ending. Come up here."

I freeze. His sweet endearment fills me with dread. He never calls me 'dear', not even when he's socialising.

"Don't be shy now. Come up here."

I turn around slowly. A gap is made in the throng of bodies, and I

Depths of Deceit

have no choice but to comply. I walk on hesitant legs, eventually coming to a standstill at my father's side.

My heart is racing and my mind is working overtime at what my father could possibly do next. I'm struggling to breathe.

"For the main event, my daughter... Harper Benson," my father starts. "Bidding starts at one hundred thousand."

The room erupts.

I swing my body around and face the person who gave me life. The only person I have left who is supposed to love me.

"Father? What... what are you doing?" I can't hold back my tears any longer.

"As you can see, she's defiant and needs whipping into shape," he continues, showing no emotion at the thought of letting me go. I'm getting nothing from him, so I turn to Evan, hoping he will help me. He looks just as shocked as me.

"Evan... please. Don't let him do this." I fall into his arms.

"I'm sorry," he whispers in my ear. My father is busy smiling at the money rolling in for me.

"You're sorry. Did you know this was his plan?"

"Of course I didn't. But I promise I'll do what I can to help you."

"How are you going to do that if you have no clue where I am?"

"I'll figure something out"

"Don't bother. You lied to me and my mother!" He pulls back from me like I've burnt him; that's when I see the hurt I've caused him, but I don't care.

How could he let this happen to me?

CHAPTER 14

KEANU

Just when I thought this evening couldn't get any weirder, Benson slumps down in the seat recently vacated by Harper.

"What is it you're looking for Keanu? Why are you hanging around in Camden? He knocks on the bar, gaining the bartender's attention. Moments later, two shot glasses appear before him.

"What makes you think I'm looking for anything? I might just like Camden." I smirk when he turns to face me. Just the sight of him and being this close to him has me wanting to reach behind my back, pull my gun free, and shoot the fucker between the eyes.

"I know your men have been to a couple of my establishments. You just so happen to like Mexican food?" He arches his brow.

"As a matter of fact, yeah."

"It stops now. I have nothing you need here. You won't find what you're looking for."

"Actually, I've found more than I was looking for."

He huffs. "What, my daughter? Please, she wouldn't be able to satisfy a man like you for long, and you'll never see her again after tonight."

For the first time since he started speaking, I'm interested in what he has to say. "Why is that?"

"None of your concern. I didn't have to ask you here, tonight, but I

Depths of Deceit

did as a sign of respect to do this face to face. Stay in your own lane. Unless you want a war."

He thinks he's got this shit handled. He hasn't. I stand tall, leaning over him, causing him to get defensive, "You started a war a long time ago. You just don't have the balls to finish it." I reach for the shot glass and down the liquid. "I'll be seeing you around, Benson."

I don't stick around. I've seen and heard enough. I address my men who follow without a backwards glance. I catch of glimpse of Harper, who appears to be on tenterhooks. Probably wondering what I told her father. She needed worry, I wouldn't give that man the satisfaction of laying a hand on her at my expense.

We breach the entrance without any drama.

"Did you find out why you were asked here?" Lincoln asks.

"Just Benson, trying to appear as he's got it all together by threatening me." I shrug, not at all concerned about his threat. He's feeling the pressure of my presence.

"He threatened you. And you're just going to let it slide?"

I stop abruptly, turn, and get all up in his business, "It was an idle threat, Lincoln. One I'm paying no mind to because it doesn't matter. He can threaten me all he wants; I'm not going to back down. You should know me better than that." I see nothing but respect in Lincoln's eyes. Loyal to a fault, but I wouldn't be where I am today if it wasn't for him. I spin on my heels, not giving them any direction. It's not needed, they follow instinctively anyway.

Benson will never admit to me what he's involved in, but he's not the only person in his organisation. Someone knows something, and I'm not leaving here without something for my troubles.

We head back to the main hall as a round of high-pitched cheering begins.

What the fuck is going on in there that wasn't before?

As I enter, I hear the words I never thought I would in my lifetime. This most definitely isn't my lane, but I'm finding out exactly what lane Benson is in and I don't fucking like it. All his secrets have been unravelled and I'm on to him, but I never expected it to be this extreme.

I've just walked in on Benson auctioning off his only daughter. The room erupts with bids. It makes me sick.

I zone in Benson and all I see is blackness. Then I look at Harper as she pleads. I know I need to be careful as my actions here will have consequences and we could be out-numbered. I'm about to risk my life or that of my men.

I'm in a room full of shady motherfuckers, but I can't be the raging monster I know I can be when pushed too far.

I've done some sick, fucked-up things in my time, but nothing on this level. We don't harm, sell, or kill women.

Why would Benson do this?

He's more fucked in the head than I originally thought. Even Evan's finding it hard not to show his disgust, but when our eyes meet, I see the shock and sickness like he's mirroring my own.

Why wouldn't Benson inform his right-hand man of his plans for this evening?

Was Benson doing this off his own back, not informing those closest to him?

Maybe he's got doubts about Evan's loyalty.

It was an undoubted shock for everyone in this room, none more so than Harper Benson herself, but that doesn't stop the disturbing fuckers bidding, not even questioning Benson's motives.

It's a bold move from Benson. Is it all about the money? Has he finally had enough of using Harper as his personal punching bag?

Does he even have a heart?

At least the other girls were drugged and unaware of what was happening to them. Harper is feeling every emotion as she stands by her father, begging him to stop what he's doing. I can hear her screams from the back of the room.

"Stop it. Please, Father. I'll do better," she cries.

"This is some fucked-up shit." Lincoln speaks at my side, not taking his eyes off what is happening around us.

"Sold!"

I'm scanning the room to see who the buyer is, but I can't see shit. "Fuck."

"Who are you looking for?" Lincoln asks, coming to stand in front

Depths of Deceit

of me and blocking my view. I can hear Harper's screams as she's forced out of the room.

"Get out of my way, Lincoln. This is a fucking shit show, but it means we're on the right doorstep where Tillie is concerned. That prick knows what happened to her. I just know it. You can't say he's not after what you've just witnessed. This wouldn't be going down if we were on my turf."

"But we're not in your part of town, boss," Yates pipes up, pissing me off more. I glare at him. He holds his hands up.

"No, but it's a little close to home for me. Why am I only just learning this now? You've been watching Benson for days now and nothing odd flagged up?" I shout.

"Boss, we..."

"We're getting out of here," I announce, not waiting for them to follow. I know they'll be behind me in seconds anyway. We make it out of the main room undetected. The last thing I want is Benson's slimy grin in my face. "Bring the car around," I demand.

"On it, boss." Dean darts off with Sam, leaving me with Yates and Lincoln.

I feel Lincoln's eyes on me. "What?"

"Is there something else you need to say?" he asks.

"If there was, I'd say it."

He doesn't say anything else while we wait for the car to pull up. It doesn't take long for Dean and Sam to appear in the Range Rover. I'm just about to get in when I hear my name being called.

"Knox." I turn to see Evan fast approaching. My men move fast, ready for any threat. "Tell your men to stand down." He holds his hands up.

I raise my arm, instructing my men to relax. They do it, but reluctantly. "What do you want, Evan?"

"I don't have time to explain everything right now. But I need a favour, and only you can help me."

"You're asking me for help?"

"Yes."

I laugh sarcastically. "You're ludicrous if you think I'm going to help you after what I've just witnessed," I spit, truly revolted.

"I didn't know he was going to offer up his... Harper. I swear to you, I was as much in the dark as you were. I wish no harm to Harper. That's why I need your help." He steps closer. "In the cafe that day... you said you could help me. I didn't understand why, and I still don't. But if you help me, then I'll help you."

I did say I could help him, but not with this. I meant more for his benefit. If what my father found out about Evan, knowing he was a good man, means he doesn't want to live this life. I'd have helped him out, in exchange for something, obviously. Which had me wondering how he was working for someone like Benson. But I'm intrigued at what he's thinking. "Help me how?"

"I'll tell you what I know." My whole body tenses. He nods, confirming what I'm thinking.

"I'm no fool, Evan." I bare my teeth at him.

"And neither am I. I know why you've been hanging around Camden. Your father was doing the same. I know it's got something to do with Tillie's disappearance. I'll help you nail it all to Benson. You have my word, Knox. Please, I just need you to trust me," he says calmly.

"I don't trust easily. You have to earn it."

"Then let me do that. Just say you'll help me," he begs.

I'm sceptical about what he wants from me, but I know a begging man who has nothing to lose has nothing to gain. That is the only reason I'm even considering helping him. "If I get a whiff of bullshit, or I feel like I'm being played, it'll be my bullet that pierces your forehead. Are we clear?"

"Crystal. So you'll help me?" he asks.

"Yes, I'll help you." I don't know what I'm agreeing to, but if it helps me get what I want, then so be it.

I follow Evan back inside, instructing my men to stay by the car as I'm not intending to be long. As I knew he would, Lincoln follows me.

"We need to do this discreetly and fast. I know all funds have been wired across for the girls, and if I know Benson, that includes Harper. We need to approach the buyer without Benson knowing. For this to work, I can't play a helping hand in that, Knox. This has got to be done entirely on your own," Evan says.

Depths of Deceit

"Why do I need to approach one of the buyers?" I'm starting to get the feeling I'm already being played.

"Not just any buyer... the gentleman that bought Harper."

"Come again?" I stop my stride.

Evan stops and spins around, his hand on a door handle leading from the main room down a hall to a more secluded room. "You're going to buy Harper back." The words roll off his tongue with ease.

"Like fuck I am."

"Keep it down or you'll draw attention. You offered to help me. This is what I'm asking."

"I didn't think I'd be dealing with some fucked-up trafficking ring when I agreed to help you. I want no part in this. I deal with drugs, weapons, and I own legit businesses, not this shit." I turn around and head for the exit.

"Please, Knox. I made a promise to protect her. I know your father's rule when it comes to women. I'm hoping that's something he passed on to you when you took over. If she goes off with that buyer, he'll drug her up and she'll be used as a sex worker. She'll be treated worse than the dogs they own, and she'll lose the small amount of dignity she has left." My feet stop moving, every word he speaks making my rage rise to the surface. "I can't let that happen to her. I'd rather kill her myself than watch her become a shell of the person I care about. It's no life for her, Keanu."

My head drops and I huff loudly, not believing what I'm about to do. If it was someone other than Harper, would I be helping him? Probably not. She's on my radar now. I turn and head back towards him.

"Don't do this, Keanu," Lincoln says, grabbing my arm, trying to stop me.

"You know I have to." I remove his hand from my arm. "I need to do this for her, Lincoln." He lowers his head, knowing my reasons. If this is what my sister went through, then Harper's fate will be the same. I can't let that happen again.

I address Evan. "If I do this, I want every-fucking-thing. No weak information just to buy yourself more time. If Benson is involved, I want everything you have on that fucker to bring him down." I don't leave him room to argue.

"You'll have it all."

I study him, looking for any signs of him lying. His features don't falter once. "Tell me who I need to speak to, a bit about him, and I'll do the rest."

I listen intently as Evan begins telling me everything I need to know for his plan to work.

"Remember, you need to get in and out as quickly as possible. I'll keep Benson busy as long as I can," Evan urges.

"This is what I do, Evan. I have a knack for persuading people." With that said, I head into the room where all the buyers are lounging, sipping champagne, and congratulating one another. It makes me feel sick. I quickly glance at Lincoln at my side, and if his face is anything to go by, he's not liking being in this room any more than me. I scan the room and find the man I'm looking for——not that it was hard. He's surrounded by people praising him for being brave enough to not only bid on the princess of Benson's empire, but win her.

Who are these sick and pathetic people?

I've heard enough. I shove my way through the scumbags and come face to face with the biggest one of them all.

He narrows his eyes. "Can I help you?" he asks, clearly not knowing who I am.

"I think it's more how I can help you, Mr Gusto."

"And you are…"

"Knox. Keanu Knox." I watch as his eyes widen. "I'll take that as a sign you know exactly who I am and I'll let your rudeness pass this once as I'm on a tight schedule."

"What can I do for you, Mr Knox?"

"I'll get straight to the point. The girl you brought. I want her." I can't believe the words that are coming out of my mouth. My father would be turning in his grave at me just being in the room with these people, let alone buying.

He almost spits his champagne at me. "You're joking? Since when have you taken an interest in girls?" He laughs.

Depths of Deceit

I'm struggling to rein in my temper. "I haven't. Just the one you happened to bid on." I smile sarcastically.

"I won her fair and square. I——"

He's saying it like he won a fucking raffle. I cut him off, bored with him and this whole conversation. "I'll add twenty percent on top of what you paid." I don't hesitate. I sense Lincoln is more reluctant about my offer.

"Twenty percent?" Mr Gusto repeats.

"Yes. Do we have a deal?"

"No. She's a mafia princess. She'll make me a hefty profit on what I have planned for her."

I hide my disgust for this man well. Every instinct I have is telling me to reach for my gun and kill every single person in this room, but if I want what Evan is offering, I need to do this his way. Plus, there could be innocent bystanders here. I highly doubt it, but I won't take that chance.

"Maybe, but for how long? The novelty of who she is will soon wear off."

I watch as he weighs up his options. "Nah. I think I'll stick with Daddy's little princess."

"You sure about that? You've just said it yourself. She's Daddy's little princess. Why would he offer up his own daughter? I wouldn't trust the deal, even if you've paid. What's stopping him from taking her back? It's not like you signed a contract or anything, right?" I pretend it's his best interests that I'm worried about, but really, I'm after intel. Is there a paper trail for this shit?

He shakes his head, seeming a little worried. "You'd have paid all the money and it'll all be for nothing. You could get a couple weeks or a year max out of her before Benson comes knocking. Which he will. Are you prepared to take that risk? Is she really worth the trouble?"

"I never thought about that. I know I've paid for her so, technically, she'll be mine to with as I please, but when blood is involved… and no official contract."

"Exactly, and I don't think anyone is going to speak out and say they witnessed the sale of a human being, are they?" I push further.

"Oh, Jesus, no. I know I wouldn't. Hmmm, it could get messy."

I make a point of checking my watch, "My offer just dropped five percent. Once I walk out that door, my offer will have expired." I turn as if I'm about to walk away. When he doesn't answer, I continue. I'm about to reach for the handle of the door when I hear him.

"Wait."

I hide my smirk and spin around.

"You have a deal, on the stipulation that if there's a fall-out between you and Benson over her, I'm no part of it."

This guy is pathetic and doesn't have a backbone. "You have a deal. Lincoln?" Lincoln digs in his jacket pocket for his phone. "Wire him the money." It takes no more than two minutes for Lincoln to load everything up and Mr Gusto to enter his details before he pockets his phone again. Evan already told me the price the buyer paid for Harper, so Lincoln gets it done quickly.

"Done, boss."

I nod. "I'd say it was a pleasure doing business with you, but I'd be lying. Enjoy the rest of your evening."

I spot Evan in talks with Benson on the way out of the main entrance. I give him a swift nod, letting him know it's done, and head out to my men leaning on the hood of the vehicle, waiting for Evan to complete the rest. I can't wait to get home so I can wash the filth off my skin from spending even a second in that room.

Waiting isn't something I'm good at, but under these circumstances, I'll be patient. In the end, I'll get what I want and Evan will hold up his end of the deal if he knows what's good for him.

CHAPTER 15

HARPER

I've been ushered into a side room with all the other girls that have been sold to the willing sickos. Even though they're all high on something, they still look as panicked and scared as I do.

My father has sold me off like a piece of meat at a farmers' market. Does blood not mean anything at all?

Everything feels surreal. I no longer have control over my own body. My chest gets tighter with each breath I take. My vision begins to blur as tears spring to my eyes. My legs turn to jelly, causing my knees to buckle underneath me. I feel myself falling to the ground and I can't stop myself.

I feel strong hands catch my fall. I look up and find Evan's worried face. Even though the room is spinning, I can see how stressed he looks.

"Christ Almighty. Harper, are you okay?" He stands me back up on my feet but doesn't let me go. I get my bearings back before I speak, only able to jerk my head in a sort of nodding motion in answer to him.

A door across the room opens, taking my attention from my panic-stricken mind for a split second.

Is this it?
Is it him?
Has he come to claim me already?

I was hoping to find a way out of this mess before my buyer came to collect me.

I start to shake uncontrollably as my new reality becomes fully apparent. When I see that it's not my buyer, I turn back to Evan with pleading eyes.

"Don't let him do this. Please, Evan. Help me," I beg with fresh tears streaming down my hot cheeks.

"I'm so sorry, Harper. I never anticipated your father would stoop this low, but don't worry. I've fixed it in our favour. But you will be going off with a buyer tonight. There's nothing I can do to change that."

What the fuck does that mean? Anger boils up in my gut.

"Evan, no. Please, you promised," I plead.

"Harper, you have to do this. You have to go. Be brave and do this for me. I promise you everything will be all right. I won't let any harm come to you. You have to trust me. Can you do that?" He grips my shoulders and bends to my level, looking directly into my eyes as he tries to convey how important this is.

I believe him when he says he was none of the wiser to my father's plans tonight. "Okay, I trust you." I wipe the tears from my face with the backs of my hands. "Doesn't mean I have to like it." I try to stand tall and compose myself as another dirty old man walks in to claim his girl.

"Good girl. Come on. I have arranged to make the handoff myself," Evan tells me as he places his hand on my lower back, ready to guide me to my fate. A fate I know nothing of. I could be heading towards danger and have no clue. No, I can't think like that. Evan wouldn't put me in harm's way. He wouldn't be risking everything now to get me out of here and with someone else. There's got to be a method to this madness.

"Can I at least go pack first?" I think quickly of the things I have to have with me; everything else can stay.

"No, you don't have time. I have to get you to the buyer."

"At least let me grab the photo of my mother. That's all I have left of her. I can't leave her behind."

Evan huffs out a huge breath of frustration at my request. "Shit!

Depths of Deceit

You're going to be the death of me. Stay here. I'll go get it." I tell him where he can find my one and only hidden treasure and find a corner in the shadows to hide until he comes back for me. I could use this as an opportunity to escape, but where would I go and what would I do? There isn't a single person I can trust other than Evan.

One by one, the other girls leave the room until there is only a handful left. I dread to think what will become of their lives once they leave my father's estate.

Where have they come from?

Someone must know they're missing.

My nerves are shot to pieces by the time Evan reappears, opening his suit jacket to show me he's got my most prized possession.

"Oh my God, thank you. I couldn't go through with this without her by my side." His smile is genuine but sad. I can see in his sorrowful eyes that he misses her as much as I do. I throw my arms around his neck, taking him by surprise. "Thank you for everything," I say into his chest.

"Don't thank me just yet." His phone buzzes in his inner pocket where my head rests, making me jump away from him. He takes a quick peek. "He's waiting. It's time to go. Be strong. I'll be in touch, I promise." His words make me freeze. My feet are no longer able to move.

"I can't do this." Fear once again takes over.

"Yes, you can. You've got this. Now come with me before your father notices something may be wrong."

That gets my feet moving.

I follow Evan silently towards the entrance of the building but come to a halt when my father's voice catches my attention. In that moment, I think he might have changed his mind, giving me hope, but that soon crushes under the weight of despair when I see him with my original buyer.

"You can't do that," my father proclaims loudly.

"Yes, I can. The funds have already been paid to you, so what I choose to do after that is up to me. Plus, he offered me more than I paid for her," the buyer replies.

"Who did? I want to speak to them," my father bellows. It then occurs to me, if my buyer is there with my father, who is Evan leading me to? Who does the waiting car with blacked-out windows belong to?

Does Evan even know?

I don't have to wait for long. The back passenger door is flung open and a familiar figure steps out. I gasp, earning the unwanted attention of my father. This isn't going to go well.

"Go. I'll deal with your father. Take care of yourself, Harper. I'll see you again soon. I promise." He kisses the top of my head.

Apprehension takes over as doubt and anxiety slice through me with every slow step I take towards the man who holds my future in his hands.

CHAPTER 16

KEANU

"You ready, boss?" Sam questions as I take my seat in the back.

"Not yet. We'll have another passenger on the way home," I say as three confused faces stare back at me.

"Keanu, are you sure about this? You've done some crazy shit in your time but, man, this one tops them all." My head spins towards Lincoln, who's sitting next to me. He knows better than to question my choices. He never does normally, but the last couple of days it's all he's done. Is he really worried about this? Dean and Sam look at each other, confused.

"I know what I'm doing." I look through the blacked-out window, and my mind wanders to the deal I made with Evan. Was I stupid for doing it? Maybe so, but that beautiful woman is playing with my head. I have an overwhelming need to protect her, yet I want to wring her for all the information I can get from her too. I've never felt such conflict in all my life. It's just not the way I was brought up. Knox men don't show or feel such emotions.

Throw in the mix some or all of the information about what happened to Tillie, and it was a no-brainer. I had to take the deal with Evan.

I can sense them all side-eyeing me, and I don't like it. "I know what you're all thinking and it stops now. I have reasons for every decision I make. Reasons I do not need to explain to any of you. I've never done anything to jeopardise my family business, and I don't plan on starting now. So, you'll take my fucking orders and you'll carry them out, no questions asked. Do I make myself clear, or am I going to have to start popping bullets at those who question my decisions?" My rage has taken a new turn. I'm questioning the loyalty of my men, something I've hardly ever done.

Sam is the first to speak. "No need to waste bullets on me."

"Me neither," Dean says.

I spin around to Yates, who's sitting at the very back of the Range Rover. "You got anything to say, Yates?"

"Nothing at all. You're the boss." He goes back to watching for any sudden movements at the rear of us.

"And you?" I aim my harsh words at Lincoln, the one guy I thought would have my back.

"You know I'm only looking out for you, Keanu. I trust you know what you're doing. You can call my questioning what you like, but I ask the hard stuff because no one else will. That's why I'm your number two, but that doesn't mean I'm not on board with whatever you decide to do. It's your call."

I should feel bad about what I've said, but I don't. I'm not having my men thinking I don't know what I'm doing and that they can get away with it and face no repercussions. I've killed for less, and I need to know I can trust the men who are guarding my life and my estate.

"Good. Now we're all on the same page. I'll hear nothing else on my choices."

The car is filled with silence. Silence I bask in, which is cut all too short.

"Boss, there's movement," Dean announces, nodding out the window.

"It's about damn time. I don't think Benson is aware I'm still here, so there may be some heated words. Keep your eyes and ears open." They all get out of the car. "Sam, start the car in case we need to make a hasty beeline."

"Boss." He inserts the key in the ignition and the engine roars to life.

Depths of Deceit

I swing the car door open just as Harper makes an appearance, closing it behind me. I lean my back against it and fold my arms across my chest. Her steps falter and she comes to a complete standstill. Evan soon ushers her on, and that's when she clocks me. I offer her a smirk in greeting. Evan says something to her before he darts off to the right. She takes the steps down to me slowly, looking all around her.

Is she looking for an escape route?

Keep looking, baby cakes, because there isn't one.

She eventually takes the last step, closing the distance between us.

I'm the first to speak. "Hello again, Harper."

"Why?" she asks.

"I have my reasons." I walk a few steps until I'm standing directly in front of her.

"I don't understand any of this." I can hear the confusion in her tone.

Commotion behind her gains my attention, and I angle my body around Harper, shielding her behind me as my instincts to fight take over.

"What the fuck are you doing here?" I see the panic written all over his face and his body language is no better. "I thought I'd made myself clear before."

"Oh, I think everything is crystal clear from where I'm standing." I see his Adam's apple jumping up and down from a distance. He's nervous. He knows I've seen enough to work out what he's involved in. I just need to prove it and find where he's put Tillie.

He's rattled and doesn't have a move to make, so he goes with the obvious one, clocking sight of Harper beside me, "Over my dead body." Benson pounds down the steps in a hurry. "Harper, you come here right this second," he orders, his eyes locking on me. I smirk at him and cross my arms over my chest once again.

He stands a few inches away from me. "Harper, did you hear me? I said come here."

"She belongs to me now, Benson," I shout over the rustle of bodies moving around to see what the hell is going on. I spot Mr Gusto making a hasty exit.

Fucking pussies, the lot of them.

"Like hell she does. She's my daughter!"

"Was. You sold your daughter. Although, no one here knows why. You made your choice. Now I suggest you turn around and crawl back to the dirty, fucked-up cave you came from." I step forward, ready for anything.

He makes a beeline for Harper. I thought I'd put enough distance between us that he wouldn't be able to touch her, but somehow, he manages to grab her wrist. Like history repeating itself, I'm back at Cheetos and spotting the bruising on Harper's wrist all over again.

"Take your motherfucking hands off her," I roar. He ignores me and begins pulling her. "I said, take your hands off her. Nobody touches what belongs to me and she's mine now." I remove his tight grip from her arm. Harper's staring wide-eyed with tears falling down her cheeks.

"Lincoln... put her in the car." I don't release my hold of her until I know Lincoln has her. She doesn't need to deal with her father anymore.

"Got her boss. You can let go now." That's all the reassurance I need.

"You can't do this, Keanu," Geoffrey says.

"I can and I have. Don't bother changing your mind and come seeking her out because you'll never get close enough." I turn and head back to the car. "Oh, and Benson... That war you mentioned earlier... well you've got one." He curses loudly, but I pay no mind as I jump into the car and wait for Lincoln to climb in the back with Yates and Dean to get in the front. "Drive," I order. The car begins rolling away. I grin as I watch Geoffrey throw his hands up in the air.

The last person I see is Evan. He watches us go and nods, even though he can't see me. I'll be seeing him again soon enough. He needs to hold up his side of the bargain now.

I hear the sound of sobbing beside me and turn to see Harper hugging herself as her tears fall onto her lap.

"Those tears for a man that just sold you?" I ask then kick myself.

"No."

I don't know what to say to her. I have no explanation for what the fuck went down. "It could be worse."

Depths of Deceit

She doesn't lift her head. "How?"

"You could be leaving with Mr Gusto, the dirty old pervert."

Everyone in the car laughs. Everyone except Harper. She doesn't speak, only hugs herself tighter.

I've never been in this position before. Besides my sister, and Betty, our family housekeeper, no other woman has been to the Knox estate. Even those I've slept with. I'd take them to a swanky hotel instead. I'm risking a lot on this, so Evan had better pull through.

I decide not speaking to her at all is the best for now. Just until she comes to terms with what's happened and what will happen from this day forward.

Fuck, I need time to wrap my head around this myself. I never stopped to think about how long she'd be staying with me or what her job role would be once we got back to the estate.

Was this a mistake on my part?

I've never made a bad judgement call before now. Does Harper blindside me from seeing anything else but her?

But this isn't just about Harper, it's about Tillie too, and I can't let her distract me from the job at hand. I agreed to this for a goddamn reason, and I'll be damned if I let her fuck it up for me.

CHAPTER 17

HARPER

The whole drive to this point has been deadly silent. I don't know how long we've been driving, but my brain has been working double time all the way.

I have no clue what's expected of me. I mean, I've heard stories of what happens to trafficked women and children, for fuck's sake. They're made to sleep with anyone and everyone multiple times a day. They're beaten if they don't do as they are told. They're treated like slaves, most of the time drugged to make them comply, and end up like mummified junkies.

I don't want any of that to happen to me. It sounds horrendous and I never thought I would ever become one of those victims.

I refused to look at Knox, not wanting to see the slimy look across his features as he tried to bend me to his will. I did think twice about getting in his car when he ordered me to, but one look at my father… I knew if I went back to him, my life wouldn't be worth living.

Then I saw Evan giving me an encouraging nod. Part of me still trusted him, so in the end, I did as I was told. In a way, Keanu was right. It could be worse. At least I know him, only a little, but he's not a total stranger and he's been kind to me during past encounters. Well, some of them. Do I give him the benefit of the doubt here? Or is there a side of him I'm yet to witness?

The skyline out of the window has changed from built-up areas to

Depths of Deceit

more segregated plots of land. Amid all my zoned-out thoughts, I realise I now have no clue where I am or where I'm heading. That makes escaping a lot harder.

Way to go, Harper. You don't have your wits about you. Maybe Father was right. Maybe you really are useless.

We pull up to a large set of gates, but I don't see a single house or building nearby. We're in the middle of nowhere, in what seems to be a very secluded area. We continue to drive up a long road before a huge expensive country manor comes into view.

I thought my dad's estate was impressive, but this is something else entirely. It's twice the size in height and width. It's in better condition too. My father had let things go where the estate was concerned. Clearly, his priorities were elsewhere. Now I know where.

The vehicle comes to a stop in a nearby garage at the side of the mansion, and I'm led out of the car and into the house. I'm constantly looking at my surroundings in amazement. I've never seen anything like it. This place is beautiful, and for a moment, I forget where I am and the reason I'm here. I'm so transfixed by the foyer that the nervousness I was feeling disperses.

I hear the voice of my captor, as I'm now calling him. I'm being kept here against my will and I'm still to figure out why.

Why him, and why now?

His voice booms out, making me jump. "I'll be in my office should anyone need me. Yates, take Sam and Dean with you. Put them to work on the search for information. I want answers and I want them soon. Also, keep me up to date with the new alliance we made tonight."

New alliance? Who's he talking about?

"Any leads, you know where to find me. Linc, you're with me."

I watch as each of the men breaks off in different directions, leaving me standing in the hall on my own. No guard watching over me. I could make my escape now. If no one is watching me then who's to stop me?

Maybe that's the point. Maybe it's a trick to see if I can be trusted to stay put unattended. If I go now and I'm caught, will they keep me prisoner, locked up in a cell in the basement? No doubt this place has one. Fear of being tossed into some dingy dungeon has me freaking out.

"Excuse me. Are you just gonna leave me here?" I blurt out.

Knox freezes on the spot. His head falls forward. He spins to face me, taking slow strides closer to me with a glint in his eye.

"You're not a prisoner here, Harper. You're in the Knox estate now." He walks back to where Lincoln waits for him while I decide what to do with myself. "Top floor is off limits. You can pick any room on the second floor. I have work to do, so make yourself comfortable as you'll be staying here for the time being."

My whole body tenses in fear. What does he plan to do with me if I'm not staying long?

"I'm giving you the benefit of the doubt here by giving you a bit of freedom, which I'm sure you never had living with your father. You can try to leave, but you won't get very far."

I open my mouth to say something but soon close it again. How did he know I was having those thoughts? His smug laugh puts an end to the conversation anyway. Then he walks off, frustrating me even further.

I wait for him to disappear from view, angry he just left me standing here alone, yet relieved he hasn't pounced on me at the first chance he got. I mean, why else would he buy me at a sex auction if not for that very reason?

Everything I thought I knew about Keanu Knox was a facade. He's not who I thought he was, and no matter how much I found myself drawn to him, I hate him now.

Have I left one nightmare and entered another?

I look around awkwardly. The hall is grand in size and nature. Not at all what I would imagine Knox's taste to be like. It has a woman's touch to it, and I start to wonder if he has a wife or girlfriend who dressed the place.

Do they know he's brought another female into their home?

Are they even aware of what he's really into?

I shake off the thought, not knowing where it came from. It's not like I care for these people anyway. Sure, I find the man extremely

Depths of Deceit

attractive, but he also just bought me like he was buying a leg of lamb from the market. He's no better than my father.

My gaze follows the staircase all the way up to the top floor and I remember what he said about it being off-limits. Colour me curious and maybe a little rebellious, but I make my way up the stairs, slowly at first, careful not to make a sound and alert anyone where I'm going. I keep an eye out for anyone who may be roaming the halls, but I see and hear no one. I head straight for the forbidden landing, wondering what makes it a no-go zone. I tiptoe to the first of four doors and poke my head in only to find an elaborate storage room filled with bed sheets and bathroom products.

"Well, that was disappointing," I mumble to myself, closing the door before moving on to the next. I open the next door to find a huge bedroom. It's decorated in manly tones, modern in design and textures aplenty. The room is tidy but lived in. This is most definitely Knox's room. I can tell by the scent that hit me as soon as I opened the door. My feet itch to move from the doorway further into his space, but my brain stops me. This is his personal space. This must be the reason he didn't want me up here. I back away softly, close the door, and move to the next one. That one proves to be just as exciting as I've found the most elaborate bathroom I've ever seen. The room is light and airy, and a huge bathtub adorns the corner of the room. Next to that stands the biggest shower known to man. The toilet itself is fit for royalty. The whole room has white walls but there are accents of gold throughout, giving it a rich feeling.

"Wow, this is amazing."

I've looked at every fixture in the room, and having spent too much time up here, I get moving. If I'm not careful, I'll get caught. Would that mean I get punished? I shudder at the thought. I've taken enough beatings from my father to last me a lifetime.

I leave the bathroom having just one room left to see. I open the last door allocated at the very end of the hall, sucking in a lungful of air as I take in the sight in front of me. It's a woman's room. It's beautiful. Not as neat as the other rooms but no less magnificent. Its size alone takes my breath away as I step into the space that looks unlived in judging by the dust lingering on the surfaces. I walk over to a set of drawers where there's a bunch of framed photos. The pictures tell a story through time from a little girl to a teenager. Some of them are of a girl on her own, but most of them with her family. I'm guessing it's her parents and a younger Knox. They look so happy and such a tight-knit family. The total opposite of my upbringing.

My eyes fix on Keanu, his smile something of the Gods. He really is a handsome son of a bitch and I hate myself for even thinking it after finding out what he's really like.

"What the fuck are you doing in here?"

I jump, almost knocking over the photo frames. His voice is laced with anger. "I told you this floor was off-limits." I back away from the photos slowly and turn around. I'm met with a furious-looking beast.

Guilt laces my veins as he stands in the doorway looking madder than Hades. He looks every bit the devil himself. His arms folded across his chest intimidatingly. My guilt turns to fear.

I'm in for it now.

My nightmare has only just begun.

CHAPTER 18

EVAN

What have I done?

Did I do right where Harper was concerned?

I know she wouldn't see it that way, but I made a promise to protect her, and it's a promise I've every intention of keeping.

Geoffrey fooled me tonight. I thought I knew all his plans for the auction, but never in my wildest dreams did I think he'd sell his own daughter.

What would he gain from doing so?

Nothing other than getting rid of a nuisance, as he called her. She wasn't the strong son he wanted or needed to keep his empire running when he no longer could, but was that really enough reason to sell her off to some slimy fucker who wouldn't care about her, only use her body to make them more seedy money to buy more girls?

Did Benson do it for the money?

I know the business took a big hit over the last two years or so, but... it can't be that bad. He's clearly got his fingers in more pies than I thought and didn't feel the need to inform me of them.

Does he not fully trust me anymore?

Have I given too much away?

He knows how I feel about this side of business. Is that why he never takes me to the meetings at Cheetos? Is he planning something bigger?

Benson's holding out on me. That needs to change and fast, otherwise I'll have Knox on my case. I made a promise to him and that's one I also intend to keep.

I made the best out of a shitty situation with what little time I had. As soon as the auction was over, I moved fast. Benson was too busy soaking up the limelight to notice I wasn't around. I made a rough as fuck plan in my head and went looking for the only man I trusted to protect Harper, praying I hadn't missed him. It sounded stupid when I first thought about it. How could I trust a man who was the enemy? Not so much mine, but one of Benson's.

I knew his father well. I've been in the game long enough, but I know the Knox family have morals and they stick to them. They never harm women or children. Leaving with Knox tonight was Harper's best chance at surviving. I just hope Keanu still sticks to that rule. I also knew Knox was hanging around Benson's neck of the woods before. He was looking for something, possibly someone. I always had my doubts about what Benson was really capable of, but seeing Keanu Knox had me trying to piece everything together. After his visit in the cafe, I did some digging of my own. That's when I found Tillie Knox went missing in Benson's part of town. I wasn't even aware she was kidnapped until I heard it through the grapevine before it was even made public. When I approached Benson about it, he told me he didn't know either and that was the end of the discussion.

In this world, there are no coincidences. Knox must have had some information leading him this way, and I bet my life's savings Benson was involved.

It was the only leverage I could use with Knox; nothing else would have persuaded him to agree to my mad plan, but it was a chance I needed to take.

Thankfully, I caught him in time and he reluctantly agreed and was in the room with all the buyers. I slipped back into the main hall undetected just as Benson finished talking to a group of men in suits and ordered me over.

Depths of Deceit

"Evan, are the girls ready to be transported to the buyers and all funds cleared?" he said without a care in the world.

"I believe so, yes. Will that include Harper?"

"Why wouldn't it? She fetched a hefty price. I'm not stupid. I made sure those funds were cleared first." He laughed sadistically.

"I don't understand. Why, Geoffrey?"

"You don't need to understand, Evan. You just need to do your job." He turned to me, looking unconcerned.

It pained me to say my next words. "You sold your daughter, your only child, like she was nothing. Don't you think she deserves an explanation?"

"I know you have a soft spot for my daughter, so I'll let your inquisitiveness slide. Harper is of no use to me. She doesn't do anything for the business. She's useless, just like her mother. All I asked for was a son and she couldn't even give me that. So, I might as well make money off her while she's still young and has some looks about her. Now, I suggest you do what I pay you to do." He turned and headed into the crowd.

That had sold it for me.

I couldn't keep doing this anymore, and I'm glad I did what I did and asked Knox to get involved. It would give me great pleasure giving Keanu everything on Benson.

The deed was done and Benson was about to find out that not everything goes to plan.

He watched Knox drive away with Harper instead of Mr Gusto. I stood behind him at the top of the stairs, trying to hide the smug grin on my face. I nodded discreetly as Knox's black Range Rover passed by me, confirming I'd get what he needs.

"What the fuck is happening? He knows too much, and I can't have that. Something needs to be done. Keanu Knox and the rest of his clan need to go," Benson roared, gaining the attention of his guests.

"Why don't we head to the office? You don't want your guests witnessing any more disruptions and thinking you're bad for business," I said as I came to stand beside him.

"Good idea."

I guided him through the main entrance towards his office as he was off in his own world and seemed incapable of doing it on his own.

I addressed the room. "Ladies and gentlemen, please enjoy the champagne on offer and tonight's entertainment."

Once we were in the office, I closed the door and watched Benson's body language.

"Well, what was eventful," I joked.

"What the fuck happened, Evan?" He slumped down in his rotating chair behind his desk, resting his head on his arm.

"I haven't got a clue. One minute everything was fine, the next you're auctioning off your daughter and I'm in the dark about it all."

"I had my reasons, Evan. That's not what I'm talking about. I mean Keanu Knox driving away with Harper, grinning like he's got one up on me." He slammed his hands down on the table with an almighty bang. "Fuck! I thought if I threatened him, he would walk away. He left, for God's sake. He fucking left."

"You can't threaten a man like Keanu. What were you thinking?"

"I was trying to get him off my tail."

"About what?"

"Oh, nothing I can't handle." I knew he was lying, but I couldn't push him, not when he was already on edge.

I tried a different angle. "What I don't get is why. Knox isn't into the whole sex trafficking business, so why cause trouble by buying Harper? There's got to be more we're not seeing," I added, eyeing him for any signs he was hiding something. He nibbled the inside of his lip. He was definitely hiding something. "Is there something you want to tell me, Geoffrey?"

"Like what?" He swung around in the chair, putting his back to me.

"You tell me. It's not like you've been very forthcoming about what's going on around here. You didn't give me any heads-up about your plans this evening and look how that turned out. If you had told me, maybe this wouldn't have happened."

He swung back around and faced me. "Maybe you're right, but everything is going tits up lately. I don't know who I can trust in my circle."

"You're questioning my loyalty, after all this time?" I acted offended.

Depths of Deceit

"I'm beginning to question everything. I could tell Knox was interested in Harper, but to buy her? There's got to be more behind his motives. Gusto was more than willing to take Harper off my hands. He had plans for her. So why the sudden change of heart?" He tapped his finger against his chin.

I stared at the man I'd known for thirty-plus years, wondering what changed in him to become this sick and uncaring person, or was it me that changed? Maybe I refused to think he could be capable of such things. He made my skin crawl. He didn't even show an ounce of regret for what Harper would be doing at the hands of Gusto.

"What did Gusto say to you?" I prodded.

"That Knox offered him more."

"And that was it?" I needed to know Benson wasn't suspicious about my involvement.

"Yes."

"Well, think of it this way. You got rid of her and still made a profit. Surely that counts for something, right?" My words tasted bitter, and it was hard to swallow the aftertaste they left on my tongue.

"I know you're right. She was weighing me down. It's no skin off my nose where she ends up, and it's not like she knows anything."

"Leave Knox to me. If he's up to something… I'll find out what."

I've never been a snitch or backstabber as long as I've been in this business, but the stunt Benson pulled tonight was enough for me to want out of this life for good. Once I know Harper is safe, I'm fucking retiring.

I'm too old for this shit and if I don't get out soon, I'll find myself with a bullet in my head.

What will Harper do then?

I would have broken the most sacred promise I've ever made and there's still so much Harper doesn't know.

CHAPTER 19

KEANU

After a quick briefing with Lincoln, I decided I needed a shower. I had just bought a human-fucking-being. This isn't the Knox way. We don't get into this shit, and it's making my skin crawl. I can't believe I even did it. I pride myself on my morals and ethics and this has gone against them all. I have to keep in mind why I did it, though.

Finding Tillie has become my life's mission, and I might be crazy, but I think Harper could be part of the answer I'm looking for. If not, she's at least a beautiful distraction.

Heading up the stairs, I get an eerie feeling running over my skin, and I've learnt to trust my gut.

I make it to my room, but a shadow catches my eye down the hall.

"What the fuck?"

My feet move at speed, but stealthily, so as not to make my presence known. My heart is racing as I get closer to the open door of my sister's suite. I freeze in the open doorway as I spot Harper over by the dresser, looking at the candid shots of Tillie.

"What the fuck are you doing in here? I told you this floor was off limits." At the sound of my booming voice, she jumps, leaping backwards away from Tillie's belongings.

Harper looks like a guilty goldfish as her mouth opens and closes, but the lack of explanation makes me angrier. I march over to her,

Depths of Deceit

taking her arm in my grasp and ignoring the electricity that seems to come from touching her.

"Ouch! Let go of me, you big brute." She fidgets as she tries to free her arm, but she's no match for me. I pull her out of the room, not letting go until I have her on the floor below and completely out of Tillie's personal space. That room hasn't been touched since she left and that's how it will stay until she's home safe and sound, after a good dusting it seems.

I let her go just as she tries to yank her arm free with enough momentum to make her tumble to the ground. I'm ashamed for manhandling her, but I don't show it. Instead, I raise my voice and use it to show her my authority.

"I warned you not to go up there and you most certainly do not go in that room. Do you understand me?" I will not budge on this, no matter her excuses.

"I... I..."

"I don't want to hear it. You stay away from that floor unless told otherwise." I open the first door on this floor. "Get in there. This will be your room from now on." I leave, slamming the door behind me.

Running back upstairs to my room, I take my shirt and tie off and undo my belt when I realise she has nothing with her. Annoyance that Evan didn't even send her with her stuff winds me up even more than it should, but he claimed to be looking out for her when he begged me to take her so it was rather rushed.

I grab one of my nicely folded T-shirts from the pile in my massive closet and take it down to her. I stormed into her room without knocking to find her in nothing but her underwear, turning down the covers on the bed with tears streaming down her face like a scared, caged bird. It's the first time I've seen her show this emotion towards me, and I can't lie, it kills me to know I'm the cause of it.

My mother would be so proud of me.

Her invisible exasperation with me makes me irritable.

The vision of her in her sexy-arse underwear will appear in my dreams tonight, that's for certain. I'm still staring at her when she coughs to get my attention.

"Do you mind?" she bites, taking on a strength her body doesn't portray. Her words trigger something in me, and before I know it, I have her pinned up against the wall, staring deeply into her ocean-blue eyes. They hold an element of fear, but not as much as one would think considering how she came to be here.

"My home. I admire what I want, and let's not forget that I own you now." I'm being a bastard, but I've taken on a new level with this. Plus, she needs to learn I'm not a pushover. We may not harm women, but if she keeps pushing my buttons the way she is, I'm going to lose my shit and give into my temptations.

"You don't scare me. You don't have a clue what I've been through."

I think back to the bruise on her wrist, and once again, guilt slices through me.

I step away from her like she's burnt me, pick up the shirt I dropped to the floor, and in a quick personality transformation, I hold it out for her to take. Call it a peace offering.

"Here. I got you this to wear for bed." She gingerly takes the garment from me. I made a hasty retreat, closing the door gently this time, and return to my room.

WAKING UP THIS MORNING AFTER A SHITTY NIGHT'S SLEEP FELT LIKE THE worst thing in the world. Five a.m. is not a time to be awake, but I couldn't settle back down. In the end, I got up and went for a run around the grounds to try and clear my mind. When I got back, I showered, climbed into a pair of sweatpants, and headed down to Betty for breakfast.

"Good morning, Betty."

"Good morning, Keanu. I saw you out running when I got up. Is everything okay?" she asked, her voice concerned.

"I'm fine," I lied. "Listen. We have an extra mouth to feed from now on. I'm sure she will be down soon." I wait for the barrage of questions I know are about to be thrown my way at the mention of a female in the house. "Do not mention anything about Tillie or what I do here. Is that understood, Betty?"

Depths of Deceit

She nods, confirming she understands the situation before a grin breaks out across her face.

"Now, don't be getting any ideas. She means nothing to me. However, she'll be staying here for a while." Her smile falls as she sulks out of the kitchen and into the garden, no doubt to pick something fresh from the veggie patch. She insisted we needed to have one. I think she just liked growing things, and my mother made sure she got it. My father gave my mother whatever she wanted and agreed to it without question. She also asked for chickens for fresh eggs every morning, but my dad drew the line at that one. I snigger at the memory as I take my place at the dining table.

I turn at the sound of someone entering the room. Under the table, my dick twitches at the sight in front of me. My mouth runs dry, and the only word that comes to mind is perfection. A new light in my dark and twisted world.

I know I shouldn't look at her this way. She's fast becoming a thorn in my side, but fuck my life, I am a man. I can't deny the effect her womanly curves have on me.

Look, but don't touch, Keanu.

CHAPTER 20

HARPER

I stand in the doorway feeling self-conscience about my appearance. He'd already seen and assessed me in my underwear last night. I may have acted like I wasn't embarrassed that he got to see this part of me already, but it was an act. I was horrified. I wanted to fight him all the way in hopes of him never seeing my body at all. I tried my best to keep my dignity intact with my smart mouth, but he made clear his intentions to ogle what he wants, reminding me why I'm here and that I'm his possession. In hindsight, I should be happy that all he did was look. I can only imagine the other girls my father sold haven't been treated so lucky. He then shocks me with his thoughtfulness in leaving me one of his shirts to sleep in before he calmly retreated, leaving me reeling with a storm of pent-up emotions.

I'm only wearing the crisp white T-shirt Keanu gave me to wear last night because I don't have any clothing with me. I left my father with just the clothes on my back. I'm acutely aware this isn't appropriate morning wear for a stranger's house, but it was either this or my dress from last night, and I opted for comfort.

I can feel eyes assessing me, and it has me wanting to cover myself up, but with what?

A shiver runs the length of my spine as I witness Keanu Knox looking at me. He's sitting in a pair of sweatpants identical to the ones he was wearing last night, and once again, he chose to forego a t-shirt

Depths of Deceit

His tattooed chiselled chest taunted me. I remember my current situation and watch, mortified, as his eyes rake up my legs and hover in on my breasts. I look down and find the source of his heated gaze. I blush, embarrassed because my nipples poked through the shirt. I cross my arms over my chest and dart for a seat at the eight-seated diner table.

I've never been more humiliated in my life, and the fact he laughs under his breath as I stomp past him makes it worse. He definitely saw everything. Thank God I chose to keep my knickers on. That's my only saving grace this morning.

"Good morning, sunshine." I spin in my seat, covering myself more now there are more people appearing. An elderly woman comes over to me, gently lifting my head with her finger. "Aren't you a pretty little thing." She smiles, and I can't help but feel warmth radiating from her.

"Betty, if you will. I'm waiting on my bacon and eggs." The woman I now know as Betty casts her eyes over to where Keanu is sitting.

"So impatient." She winks at me, releases my chin, and goes to the stove. "Hang fire. It's almost done."

The smell of freshly ground coffee filters through the air and has my taste buds dancing in delight. Mix that with the smell of bacon and it's a heady concoction, almost as good as Knox's aftershave… almost.

"Would you like something to drink?" Betty asks, not taking her eyes off the food sizzling away.

"I'm glad you asked. Coff—"

His words are cut off. "I was speaking to our guest. Did you leave your manners in bed this morning?" I watch as she narrows her eyes at Keanu. I can't help but chuckle, which stops immediately when Keanu swings his beady eyes my way.

I think Betty and I are going to get along well. Having her on my side and giving Keanu Knox the notorious mafia boss a run for his money has me feeling brave.

"Coffee would be great." I cock a mischievous smirk Knox's way.

"You like bacon and egg bagels? If not, I can make you something else, dear."

"No, that sounds great. Thank you."

"Why are you giving her special treatment, Betty? I don't want her getting used to it. You never offer the lads something different. They normally get what they're given."

"That's because you're all animals and will eat anything that's put in front of you." She spins around with two plates in her hands and heads to the table. "Plus, it's been a while since I've cooked for someone other than you and your men." I don't miss the moment Keanu's whole demeanour changes. His hackles have gone up and he's giving Betty a dangerously dark stare.

Am I missing something?

A plate is placed in front of me and another in front of Keanu.

"Things change." There's a sadness in his tone that I've never heard before. Almost a vulnerability to him.

Does this man even have a soft bone in his body?

Betty pats his shoulders and speaks tenderly to him. "Patience, Keanu. I believe in you. You'll have it all figured out soon enough and everything will be as it should." She kisses the top of his head and goes back to cleaning up.

His eyes find mine and I look away, feeling like I've imposed on something sacred. "Eat, before your food goes cold," he orders.

My hands move of their own accord, his order obeyed. I didn't realise I was so hungry until the first bite hits my taste buds. It tastes amazing, and I praise Betty for her cooking skills.

"What are your plans today? I hope you've made some room for shopping," Betty asks over the sound of dishes clashing as she loads up the dishwasher.

"Shopping? Betty, I've never done the food shop in my life, and I'm not about to start now," he says, confusing etching his face.

"Not for food. For clothes." She laughs.

"Is this your way of telling me I need new clothes?" He narrows his eyes. "Because I happen to like my style of clothing."

"Not for you. For the beautiful lady you have staying here. Unless you think it's okay for her to be wearing your clothes?"

His eyes widen. His half-eaten bagel drops to his plate and his chair scrapes the floor when he stands. "For fuck's sake. Me? Why can't you take her?" he shouts, clearly frustrated.

Depths of Deceit

"Language, and because you're the one with the platinum card." She throws me a wink again.

I would say she enjoys rubbing him up the wrong way.

"Can't I just give you my card and you take her?" he asks.

"No. I have my own errands to run today." I get the feeling she's lying to him.

"I don't mean to be rude, but I am here. I don't want to be a burden on anyone. I can wait for a more convenient time if——"

"There won't be a convenient time. You aren't meant to be here anyway," he roars.

I can't lie and say his words didn't hurt me because they did, but more than anything I'm angry. "And I never asked to be here. Yet, here we are." I shout back. "If you didn't want me here then you shouldn't have paid for me," I add.

Betty gasps, like what she's just heard, shocked her.

Keanu inhales deeply before releasing it loudly. "Betty, can you leave us?" He doesn't take his eyes off me.

"Play nice." She offers me a sweet smile in passing. "It was lovely meeting you——"

"Harper," I finish for her, only just noticing she didn't know my name. "Thank you for breakfast."

"It was my pleasure, dear." She scurries from the room, leaving me alone with a menacing-looking Keanu.

"What did I tell you about your tone, Harper? You want respect around here, then it needs to be earned. I suggest you remember your place and whose roof you're under. Things could have played out differently for you had I not intervened. You should be thanking me, not giving me a pathetic attitude."

Who does he think he is?

"Thanking you? Please! I've left one hell hole and found myself in another. You're just like my father, possibly even worse." I regret the words the moment they leave my mouth.

He marches towards me and grabs my arms, lifting me out of the chair, and pushes me back a few steps until my back hits the wall behind me, taking my breath away. "You're right. In some ways, I'm worse than your father. I'm the dark shadow that haunts people's dreams. I can be your worst nightmare if you cross me. You don't know a goddamn thing about me to pass judgement. But keep talking shit like that and you'll find out what I'm really capable of."

"Oh, I think I'm getting a taste of what the real Keanu Knox is like, and I don't like him."

He angles his head, his face close to mine. "You're not meant to like me. Means I'm doing my job right."

"You won't break me. You think I don't know what you want from me. It'll never happen. I won't let you take my voice away." My chest is rising and falling rapidly.

"One, you don't know anything, and two, I won't need to break you because you'll break on your own. You'll be begging me to take you. As for your voice, you'll lose it when I have you screaming my name in pure fucking ecstasy."

I don't know what comes over me, but my hand connects with this face. I gasp in shock. Never in my life have I slapped someone, let alone someone who could kill me with his bare hands and hide my remains, never to be found.

His head whips to the side and is still downcast, staring at the floor at our feet. He huffs and puffs like a caged animal.

"I… I'm so sor… sorry. I don't know—" I let loose a scream when he bangs his hands on the wall at either side of my head.

"That will be the one and only time you do that. The next time you even think of acting out like that again, it will be your last mistake." He stares at me long and hard. I'm frozen to the spot, paralysed by terror.

Then he walks away without a second glance.

What the fuck is wrong with me? Do I have a death wish?

More importantly, why am I so goddamn turned on?

CHAPTER 21

KEANU

I leave Harper without looking back.

The bitch fucking slapped me. *Me!*

Part of me is a raging bull seeing nothing but red, but as I watched her chest rise and fall in trepidation, I couldn't help but find her attractive. At that moment, I could have taken her and she'd have enjoyed it, but I wouldn't do that… at least, not until she asks me to, and she will.

Has she just found her backbone?

I storm off to my office to give Lincoln a heads-up on the change in plan.

When I tell him I'm taking Harper out for clothes, he stifles a laugh but fails to hide it. I want to throttle him as it's already embarrassing enough, never mind the inconvenience of it all. When I dart my eyes to him, his laughter dies down and he suggests the same thing I did about Betty taking her. I inform him Betty already has plans, even though I get the feeling she was trying to pull the wool over my eyes. I tell him I'll take Sam and Dean with me as I want him to continue the search for information. Just because we have Evan working with us now doesn't mean I'll stop everything on my side. For all I know, he could still be playing me.

After wishing me luck with yet another snigger, I flip him the bird and head to my room to change into something more suitable, but before that, I splash some cold water on my face to cool myself after what happened with Harper only moments ago.

She should count herself lucky she's not a man, because if she were, she'd be dead.

I could tell the moment her hand made contact with my cheek, she panicked and regretted it. Her shocked expression said it all. I bet that was the first time she's ever stood up to someone in her life. She even tried to apologise, but at that moment, I didn't want to hear it. I was mega pissed at her actions and words, but a huge part of me was proud of her. She was growing a pair of balls, and in this world, you needed a big fucking pair just to survive. The fact I feel any emotions for her confuses the hell out of me, and that's why I left her. I wanted to cause her some serious bodily harm, in the best fucking way, but I couldn't do that. If I'd stayed and felt her breasts brushing against my chest any longer, I would have ripped the t-shirt clean off her body, torn her knickers off in one fluid pull, and taken her there and then. I didn't because that would have only complicated the situation and proved to her that I brought her for the things she was insinuating.

I ring down to Betty and inform her of my plans, instructing her to have Harper dressed and ready. She gave me a bit of lip, asking what the hell she was meant to dress her in, but I didn't care, so I yelled, 'Just sort it' and ended the call.

I head to the walk-in closet in search of some clothes. I opt for a plain Armani t-shirt and some Hugo Boss dark denim jeans and finish it off with a pair of designer shoes. I squirt a large dash of aftershave on my neck and quickly style my short dusty blonde hair.

I glance in the mirror and decide I'm done before heading back down to the main floor, where I expect Betty to be with Harper.

Like I knew I would be, I'm met by silence. Why does it always take women so long to get ready?

It was the same when Tillie was here and we had to go somewhere, we were always waiting on her. Just like mother. 'Like mother, like daughter' my father would say.

The thought of Tillie has my mood turning sour, more than it was already. I know time is running out, and the longer she's out there

Depths of Deceit

somewhere——which I know she is——the more chance we won't find her at all.

Sam and Dean make their presence known. No doubt Lincoln has already informed them of my plans. They both give me a stern head nod in greeting but don't say anything. They know the score.

"Have the car ready. I'll be out in five minutes." They leave to follow through on my orders as my patience is wearing thin. I'm about to head up the stairs and demand they get a move on, but as my foot touches the first step, Betty comes into view.

"It's about fucking time," I bellow.

She rolls her eyes. "Don't go mad. I was low on options."

"You telling me not to be mad tells me I'm going to be mad." I remove my foot from the step when Betty greets me at the bottom. She looks back at the top of the stairs and narrows her eyes.

"Come on, dear. Don't be shy." I look from Betty to where she's looking and back again. She gives me a nervous smile, and it puts me on edge.

"Oh, hell fucking no," I roar, my fists clenched tight. "Turn around and put something else on."

Betty places a hand on my arm. "Keanu, where did you expect me to get clothes from in the short amount of time you gave me?"

My heart is beating out of my chest as Harper descends the stairs hesitantly.

"Should I go and change?" Her soft, poetic voice hits my ears.

Betty and I speak at the same time. "Yes—"

"No, dear." Betty disagrees with me. She narrows her eyes before helping Harper down the last step. "You look lovely. Doesn't she, Keanu?"

She's wearing a baby blue summer dress that stops just above the knee and a pair of white gladiator sandals that go up her leg. The fact that they're Tillie's clothes changes everything.

It's a massive shock to the system and solidifies the fact my little sister isn't here where she's meant to be.

I'm grounded to the spot, unsure of what to do for the first time in my life.

"Keanu?" Betty's voice comes from a distance. It's louder the second time I hear it. "Keanu."

I shake my head, clearing my vision and restoring my hearing.

"You should get going." She gives me a weak smile.

"I can always put the dress I arrived here in back on. I don't mind," Harper says.

"That won't be necessary, my dear." Betty nudges her shoulder against mine.

I release a growl. "The car is waiting out front. Go," I say harshly without looking at her. My eyes are trained on Betty.

Betty pushes Harper along. "Have a good day, Harper."

I wait until she's out of hearing distance and zone in on Betty. "We'll continue this conversation when I return." I don't wait for her to reply.

Now, I just needed to remain calm and not look across the car at Harper dressed the way she is and smelling like my sister once did.

God, give me strength.

CHAPTER 22

HARPER

The moment Keanu gets into the car, I figure it's best to stay quiet. The last thing I want to do is anger him any more than I already have.

It's strange. I was used to silence at home, so I'm normally comfortable with it, but this seems awkward somehow. I get the feeling he wants to talk, but he can't look at me. He hasn't glanced my way once, and we've been in the car for almost ten minutes. It seems longer in silence.

Betty had told me the clothes belonged to a girl who used to live in the house. It had me wondering if they came from the room I was in last night, as Knox had the same reaction to my being there too.

We pull into a huge underground car park that belongs to Harrods.

"Get out," he snipes.

"You know, I didn't ask to be here. You bought me, yet you're acting like I'm an inconvenience to you. Why not just send me back home? You've obviously changed your mind and no longer want me here." I know I'm poking the bear, but I'm past caring today.

He laughs at me. "You're not going anywhere other than shopping with me, so let's get this shit over with. I have other stuff I should be doing today." He waves his hand in front of him. motioning for me to go ahead. I reluctantly put my feet into gear.

We walk side by side, his men following close behind us. To

everyone around us, we're just another couple walking from the car towards the store. "What do you need?" he asks like I haven't just pissed him off.

"I don't know. Sleepwear, underwear, clothes, toiletries, that sort of stuff." I shrug. It's not like I'm used to going shopping like this. Normally, it's just me and Chelsea, and I only buy things I know my father wouldn't think of, like ladies' products. I very rarely buy new clothes as my father would never approve of them. The only time he gave me money to buy something was when I needed to look the part, and he gave me specific details on what he expected me to buy.

"All right, this place should have everything you need. Follow me."

I do, not wanting to annoy him again. We come to a stop inside the grand building.

"Holy shit," I murmur, making the doorman roll his eyes and scowl at me for being so vulgar in front of the wealthy clientele.

I read online once that this place has three hundred and thirty departments and over five thousand brands set over eight floors.

We follow the signage for the women's wear on the first floor. It's all becoming too much, though.

"Um, Knox... I appreciate you bringing me here, but this is not the sort of place I shop."

He assesses me, bewildered. "What do you mean? Surely Daddy gave you his credit card." I drop my gaze. Clearly, Knox thinks I had more privileges than I did. Do I really want him to learn the truth? It seems he's forgotten he bought me from my father. That in itself shows I couldn't have been loved or doted on.

"Who did you purchase me from, Knox?" I question.

"My mistake, and what you should be asking is why did he choose to sell his own flesh and blood, Harper?"

I shrug off his questions as he did mine, not knowing how to answer. I have no clue what he stands to gain from selling me like a cheap whore. I didn't know that was my father's plan until it was too late. It's not like I've had time to think about it. I was too occupied about where my life was heading and what would be in store for me.

"Knox, you have one hell of an imagination. I'm no more a princess than you are a saint. I never had my father's love, let alone his credit cards."

"You're staying at the Knox estate now, and you won't be seen in cheap tat. I have a rep to protect." His words ring in my ears, and I try not to laugh at them. I'm kind of glad he doesn't look at me with pity. I don't want him to feel sorry for me. Once my mother died, I came to terms with how my life was. There's no point dwelling on it. There was nothing I could have done to change it.

"Let's get you sorted with some clothes and whatever else you need and get the hell out of here."

We get off the escalator, and I begin looking for something comfortable to wear when an elegantly dressed woman with a pretty face and perfectly manicured fingernails saddles up beside Knox. She flashes him her best flirty smile, not seeming to notice I'm here at all.

"Hi, My name is Cherish. I will be your personal shopper today. As you're in the women's department, I presume you're looking for a gift for your mother, wife… girlfriend?"

I roll my eyes at her blatant attempt to be flirtatious.

"None of the above. This is Harper. We'll be shopping for her today. A whole new wardrobe is needed." Knox winks her way. The assistant turns, looking me up and down like I just came off the bottom of her expensive shoes.

"Looks like I have to earn my wages today," she grumbles under her breath, but I heard her. Just another sign I'm not the type of person who would normally shop here. Doesn't mean I want her to know that. I remember reading the first page of the website and being intimidated by that alone. I came off it, knowing I would never be able to shop here, but now I'm standing inside it, I might as well make the most of it.

"Pardon?" I say, unwilling to put up with her shit.

"Oh, I was just wondering about your size. I may have to check," Cherish smugly retorts while Knox is checking out her arse. He's such a typical bloke.

I give her my sizes anyway, then she asks what sort of garments I like to wear, but I have no clue what he wants me to get. I slide a glance over to where Knox has taken a liking to his phone. He must sense he's being watched as he looks up.

"Get whatever you want." He shrugs, and I shrug too, only towards Cherish.

"In that case, let's start over here, in Gucci." Cherish grabs a clothes rail and starts piling dresses, shirts, tops, leggings, and trouser suits aplenty. Then she gets some shoes. High heels, trainers, cute little flats line up along the shelf at the bottom of the rail. I have no clue where I'm going to wear any of this stuff, but nothing is stopping her now she's on a roll. Once she's done, I'm taken over to the changing rooms. There's so much stuff here it'll take me all day to try it on. I decide to pick the stuff I think I'll like, forgoing the rest.

I climb into the first dress and look in the mirror. It's nice, but I'm not sure if it's for me. I step out to where Knox is waiting on me to seek his approval, but I can't see him around.

"Oh, no. That one makes you look a little... fat. Try the next one." Cherish pushes me back into the changing room before I can call her out.

Maybe I do look a little plump in it, but I'm not letting this bitch tell me what I should or shouldn't wear. "I'll take it." I see her recoil slightly in the mirror, but she doesn't say anything.

The next half hour goes pretty much the same way. She picks fault with everything I try on. It's too pink for my complexion, or it's not long enough to cover the cellulite on my thighs. I'm about to lose my cool but remember what Knox said about his reputation and decide to pull him away to talk to him in private.

"Knox, can you come help me a second?" I flick my chin in the direction of the changing room. He looks at me with a cocky smirk, one I want to wipe off his face. I ask Cherish to give me a moment. She's reluctant but slides off.

He comes over, rubbing his hands together. If he even thinks he'll get an eyeful in here let alone cop a feel, he has another think coming.

I close the door behind him.

"What's up, baby cakes? Need help getting out of that dress, huh?" He comes closer, eyeing me up.

I suddenly have a shortness of breath at what he's just called me,

Depths of Deceit

but I catch myself and pretend I didn't hear it. "Dream on." I push him away gently. He sniggers, unfazed by my rejection. Nothing seems to affect this man.

"If you want me to find some clothes and get out of here quickly, you need to tell Cherish to back the fuck off." God, just saying her name is enough to make my skin crawl. "She's picking fault with everything I've tried on and she chose all of it." I'm fed up and in need of a good cuppa. I just want to get out of here.

"Fine, that suits me. Get changed and I'll ditch her." For the first time since meeting Keanu Knox, I smile, and it's genuine.

The rest of the day flies by. We make our way from one department to another without a hitch. We leave Gucci with a couple of dresses that I actually like. Fuck that bitch and her snooty comments. We head into Jimmy Choo, then Dolce & Gabbana—the list goes on. I leave each department with at least one item.

I have everything from designer suits to designer dresses, from loungewear to killer summer dresses. I have shoes and trainers for every occasion and outfit. I have even managed to sneak in some sexy underwear. Not that anyone will see it, of course.

I'm hungry and still in need of that cup of tea. By the time I'm done, I feel ready for bed, or whoever's bed I'm sleeping in at the moment.

"Ready to get back home?"

I freeze at his choice of words. Home. I panic, thinking he'll take me back to my father but realise he means his home. I disguise my horror as we pick up all my bags adorned with each brand name on the side. His men are also weighed down with bags. I feel bad about the amount of stuff Knox has brought me. I have so much that there's even a man dressed in the Harrods uniform with a bellboy trolley loaded with all my items, waiting to take it to Knox's car.

For someone who's constantly telling herself she's not a princess, he sure has treated me like one today, and because of that, I'm having conflicting feelings about him. He's a mystery to me. Just when I think I have him all figured out, he throws me off.

We make it to the car park, and Knox's two men load up the car using every available space before getting in and starting the engine.

Just like on the way here, we sit in silence, only it's more of a comfortable one. Neither of us feels the need to speak or mask the silence with music.

Knox suddenly breaks the quietness and almost knocks me sideward with what he utters next.

"Her name's Tillie, and she's my younger sister."

CHAPTER 23

KEANU

"Her name's Tillie and she's my younger sister."

I say it quietly, but the gasp she releases tells me she heard me. She doesn't say anything, and for a few more seconds, I stare out the window before I turn my head and look across at her. I know the information I've told her doesn't really explain much, so I continue. "That's whose room I found you in last night, and whose clothes you're wearing." I take a deep breath and then release it. "Around sixteen months ago, she went missing. Not long after that, my father died, but I've never stopped looking for her. And I won't until she's back home, where she belongs." I watch as a lone tear falls from her eyes. I reach over to her. She flinches, but I lean a little further over and wipe away the tear before it falls from her face. "Why are you crying?" I ask.

"Because it's so sad. I can't imagine what you must have gone through… what you're still going through. Do you have any idea where she might be?"

I got all the answers I needed from her by her reaction. She doesn't know what her father is really like, let alone that he might be involved in Tillie's disappearance. Part of me is glad she's not involved; it makes her presence more tolerable, but I'm gutted she can't give me information either. Evan might be my last hope in finding out anything useful, unless I go at it all guns blazing, but that won't help anyone.

"I may have a lead, but it's not for you to worry about. I just wanted you to understand why I reacted the way I did. I don't want to fight you at every turn, Harper. I have my reasons for you being here, but it's not what you think. I'm not into the trafficking business. I never have been and I never will be. I may run some illegal businesses, but I also have legit ones too. I'm not all bad, and neither was my family, even though we have a reputation that precedes itself. I'm a mafia boss, after all, and sometimes you have to become the devil in order to succeed."

I don't expect her to say anything else, but she does.

"Thank you... for telling me about your sister. I know that can't have been easy, trusting me with that. Especially after what kind of party my father threw. But I want you to know, I'm nothing like him."

I believe her. But that doesn't mean I can trust her. Not fully, anyway. We seem to be on the same page for now, and I want to keep it that way. The less time I spend arguing with Harper, the more time I'll have on my hands to bring her father to his knees and watch his empire fall along with him. I have no intention of telling her this just yet. She's made her dislike towards her father very clear, but I don't think she's ready to hear about his looming death.

More secrets, more lies.

We arrived back at the estate in record time. A new feeling surrounded us. Peace and understanding. It's a start, and I can work with it.

Betty appears to help my men carry all of Harper's things to the room she's been staying in. It takes them a couple of trips, but the task is completed in no time.

I haven't forgotten what I said to Betty before I left this morning, and by the look on her face, she knows she's in for it.

"Is it okay if I go and put my clothes and other belongings away?" I turn towards Harper as she reaches my side.

I'm shocked she's asked for permission to do something. "Of course. Dinner will be ready at seven. Make sure you're down by then."

She nods and climbs the stairs two at a time. She reminds me of my sister; she used to do that when she was excited or happy about some-

Depths of Deceit

thing. I miss having my sister's presence in the house, but hopefully, it won't be for much longer. Some people may call me crazy for continuing my search for her. I know it's been a long time since she was last seen but I know she's still alive. I can feel it, and so did my father. I won't be giving up until I know for sure what happened to her or I find her.

"Betty, a word. Now." I pace off towards the kitchen, knowing she's following.

"About this morning. I wanted to apologise—"

I hold my hand up, halting Betty. "You have nothing to apologise for. It was me who was out of line. You did the only thing you could, and I should have known to expect it. It was just a shock, and I took my anger out on you and Harper. It was wrong, and it won't happen again." She's the only person I ever use my soft voice for. I guess you could say she's the mother hen around here, and that's why I can't stay mad at her.

"Apology accepted." She rubs my arm gently before picking up a dishcloth and getting back to work. I turn to leave, but she has other ideas. "I don't know much about Harper, but whatever she's doing to you, I'm liking it." She smirks over her shoulder.

"What are you getting at, Betty?"

"I see the way you look at her. She'd be good for you. A perfect match. Your darkness could do with a little lightening up, and I think she can give you that."

I burst out laughing. "Betty, I think you're getting ahead of yourself. There's nothing between me and Harper and there never will be."

"If you say so." I don't like the way this conversation is going, and Lincoln is my saving grace when he pops his head in the room.

"Boss, we've had word from Evan. He thinks he could be onto something but might be radio silent for the next few weeks."

I use that as my cue to leave and head to my office to get some work done.

The whole time I spend in my office, Betty's words play over and over in my head.

CHAPTER 24

HARPER

It's been four weeks since I've been at the Knox estate. It's not what I had been expecting, not that I knew what I was expecting, really.

I knew people were bought and sold off like cows at the cattle market. I knew they were often used as slaves or sex workers, having no choice but to do unspeakable things to survive. That was if they did survive. It would be enough to break any strong-willed person, but that's where my knowledge ends.

What confuses me the most is why my time here hasn't been anything like that at all. It's been the complete opposite. I'm not foolish enough to think a man like Keanu Knox isn't dangerous, but he's shown me no sign of the devil he's claimed to be. He's spoken back to me with venom lacing his words and giving me orders, but he's never laid a hand on me. He took me shopping. He shared a little information on why he kicked off over what Betty gave me to wear. He set me up with a Kindle when he found out I liked to read and made sure there were physical books delivered for me too. I even get to help Betty in the kitchen with the cooking just for something to do. I'm starting to like the fact that I feel useful for something. It might not seem much, but to me… it's everything.

Maybe Keanu was feeling the truth about him not being in the

Depths of Deceit

same business trade as my father. He didn't need to tell me that, but he chose to anyway, and I believe him.

My cooking skills before were questionable. I got by because I had to, but it all came from a jar. Now, I can cook spaghetti bolognese and curries from scratch, and bake fresh cookies and the fluffiest cupcakes you have ever seen.

I sleep soundly on a mattress made for a queen, and I have the softest duvet that smells of lavender and fresh flowers. I get to take hot showers or soak in a huge bathtub in my own en-suite with no interruptions, or fears of my father coming to hurt me for something I did or didn't do. I even get to sit at the dining room table with everyone and not worry of being sent to my room for the smallest disrespectful comment that I never said. I don't get belittled or told I'm good for nothing and will never amount to anything. It's nice to feel wanted and appreciated for once.

I never thought this would be my new way of living. I'm not exactly a woman in desperate need of saving. I've not got to worry about someone taking my body and using it as they wish. I'm not being treated like a piece of shit on the bottom of their shoe. I can be myself and not worry about being beaten black and blue for no reason, and I've managed to keep my dignity and some pureness where others in my shoes wouldn't have been so lucky.

I know Knox is still a stranger to me, and he did buy me, for reasons I still don't fully understand yet, but he's treating me like a human being when no one besides Evan ever has.

Do I really want to run from what I have here?

At the start, I thought about trying to make my escape all the time, however, the days went by, and I realised.... what would I be running back to? A life of abuse from the one man who is meant to love me unconditionally. Why would I willingly put myself back there?

Back home, my room was my prison cell, only being let out to see Chelsea, and that was with an eye watching over me to make sure I didn't step out of line. The thought of my best friend brings a tear to my eye. I miss her so much. Will I ever be able to see her again?

Will she be worried about me? What excuse has my father given her for me not being around anymore? When all of this has blown over, I'll reach out to her. For now, she's safer not knowing.

Here, my prison is a beautiful building with more rooms than I need. The grounds are gorgeous to walk around. I can do it without a guard looking over my shoulder or telling me what I can and can't do. Don't get me wrong, I'm under no illusion that my every move isn't being watched. I've spotted the cameras dotted around the place, hidden amongst the trees and within the water fountains.

Knox's men aren't afraid to speak to me either. Granted, the most we've spoken about is how my life was back home. They ask questions about what I got up to, but mostly, they would ask about my father and why he chose to sell his only child. I guess they were curious. I get it because I've thought about it every day too. I've questioned him in my head every night in bed when my mind won't settle and I have too much time to think about things. I never get the answers. Story of my life.

Knox has been around at meal times but sparsely in between. He always seems busy doing something either hidden away in his office or off the premises.

Betty has become a good friend to me, like a mother figure. She tells the boys off if they get up in my face over something. She reminds me a lot of my own mother from what little I can remember of her. They share the same kind and caring soul. Eyes that have witnessed so much but can't hide their emotions.

Today, she's teaching me how to make another classic dish—chilli con carne. Apparently, it needs time to slow cook for a few hours. The upside is it's a one-pot. I have no clue what that means, but that's what she said.

I make my way down the stairs when voices in the distance catch my attention. I know that voice. I strain my neck further… that's Evan. Excitement fills me and I run down the rest of the steps as fast as I can without falling down them. I head in the direction of the voices and see Knox and Evan's retreating backs, casually strolling into Knox's office.

"What the fuck?" My head spins. Has he finally come to get me? Do I want him to come and take me back to that God-awful man I once

Depths of Deceit

called father? Either way, he said he'd be in touch. I just didn't know he would be in touch with Knox first.

I want to knock on the door and demand answers, but I know I can't do that. Knox and I are on good terms, and if I go in there making demands, it'll ruin everything. I'm earning his respect as he is mine. Plus, I have to trust Evan in this. He knows what he's doing. At least, I hope he does.

I sulk into the kitchen where Betty is humming her way around each cupboard, pulling items out and placing them on the countertop.

"Hey, Betty. I'm ready to learn. Where do you want me?" I smile, eager to do something other than think about what's going on in that office right now. The possibilities are endless.

"Hello, dear. I'm almost ready. I just have a couple of things I need to get done before we start. My brain's getting too old for this. If I don't do the chores in order, I'll only forget to do them."

This woman makes me chuckle. I don't care how old she is, Betty is as sharp as a tack. She sees and hears everything but says nothing. I'm guessing that's one of the reasons Knox keeps her around.

"I don't mind helping you. What can I do?"

"Child, you're a blessing from God himself. Can you empty all the bins while I hoover?"

"Of course. I'll be right back." I take a black bin bag and go from room to room until I come to a standstill outside Knox's office. My footsteps falter knowing they're in there. I should turn and walk away. I'm sure Betty wouldn't mind if I left Knox's bin for one more day. Only, curiosity gets the better of me, and before I can talk myself out of it, I knock and enter without being granted permission. I instantly regret it when my gaze connects with Knox's stormy blue eyes, his face like thunder.

"What are you doing, Harper?" My eyes flick from Knox sitting in his office chair to Lincoln, who's standing behind him, looking equally as angry. I swing my gaze to Evan's softer, more caring, gentle features, where he sits on the couch.

"I... I'm just helping Betty out. She asked me to empty all the bins," I blurt out, looking back to Knox.

"Well, get on with it and get out." My feet move quickly, eating up the space between the door and the desk. I come to a stop at Knox's side, reaching for the bin. Knox stops me from lifting it, firmly taking hold of my wrist. I hold my breath as he leans closer. "Next time you knock on my door, have some respect and wait for permission. You don't just barge in. Now get out."

I quickly empty his bin and practically run out of the room, not even sparing Evan a second glance. I close the door behind me, slump against it, and let the breath back out.

"What the fuck were you thinking?" I whisper.

I grab the black bin bag, but in my hastiness to move, I send the rubbish flying. I huff in annoyance and begin picking up all the white paper. I swipe the last piece up from the floor, intending to place it in the bag, but my father's face and name glare up at me. His slimy smirk mocks me. I contemplate whether to unfold the screwed-up paper and see why Knox is so interested in him and maybe get some answers, but when I hear a scuffle behind the door, I panic and throw it in the bag, scared out of my wits at getting caught red-handed snooping.

Do I want to find out what my father is really like?

It's not like it'll change anything.

CHAPTER 25

KEANU

"Evan, take a seat." I point to the long sofa on the far wall on the right as we walk in. Lincoln is already there, sitting on a lounge chair on the opposite side of the room, one leg on top of the other.

"I take it with you being here, it means you have something for me?" I ask, getting straight to business.

"I do. I would have been here sooner, but I had to go in deep just to recover something useful."

I spot a file under his arm. "Is that it?" I nod my head at the folder he's clinging on to.

"Yes. It's not the grand reveal of everything, but I think it's something you need to look into, as I can't do it myself. It'll take me too long. I know you're not a patient man, Knox." I nod again, confirming he's right. "Also, I'd get caught and it would raise too many questions."

"So… what have you got for me?" I hold my arm out for him to pass the file across to me, but he doesn't. I know he's on edge. His stance tells me as much. He's on guard, as I am. Has Evan got more tricks up his sleeve?

I'm about to demand he hand it over when there's a light knock on the door. "Not now——" My words are cut off as the person behind the door doesn't wait to be granted access.

What the fuck?

No one enters my office without permission. The room is eerily silent when Harper glides into the room. She says she's come to empty the bin, but as she approaches, I grip her and utter a warning never to walk in uninvited again. She scurries away once she's done.

I don't care if I was harsh. I have rules for a reason, and she will fucking follow them as everyone else does. Maybe she's having too much freedom in this place and she's getting complacent. That stops today. I'll deal with her later.

I sense Evan glaring at me. "You got something to say?" I narrow my eyes.

"I thought Harper was safe here. From what I've just witnessed, she clearly——"

I stand abruptly, banging my fist on the desk. "You don't come into my home and question my loyalty. I gave you my word that I'd keep her safe. I've not broken that promise to you, but I won't have her disrespecting my rules. She's had more freedom here than she's ever been given before. As you could see, there isn't a single fucking mark on her. So I'll ask one more time before I terminate the deal. What's in the file, Evan?"

He glances between me and Lincoln, eventually giving up the secrets and handing me the file. I snatch it from his hands, anger and hostility still running through my veins.

I open the file and flip through each page, giving them a scan. Every page has a different address and details about the grounds, its square footage, and if it's abandoned or up and running.

"Do all of these belong to Benson?" I ask. I own a few buildings myself, and one or two off-the-book locations for security reasons, but for someone like Benson and what he's known for, there's no way he'd need all these buildings. Half of them would be sufficient.

"Yes. I did some digging, and all but three buildings listed are in Benson's name." He stands, pointing to the paper in my hand, seeking approval. I slide them over and he begins looking through them, handing me back three pages. "Those three are owned by someone else."

Depths of Deceit

"Who?" I can feel my blood pumping at all this new information. I might actually be getting somewhere.

"Look at the name on the deed." Evan's voice drops.

When I see the name he's referring to, I see red. My blood is pumping for an entirely different reason. "Are you fucking kidding me?" I roar, grabbing Evan by his collar and ramming him into the wall. "You told me I could trust you." It takes everything I have not to bust his face up.

"Do… you… think.." I loosen my hold around his throat so he can speak. He rubs it before he continues. "Do you think I'd ask for your help if she was involved?"

"How do you know she isn't?"

"Because I know her. I've known her since the day she was born and she isn't capable of it. She's been with you for a month. Does she come across as a monster to you?" I don't answer. "Her father is using her name as a front. I bet these buildings are where you'll find more answers, not with Harper. I doubt she even knows she owns acres and acres of land between the three buildings."

Evan has a point.

I'm trying to piece everything together.

Is he telling the truth?

Having Harper here plays right into Benson's hands, but she has no way of communicating back to anyone.

I highly doubt Harper is the type of person to be able to pull this off. She can't lie for shit. The night of Benson's fucked-up party, she was told to butter me up. She couldn't even do that. She was so far out of her depth then; she'd be drowning by now.

There's only one way I'll be able to find out for sure if I can fully trust Harper and that's if I question her myself, and I will, but first, I need to finish up here.

Evan left a few hours ago and I'm still in my office, unable to wrap my head around what I've found out. I'm still trying to figure out who I can trust and who might be playing me. I could easily put my mind at rest if I just went and saw the person who can confirm things for me, but I'm afraid of what I'll do if my suspicions are correct.

I've been avoiding Harper on purpose, deciding to down multiple fingers of whiskey to numb my thoughts instead.

I told Lincoln I wanted to be left alone and that I wasn't to be disturbed whatsoever. I even skipped dinner, having lost my appetite. I glance at the clock on the wall reading ten pm. I've been sitting in my office for four hours straight thinking of every possible way I could address Harper, and every idea I'd come up with wasn't acceptable.

"Fuck's sake." I down the last drags of whiskey left in the glass and stand, giving myself a slight head rush. Surprisingly, I only feel a little bit tipsy.

I've wasted enough time tonight, and I'm not going to find the answers I'm seeking at the bottom of a whiskey bottle. The only thing I'll find there is a hangover from hell.

I march across the landing and towards the stairs leading to Harper's room. Without thinking, I barge through the door uninvited; and I'm the one shouting shit at her about respect.

Fucking hypocrite.

I scan the room after not receiving any backlash from my abrupt entry, but the room is empty.

"The fuck?" I spin on my heels, ready to give my men a round of abuse for not having eyes on her, but just then I hear running water. She's in the bathroom. I could walk straight in and demand some answers, but something stops me, and I sit in the armchair in the corner of the room, getting comfortable as I wait for her to finish up in there. I'm not leaving this room until I get what I'm after.

By the time the water stops running, I've lost all my patience. I'm set to make my presence known, only she emerges from the bathroom wearing nothing but a fluffy white towel wrapped around her, fresh from the shower.

She hasn't seen me yet, but then again, why would she? It's not like she's expecting the devil in disguise to be sitting in her room, silently watching as she goes about her business and drops the towel.

She drops the fucking towel.

Depths of Deceit

A growl deep within my throat has her screaming in fright and reaching for the recently discarded cloth. She quickly wraps it back around herself, but it doesn't matter, I saw everything, and now... I can't un-see it.

She's got a body made for sin. A body to make any man weak at the knees. The things I'd do to her if only she'd let me. I'd ruin her for any other man and not feel any remorse.

"Jesus Christ. Keanu? What are you doing here?" she asks, catching her breath.

"I came to see you." I don't elaborate any further. I'm still reeling in admiration of her nakedness.

"What for?" She tightens the towel around her. "If this is about earlier, I'm sorry. It won't happen again."

"Too right it won't. I don't like repeating myself, Harper. My men follow the rules with ease, so you need to do the same." My tone is harsher than I intended, but I need to stress the point. I can't have her walking around the estate thinking she can do what she wants, but that's not what has me feeling angry. It's what I learnt from Evan that's driving my frustration.

"I said I was sorry!" She raises her voice and it has my hackles up.

"Who do you think you're talking to?" I lean forward in the chair slightly.

"You. What do you want from me? One minute we're getting along and the next you're down my throat. I'm fucking trying my best, Keanu." She's feeling brave, standing her ground, but the moment I prowl towards her, she cowers slightly.

Everything comes rushing at me all at once. My sister still missing, Harper's presence here and wearing Tillie's clothes, the file Evan presented me today, and it all being linked to Benson and quite possibly her. "Did you know?" I roar in her face when I reach her.

Her scared eyes stare back at me, searching for clues, and the whole time, I'm doing the same to her.

She takes a step backwards. "Did I know what?"

"What your father was doing?"

"No one knows what my father does. Not unless he wants you to."

"You being here... was that part of the big plan? When you took me to the bar at the party and tried to play me, trying your hand at flirting with me, huh? Are you playing me now, Harper? Are you trying to get me to reveal all of my secrets and then go running back to your daddy like a good fucking princess?" I step into her space again. We're so close my nose is practically touching hers, and I can smell the coconut oil lingering on her skin.

"No... I... I'm... Of course not. I'm not involved in anything my father does. Do you think I could be capable of any of that? Do you really think I'd be okay with him selling me off to the highest bidder? And what would the chances be of me ending up with you? If I were a princess as you keep saying, do you believe I'd have lived the life I have? I did as I was told because I had no other choice, Keanu. As my father pointed out plenty of times, I was useless to him. I was never the child he wanted, and I paid the price for that in blood and tears."

"How can I trust you, Harper?" I brush a strain of her wet hair from her face that has falling loose from a towel, staring deeply into her eyes, praying she gives me a sign to show me she is trustworthy.

She places her hands on my chest, one on each pec over my shirt. "The same way I need to trust you. I like it here. I've never had this freedom before, which sounds stupid when I'm constantly being watched, but I can live with that. I've become fond of the people here. Betty is teaching me how to cook and I finally feel like I'm good at something. I'm finally useful. I have a voice here. Granted, I don't always say the right things and end up annoying you." She laughs awkwardly. "Why would I want to throw that away?"

"I'm trying really fucking hard here. When you give me attitude, all I want to do is teach you a lesson and smack your arse, but I'm afraid I'll break you. You're fragile. I'm not used to that in my life." I rest my forehead against hers and close my eyes, breathing in her scent.

"I'm not as fragile as you may think, Keanu."

I sigh. "Choose your next words carefully, baby cakes."

"What if I don't want to be careful anymore? What if I want to start living? I've been sheltered my whole life. Maybe I'm ready for more."

"You might be ready for more, but you're not ready for me." My hands find their way to the towel that's hugging her slender hips, begging for me to remove it.

Depths of Deceit

"I don't know what's happening right now, but I know I want it. I need it, Keanu." She starts to open the buttons on my shirt tantalisingly slowly. She's nervous. The fact her hands are shaking says it all. Yet, she doesn't stop until the last button is open and she makes eye contact with me, her eyes saying everything she can't say out loud.

I'm fighting a war with myself. Should I? Shouldn't I?

I know I should have walked out the moment she came out of the bathroom in the damn towel, yet I couldn't. She's held me captivated from the moment I first met her, and having her here, in my home, has knocked me sideways. There's no denying how attractive she is. Her innocent beauty calls to me like a moth to a flame, and that flame is burning stronger the longer I'm around her. I don't know what this is between us. Hell, I've never felt a connection like this with anyone before, and I don't want to sever it.

Her words cut through my thoughts. "I know you feel it too."

I can't explain to her what I'm feeling as I haven't got a clue. I don't know if what I'm about to do next will jeopardise the way things are between us, but I can't hold off any longer. I grab the end of the towel that's tucked inside by her breast and slowly loosen it.

Her breath hitches as my fingers connect with her skin briefly. The towel falls to the floor and the air around us intensifies at the magnitude of what's about to happen.

My eyes rake over her perfect body. Slender neck, peaked nipples begging to be sucked. Her thin waist and toned stomach. Her bare mound on full display, eager to be licked and fucked. Her silky smooth legs and back up. She's pure perfection. A body that, after tonight, will belong to me.

Should I stop it before it begins?
Yes.
Does that mean I'm going to?
Hell fucking no.

CHAPTER 26

HARPER

Knox grips the damp towel and ever so slowly removes it from my body. The cool air turns my nipples into sensitive, stiff peaks. My breath catches in the back of my throat, his eyes ablaze with a thousand fires. His hands glide over the clammy skin on my thighs, making my flesh break out in goosebumps.

I know what we're doing is wrong on so many levels, and I should stop him, but the truth is, I don't want to. I long to feel his touch, his lips on mine, and to be wrapped up in his arms. I've dreamt of such a feeling for a while now.

I don't have to think about it too deeply when Knox hoists me up in the air and throws me down onto the bed. My wet hair falls out of another towel that was twisted in it, making the covers wet beneath me, but I don't care.

Knox takes hold of my ankles and tugs me abruptly to the edge of the bed, causing me to squeal loudly.

I lose sight of Knox for a second, but he soon appears between my legs, sniffing my core as he climbs my naked form. His mouth clamps onto my breast as pain mixed with pleasure emanates from my nipple to my throbbing clit.

I buck under him, making my hips push into his exposed chest. His hand snakes over my other breast, kneading it unforgivingly in his palm before he slides up to rest around my throat. It's a power move but not a painful one. He's letting me know even in a situation like this he's still in control. I know I probably shouldn't, but I can't help but be turned on by the power he has over my body. How he can make it sing like a choirmaster that makes beautiful sounds come from voices alone, no orchestra needed.

He lets go of me, reaching down to unbuckle his belt, but I'm too impatient. Reaching for his shirt, I push it over his shoulders and down his arms. The growl that leaves my throat is not one I recognise, but it must do something for him, as he flips me over without warning, pulling my arse into the air. I'm on full display for him.

His fingers circle my clit, working me up; I can feel the pressure building. I push back against him, wanting him. He inserts two fingers, pumping them in and out a few times, and I can't take it anymore.

"Keanu...please," I beg.

"Not yet." He removes his fingers and lines himself up, pushing in until he's balls deep with a grunt. He fills me and hisses. "Oh, fuck."

My fingers clutch the bed sheets tightly as my muffled cries soak into the mattress.

His hips are relentless as they piston into me with a force I've never been taken with before. This is how I imagined sex with someone like Knox would be like, and I like it a lot. It's hot and steamy, and oh-so-forbidden. The roughness mixed with the smooth and gentle glide of his cock inside me is my new slice of heaven. It's turning me on more than anything I've ever experienced before, and I know he's only just getting started.

I can feel my orgasm building up with each drive in, and I know it won't be long before I'll come to an explosive end.

"Come now, Harper," he demands, thrusting into me faster and harder. My body responds to his words, and with one final thrust, we come together, me milking his cock dry and him with a death grip on my hips.

"Keanu…" I scream his name like the word offends me.

"Holy shit." He hisses as the last drops of his seed spill out. He stays still for an awkward moment before roughly pulling himself free of me. The chilly air coats my arse cheeks as he lets go of my hips without warning, letting my body hit the bed unceremoniously.

Without so much as a word, he walks butt-arse naked into the bathroom.

"When did he lose all his clothes?" I whisper to myself, confused and slightly amazed.

I hear the toilet flush and then the water rushing into the basin. I look away from the door, knowing he'll be back any moment now, but I don't want to appear like I'm waiting for him. I throw the blankets over me, suddenly feeling the need to cover up just as Knox re-enters the room.

"I don't think so. That was just the warm-up. I'm not done with you yet." He pulls the blankets off and casts them aside. "This time, I want to see you come apart at the seams."

My mind starts to spin. He wants to fuck me again. I barely had any time to recover from what just transpired between us.

He once again positions me the way he wants me. He lies me down flat on my back, lifting my legs, and throws them over his shoulders, entering me hard and making me feel all the sore spots from where he connected the first time. He withdraws slowly. I feel every inch of his cock sliding from my folds.

Knox's growl is animalistic, primal even as he slams back into me so hard my body shifts up the bed. My heart pounds in my chest like a drummer has set up camp there. My nipples harden and the force of his cock pounding into me turns me on more. I've never been taken so roughly and unforgivingly before, and he seems to be upping the ante on how far he'll go.

Knox grunts with each forceful stroke, the clapping of our skin adding to the soundtrack of our encounter. I'm now so far up the bed that my head keeps hitting the headboard. Keanu lifts my hips so he's still seated in me.

"Keep your eyes on me." There's no room for discussion, so I just keep my gaze trained on his. All the while, there's no let-up on my pussy as it takes a pounding of epic proportions.

His fingers graze over my hip bone, following the shape of my body until he reaches my throat once again. His fingertip delicately wraps around my neck as my pulse point bounces against his now firmer grip. It's not enough to hurt me, but enough to let me know

Depths of Deceit

who's in charge. His other hand takes hold of my hair, pulling it hard down my back and forcing me to strain my neck so I can still see him from the corner of my eyes.

The whole thing changes our angle, taking me to new heights. My screams become louder, my fingers clench a little harder and his thrusts increase drastically. My orgasm hits me more vigorously and rapidly this time. He comes seconds after me, pulling my hair tighter, falling onto me to empty his seed. He pauses, making sure I take every drop while we're breathing heavily to slow our heart rates.

Once done, he gets up and haphazardly puts his trousers on. I can see he has something on his mind. I don't think he came in here to do what we just did. I see his demons; they're in his demeanour everywhere he goes. I don't have it in me to care that I was used, though. I wanted it just as much as he did… if not more.

I consciously cover myself back up, knowing what's about to happen. I should feel used, but I don't. What we just shared meant something. At least, it did to me. "I know you didn't plan for this to happen, but it did. I know you probably used me too, and a part of me is okay with that." He pauses just as he's about to pull up his zipper. His troubled eyes find mine, but they don't give anything away. Something was obviously bothering him when he came in here. I don't know what that was, but the menacing look that was in his eyes before has cleared. I know I helped in removing his troubles. "I'm not going anywhere anytime soon. When those demons of yours get too hard to handle, you know where to find me."

Realisation dawns on him. He gets what I'm insinuating.

He pulls up his fly and grabs the torn shirt before walking over to me. I panic, thinking I've stepped out of line, but he shocks the hell out of me when he places a soft, lingering kiss on my forehead. He throws me a cheeky wink and turns his back on me without another word, leaving me to mull over all the emotions in my head.

He took what he wanted without any remorse or care towards me, which I'm surprisingly okay with.

But there's one thing I'm struggling with…

He's left me wanting so much more.

CHAPTER 27

KEANU

It's the morning after I lost all control with Harper and took her body so unforgivingly. I could have taken it slow with her after everything she's been through, but I chose not to. I haven't had a wink of sleep. I was overthinking everything. Every touch, every scent, every moan, and it had me in a spin. I didn't know if I did right or not, but the second I had her laid out on the bed, all irrational thoughts left me and I wasn't thinking about the consequences of my actions. She wanted it to happen as much as I did.

I took her with no mercy. I didn't hold back on her. I gave her what she wanted and what I needed. I was so irritated when I first walked into her room at the thought of her playing me. It weighed heavy on my chest, but the moment I touched her and took her so degradingly, it all disappeared. My mind was clear of everything except her. I used her for my own gain and she took it all, never once asking me to stop. She amazed me, and I know one night like that with her will never be enough.

"Are you even listening to me, Keanu?" I look across the kitchen and locate Betty.

"Sorry, what did you say?" I'm too busy thinking about Harper over breakfast that I haven't heard a word.

"I said Harper seems to be settling in well. Do you know how long she'll be here for?"

Depths of Deceit

I'm about to answer with 'I don't know', but the words hang limply on my tongue as Harper makes an appearance.

She waits in the doorway, seeming unsure of herself. I offer a small smile and nod to tell her she can come in. Knowing she's still wary of me after last night turns my dick to stone. I worshipped her body in every way imaginable, yet she's still timid around me.

Betty spots her standing there. "Oh, morning, dear. Are you hungry? I've made croissants."

"That sounds great. I'm starving." She casts her eyes at me, and I don't bother hiding my smirk.

"Seems you did something last night to work up an appetite." Her blush makes it all the more satisfying. "I wonder what that could have been?" I add. She blushes a deeper shade of crimson but doesn't bite back.

"What are your plans today?" I ask her, changing the subject.

"Me? I don't have any plans. I was just going to take a stroll down to the bottom of the yard. I noticed from my window that there's a small forest with a building of some sort."

I glance at Betty, who's standing behind Harper. She's staring at me. I know what she's thinking. That little building she's talking about was built for Tillie. She used to spend more time in the woods than she did in the house, so our father had it built so she had somewhere warm to sit when it got cold or started raining in the winter. She eventually decorated the hut into something she could relax in. It was heated, had a shelf full of books, and a desk full of arts and crafts where Tillie would sit and draw. She loved to draw.

Harper must have felt a little reluctance from me. "Sorry. Should I not go in there?"

I shocked myself by what I said next, "No, it's fine. Just don't break anything or move anything around."

"Honestly, if it's too much trouble, I'll stay away. I—"

I cut her off before I changed my mind. "Harper, I said it's fine." My tone was a lot harsher than I intended and she withdrew into the chair slightly.

"Ignore him, dear. The hut you mentioned was Tillie's safe place. She would spend hours down there, reading, drawing, or just sitting and admiring the beauty of her surroundings. No one entered the hut without Tillie's permission." Betty smiles softly at me, no doubt remembering how Tillie would react if she was ever disturbed. It's also a good job I told Betty that Harper was aware I have a sister. Otherwise, I'd be giving her a murderous glare right about now. "I think you'll love it down there as much as she did." She stands behind Harper, laying a hand on each of her shoulders. "Won't she, Keanu?"

I busy myself by looking at my phone. "Sure." I don't want to stop her exploring the grounds. She needs something to do, and I can't stop people from touching Tillie's things forever. But that doesn't mean I have to like it.

"Only if you're sure. I can always find something else to do."

"Harper, I've said it's fine already. Just accept it before I change my mind."

"My lips are sealed." She even pretends to close her lips.

Sealed shut for now, but they won't be for long, as I have ideas on what I'd like to do to that mouth. I know she sees the smirk gracing the corner of my mouth. She arches her brow at me, questioningly.

Betty is none the wiser about what's going on, and I'd like to keep it that way, especially since she's concocted her own story about the two of us.

We eat our breakfast in silence, and I see Harper glancing at me from across the table, but I don't give her the satisfaction of seeing my eyes. I know if I look at her, I won't be able to control myself. The fact she's wearing tiny sleep shorts and a little strappy vest top has my dick pressing against my trousers under the table. I don't think Betty would appreciate me bending Harper over the kitchen table and fucking her into next week.

Thankfully, I'm put out of my misery when Harper excuses herself from the table after thanking Betty for breakfast. I turn my chair when she strolls past me, and a growl leaves my mouth when I get a glimpse of her backside. Her arse cheeks are popping out the bottom of her shorts, only just, but it's enough to send me over the edge. She must have heard me because she looks over her shoulder coyly before darting off in a hurry.

The little fucking minx is testing me by wearing something like

Depths of Deceit

that. She'll pay for that later. But first, I need to head into my office and follow up on a few things.

I'VE BEEN IN THE OFFICE FOR THREE HOURS, GOING OVER SOME OF THE stuff I'd let slip since Harper's arrival.

I organise a pick up from the shipment that will be arriving at the docks in the next couple of days. It's a big shipment of cocaine, and I need to make sure the handover goes to plan. I deal with the amount of cocaine that goes out on my streets to avoid it getting out of hand. No other dealers hang out on my turf, and if they did, they know what would happen. I've never claimed to be a saint, and at least this way I know it's clean-cut drugs on the streets and it's under my control. The only narcotics I deal with are cocaine and cannabis. If I find anything else is on my streets, I know someone else has been in my part of town and I don't allow it. Luckily, I've only ever encountered one drug dealer in my town, and it was when my father was still alive. I remember him hitting the roof because they were dealing a high amount of heroin. We found six dead bodies in the space of two weeks who died with that shit in their veins. It took us two days after the last body was found to find the dealer. He wouldn't give us any names or details about who he worked for or why he chose our part of town. He was tortured for days and still didn't give up anything. In the end, my father lost his patience, knowing we wouldn't get any information out of him, and killed him.

Once that shipment information was sorted, I checked all the accounts, making sure my money was where it should be and that it added up. When you run legal and illegal businesses, it's easy to lose track of where your money is, but not me. I'm always on top of that shit. I finish off by counting the stacks of money in the safe. It's a pretty big safe, and money isn't the only thing I keep in there. I have a spare Glock and magazine. My father's most prized Omega Speedmaster gold watch still sits in the original wooden box. Both my mother's and father's wedding bands and my mother's engagement ring are in there too. It all has value, but that's not why it's in there. It's more the sentimental value. Only Lincoln and I know the code to the safe.

I lock the safe back up just as Lincoln enters my office. "All done?" he asks, referring to my checks. He knows I like the office to myself when I'm dealing with the accounts or safe.

"Just finished," I tell him as I put the wooden cabinet door in place, shutting the safe away.

"There anything you need?" he asks when I sit back down in my seat, turning around to face him.

"No, I'm covered here. Have you heard anything else from Evan?"

"No. He's been radio silent for a few days, but it could just mean he's deep in shit again. I'd give him another day or two. If we don't hear anything then we'll go to him."

I nod firmly. "Any more on the search?" I ask in hopes that one of these days he'll have good news.

"Nothing, boss. But we'll continue to search until you tell us otherwise."

I'll never tell them to stop, ever. Not until she's found. "What are we missing, Linc? I mean, what else can I do?" I sigh deeply.

"Evan might be the missing piece to this puzzle. If anyone can give us information about Benson, it's him. Just give him some time. I know you're finding it hard, but do something else to keep your mind occupied."

Harper immediately springs to my mind. "Thanks, Lincoln."

With that said, he's walking out again. It's his shift to watch the front of the estate and take one of the others off for the evening.

I drum my fingers along my desk, debating whether I should go to Harper. My thoughts are conflicting. Should I stay where I am or look for her? I know what I want to do, but I shouldn't. That wouldn't be fair on her. But she did say she's there whenever I need her.

"Fuck it." I'm out of my chair and climbing the stairs two at a time, heading for her room on the floor above. This time, I knock, but there's no answer. I open the door and call her name but get no reply. I walk further in, checking the en-suite in case she's in there, but she isn't. I wander back into the room, wondering where she could be. Then I recall the conversation from breakfast. I go to the window and search for the hut from here. Sure enough, I spot the light on through the trees.

I contemplate going down there for two reasons. One, I've not stepped foot in the hut since Tillie went missing, and two, I don't want to disturb Harper just so I can have my wicked way with her again. I don't know what's come over me lately, but I feel like a starved animal trapped in a cage, and the person who feeds my hunger is Harper. The desire running through my veins for her is a rush in itself. I've felt more alive since she came into my life than I ever have. I may deal with drugs for a living, but she's the only drug I need, and one I'm fast becoming addicted to.

I'm thinking more with my dick than my head. If I was thinking with my head then I'd know it was a bad idea to get involved with Harper. Once Evan pulls through on his part of the deal and Benson is out of the picture, I'm pretty sure he'll take her home or somewhere new.

Do I want things to go back to the way they were before I met her?

Could I really say goodbye to her after the feelings I've developed for her and pretend it meant nothing?

If I was asking myself these questions a few weeks back, then the answer would most definitely have been yes. I didn't need or want the distraction from the job I needed to do. And she was nothing but that. A beautiful distraction. When I first met her and found out she was Benson's daughter, I told myself she would never mean anything, only that she could be useful, just another person I would need to deceive to get what I wanted to find my little sister. I talked myself into believing that's all she would be. I'd have her eating out the palm of my hand, then I'd be done with her.

But now... she's become a beautiful distraction. One that fooled me into believing she was going to behave a certain way. Cause me trouble and be a pain in my arse. However, she hasn't made a single move to make me think she knows anything and she hasn't tried to run. I don't believe she really knows what her father's dealings are.

I thought she was going to be nothing more than a nuisance for me, but she's turned out to be something completely different. She'd saved me from drowning in the depths of sorrow that come with being who I am and made me feel like I have more to live for other than being Keanu Knox, whereas before I was just existing.

How is that even possible after the short amount of time I've known her?

I bang my hand against my temple, ridding my mind of the nonsense I'm thinking. I don't know where it's come from or why I'm thinking about it all now. I know none of it makes any sense.

Retreating from the room, I descend the stairs and go through one of the doors around the back of the estate. I head down to the far side where the forest of trees starts, twigs snapping under my shoes with every step I take towards her, the morning chill brushing against my face. It takes me a good five minutes to breach the hut, and when I do, my breath is knocked from me. She's casually lying on the handmade wooden bench that's covered in thick wool blankets with cushions scattered around her. She's barefoot, her slender legs on full view, and her woolly dress has slid up to her waist, revealing some sexy as fuck lace knickers. Seeing her bare legs and underwear leaves little to the imagination. Her hair is tied up in a messy bun and she's reading a book. She hasn't noticed me standing to the side of the door.

I take a few steps closer. "What are you reading?" I ask, leaning against the door frame and placing my hands in my trouser pockets.

She almost throws the book at me in panic from being startled. "Jesus, you gave me a fucking heart attack. You're always creeping up on me." She places her hand over her heart dramatically.

"Who said I was creeping?" I arch my brow.

"Is everything okay?" she asks nervously.

"Why wouldn't it be? What's your book about?" I ask again.

"Nothing you'd be interested in." She tries to hide her face behind her hand, closing the book.

"The fact you're embarrassed to tell me has me more intrigued." I hesitate in the doorway, in two minds about whether or not to go inside. "Don't leave me hanging."

She huffs. "It's a dark romance. The Santiago Trilogy by Catherine Wiltcher." She blushes crimson.

"And?"

"I'm not that far into it."

Depths of Deceit

"What do you know so far?"

She flips her legs down off the bench, sliding the dress down her thighs quickly. "So far... the main character has been kidnapped by a man. By the sounds of it, he's someone to be fearful of. She doesn't know who he is or what he wants. But she offers herself up in order to save her father from being murdered in his hospital bed. She knows he's a dangerous man, that much is clear. They have a love/hate relationship, as you can imagine. That's all I know so far."

I release a throaty grunt as I push myself from the doorframe and head inside the hut. I perch on the seat next to her and take the book from her hands. I look at the cover, flipping it over to see the back. Other than a red heart and the words 'a dark mafia romance', the cover gives nothing away.

"A similar situation to what you currently find yourself in?" I lift my eyes from the book to gaze up at her, smirking devilishly.

"No, not exactly. She was taken from a hospital. She wasn't bought."

"But the guy who kidnapped her... he's mafia?" I ask, ignoring her choice of words.

"Yes."

"And he's dangerous?" I'm trying hard not to smirk again.

"Yes, so she believes." She's not grasping what I'm getting at.

"And I take it she finds him all mischievous and intriguing."

"Oh, God, yeah. Any woman would. I mean... he's dangerous, captivatingly handsome, yet rugged at the same time. He knows exactly what he wants and isn't afraid to go after it. He's someone who has everything he needs to protect her, and I bet he does so wholeheartedly. I've not got that far yet. The fact he has money is just a bonus." She's talking without thinking about what she's saying. It's the first time she's spoken so... freely.

"Is that what you want?" She bites her lip subconsciously. "A knight in shining armour, yet someone who can kill a man for you without a second thought and treats you appallingly but you find his unspeakable behaviour a massive turn-on?"

"Yeah, pretty much." She gasps the second the words leave her mouth.

I don't give her time to retract it. I drop the book on the floor, and it hits the ground with a huge thud. I grab the back of her head and crash my lips against hers. She turns her body so it's angled towards me and kisses me back. She opens her mouth, inviting me in, and that's all the approval I need.

I grab her around the waist and hoist her onto my lap, her thighs brushing deliciously alongside mine. My restricted cock lines up against her pussy.

The smell of coconut lingers on her skin. It's intoxicating and feeds my desire for her.

She grinds herself on my cock, our lips clashing in a hunger-fuelled frenzy, our tongues dancing together, and neither one of us stops for air.

Her hands slide up my chest and around the nape of my neck. Her fingertips trail the edge of my hairline before her palms flatten and dive straight into the longer strands. This simple act has been done many times before, but with Harper, it feels different. It makes me feel different. I don't want to be as domineering with her as I have with all the women before her. I want to give her so much more, make her feel things neither one of us has ever felt before. The thought makes me want to beat my chest.

Me Tarzan. You Jane.

What the hell am I thinking?

She could potentially be the daughter of the man who took Tillie. Everything we have so far points back to him. I shouldn't be feeling these things. I keep telling myself that she doesn't know anything. She's innocent in all this.

Does this mean I can have her free and clear? Damn fucking right it does. I snap out of my own head to the sounds of a very close-to-coming Harper.

"Fuck, stop," I hiss. "You deserve to come better than just from a dry hump."

In a split second, I have her on her back on the length of the bench. I bunch the thick material dress up high, over her breasts. Her knees are bent and her feet are together with a slight smirk on her face. She's playing games with me, and it turns me on even more.

Depths of Deceit

I gently place my hands on her knees before I savagely spread them wide, causing her feet to fall off the sides of the wooden bench with a gasp. I hover over her and admire her sexy, slender frame. It's beautiful, but it's hidden behind the flimsy material.

"This picture would be a whole lot better with these off." I grunt, whipping the dress off her head and unclipping her bra to expose her breasts. Her chest rises and falls quickly as she pants heavily, almost matching the throbbing of my erection. Her knickers don't fare much better as I rip them at the seams before holding them up in the air for her to see while I check out the bare mound it concealed.

My heart races at the sight before me. I've always appreciated the natural beauty of a naked woman, but never before has a woman made me react this way.

She's mine now. Her body belongs to me and me alone.

"Are you just going to stand there gawking?"

Her words tip me over the edge. My clothes are removed quickly, and I dive on her like a horny fucker desperate to get his dick wet. I gently graze my fingers over her sensitive parts, her juices overflowing. I'm not always a complete animal, I know she needs a little foreplay before I enter her.

I slide my hand further down her mound to find her soaking wet, ready for me. I circle her sensitive nub again before sliding into her delicious pussy. Her walls coat my dick tightly, sensually hugging it. The action drives me crazy with need for her.

Using one arm to brace myself over her, I use the other to run my calloused hand over every inch of her, starting with her thigh. I grab the back of her leg harshly to spread her wider, allowing me to thrust deeper and harder.

"Holy shit, Keanu," she whispers as I forcefully push my way into her. I momentarily freeze at her use of my name. It's like she's sucked all the air from my lungs.

"What... what's wrong?"

I lean down to take her beautiful pink nipple in my mouth, changing the angle, but from this vantage point, I can cause friction to her clit with each stroke into her.

I roll my tongue over the tight bud between my lips then sink my teeth into the flesh surrounding it.

"Oh," she purrs on a long breath, and I swear my dick just grew another inch. She likes it. I knew she liked it a little rough from last time, but fuck. I knock up a few notches with how hard I bite her nipple and she fucking mewls at it like I'm merely stroking her.

I pound into her hard and fast, taking things up again. I roughly knead the breast I just gnawed on while my mouth moves onto the untouched side. I give that one the same treatment, only this time, her back arches, pushing her chest further into my mouth. Her hands find my arse as she tries to force me in deeper. Her nails dig into my flesh, and I welcome the sting.

"More," she pants.

I hear the wooden bench crying out under the weight of us and the fact I'm pounding myself into her sweet pussy so hard. It sounds like the bench could break at any minute. With that in mind, I grab her thighs.

"Hold on." It's all the warning I give her. I hoist her up and swing her around so she fully has a hold on me. Her back slams against the nearest wall before I crush my lips onto hers and swallow her squeals. Her vice-like legs secure themselves around my waist, anchoring her to me. Her tongue duels with mine, matching my enthusiasm.

Her nails scratch at my back like razor blades scorching my skin. I reach for them and pin them one-handed above her head.

I feel her tightening around me as I sink my teeth into her neck, this time feeling the need to leave a mark as I rake my teeth anywhere I can reach.

"Yes, yes. Give me more," Harper bites out through gritted teeth as my relentless thrusting becomes frantic.

I wrap her hair in my fist and tug hard, exposing her neck more. She's never looked more beautiful to me.

"Ah, Keanu, fuck…" I know what she's going to say because I can feel it, and I'm just holding on.

"Come," I command.

With just that one word, she floods my dick with her essence as I continue to assault her pussy, chasing my own release.

Depths of Deceit

Harper screams in pleasure as she comes. I swear she could be heard from the main house, but I don't care.

I come hard with a loud growl, twitching and jerking inside her, making sure she has every drop of my seed. Our joined juices leak from her, covering us both and making a mess as my cock falls pendulous. I need to get us to a shower as soon as possible.

I look down at her, taking in the state of her chest. My teeth marks are all over her, along with angry red finger marks where I'd grabbed at her. I bet if I looked, her arse cheeks would have the same marks too.

Harper's gaze follows mine, but she doesn't bat an eyelid at the marks.

"Always a pleasure, Mr Knox," she says, but the way she says it has me hard as stone once again.

Not one to waste a good hard-on, I flick my eyes up to hers. The glint there tells me all I need to know. I buck my hips and take her seven ways to Sunday right here in the hut.

CHAPTER 28

HARPER

I've been staying with Keanu at the Knox estate for almost two months now. Who would have thought I'd be enjoying myself? I read him all wrong when I first arrived. I thought he was just another devil in disguise, who used people for his own gain. At first, I believed he was doing just that with me, but it's become so much more. We've become each other's saviour in a way. If he's stressed or if he's had a hard meeting, then the first thing he does is come and find me, and I give him the release he needs. I willingly let him use my body in any way he likes, and I enjoy every single touch, every stroke of his calloused hands, every lick of his tongue, and every grab and slap of the arse he gives me. I've started to ache for him.

At night, when I get that familiar ache of need at my core, I slip my hand down between my legs to my slick folds while imagining it's him. My body craves more of him and so does my heart, but I know I'm just a willing participant for him. Living under his roof, I'm just easy access, I guess. I don't think he'll ever see us the way I want us to be.

I need to get out of this head space. I need to get up and do… something.

I shower and dress quickly. Once I'm done, I head out of my room and wander aimlessly through the halls of the estate, not knowing what to do. Betty has already done her jobs for this morning and is

Depths of Deceit

now preparing for dinner. I didn't want to get in her way as she already told me before she needs to do things in order, her way. Otherwise, she'll forget.

I hear chatting from behind one of the doors at the far end of the corridor. It sounds like Lincoln and Yates. I don't want to seem like I'm imposing on their conversation, so I make my presence known.

"Hi, Lincoln. Hi, Yates," I sing happily.

"Harper?" Lincoln says my name like it's a question. I've come to the conclusion he doesn't think much of me. He hardly ever speaks to me, and whenever I walk into a room, he walks out. "What are you doing?" he asks.

"Nothing. I was bored in my room," I tell him, slightly snarky with him. I've given him no reason not to trust me, yet he treats me with no respect.

"And that gives you the right to snoop around?"

Yates casts his eyes downwards, clearly not wanting any involvement in this argument.

"I wasn't snooping around. I came around the corner at the same time you came out of the room. It was just a coincidence."

"No such thing as coincidences around here." He narrows his intimidating gaze on me.

"Jesus, did you have bitchflakes for breakfast?" His lip twitches, but only slightly. If I had blinked, I would have missed it.

I'm all set to give him a piece of my mind and ask what the deal is, when a voice booms, echoing off the walls.

"Lincoln." All our heads turn. "My office, now." Keanu doesn't hang around and neither does Lincoln. The only difference is Lincoln looks over his shoulder at me and bares his teeth.

"What's his problem?" I turn, asking Yates.

"Don't worry about it. He's always brooding over something and he's just doing his job in looking out for Keanu. It's one of the things he's good at," Yates replies, heading back into the room he came out of before.

I pop my head around the door frame. "Wow." I'm in awe. "What is this room?" I scan it in all its glory. There are screens covering one wall, which I assume are the security cameras around the grounds, then on the other side of the room is a major computer system setup of some sort. Two computer screens, a laptop, keyboards, and a super-sonic-looking mouse. Wires are connected all over the place, leading to one unit with loads of blinking lights. I couldn't even tell you what any of this stuff does. "What's this for?" I pick up a thin black hard-wearing box, open it, and find what looks like six sets of wireless earbuds. Are they listening devices?

"Don't touch anything, and you're not supposed to be in here. If Keanu or Lincoln find you here, I'll be six feet under." Yates takes the box from my hands and places it back down.

"Is this your setup?" I ask, ignoring his request for me to leave.

"It certainly is." I can tell he's proud. "I might not have been here long, but in order for me to do my job, I had to move a few things around. Keanu wasn't happy at first, but he got used to it and let me do my thing. Over there is the security system, and each screen is directed at a different point on the estate, but all exits and doors are covered, and even the perimeter around the grounds. It's all linked to an alarm system, so if it detects even the smallest movement, it sends us an alert. Everyone who works here has their face scanned so the system recognises us and doesn't go off every time we walk by them, yours included. But if it scans an unknown face, the alarm is sounded and everyone knows about it as it's fucking loud." He smiles up at me from his bucket seat and I chuckle before he continues, totally in his element. "On this side is where I gather all the important information I need to keep Keanu happy, or at least I try to. Lately, it hasn't been a success. It seems whatever I try, I'm not catching a break."

"What is it you're looking for?" It's an innocent question, but the way he regards me puts me on edge. "It's something to do with my father, isn't it?"

I get my answer when he looks away from me and closes down all the screens on his side; not that I knew what any of it was. I don't want him to push me out of the room as this is the first real conversation I've had with him. I know he's younger than me, but he's mature for his age and he makes me laugh.

"What's it like working for a man like Keanu?" I perch my arse down into the chair next to him, closest to the monitors showcasing the

Depths of Deceit

grounds. I pretend I'm engrossed in them and not eager to learn something new about Keanu.

"Despite what people think about him, he's a good man. He's fiercely loyal to his men. He'd put himself in front of a bullet for any one of us and we'd do the same for him because he's earned that respect from us. He might be dangerous and feared by most, but he's still human and wants what most people want. It's just harder for him because of who he is."

My heart beats faster with every word Yates says. It's not like I didn't know the type of man Keanu is, but I forgot that he's just like everyone else in some ways, and maybe having normal things in his life is harder than it is for others. I know he doesn't trust anyone easily. Has he ever had a relationship before? How would he when all his time is taken up running this place and keeping his men alive? He doesn't seem like the type of guy who is ready to settle down, but surely he's thought about his future and who will take over the business when he's no longer able to handle it.

"I know what you're thinking there, Harper," Yates says, interrupting my thoughts.

I blush. "And what's that?"

"Knox loves what he does and I doubt anyone can change that. The only way Keanu loses all this," he gestures around with his hands, "will be when he's dead." Yates's tone turns the conversation a little sour, and I don't want to talk about it any longer.

"There had better be a fucking good reason why you're in here." Keanu's rough, deep voice has me jumping out of my seat and standing up straight.

We might have been intimate together once or twice, but the darkness in his eyes and his demanding presence still make me a quivering mess. I know he'd never harm me, but that doesn't mean I don't fear him.

"Boss, we were just——"

Knox never takes his eyes off me. "You were what?"

"We were just talking about what to do if the perimeter alarms go off," I blurt, thinking quickly.

"Sure. And what's that?" He folds his arms across his broad chest, maximising his bulging muscles and the intricate artwork tattooed over them that I've come to love running my hands along.

"We didn't get that far, actually. Because you showed up." I grin, rather impressed with myself for my quick reply. Normally, I'm crap at lying, but have I just fooled the mighty Knox?

"You're a fucking shit liar, Harper." I swallow what feels like a golf ball-sized lump in my throat and my grin falls. "You give yourself away when you bite your lip." He prowls towards me, only stopping when we're nose to nose. "Don't ever lie to me again. Big or small. A lie is still a lie. It'll serve you well to remember that." He grabs a tight hold on my wrist and pulls me from the room. He wordlessly takes me up the stairs and hoists me into my room.

"You want me to trust you, yet you're still lying," he yells, slamming the door behind him. "How do you expect that to work, huh?" I stare at the ground and rub my arm, purely for something to do. "Answer me!"

I flinch at his tone. "I... I'm... sorry. It won't happen again, I swear. I didn't want to get Yates into trouble for my mistake——"

"Yates has a mind of his own, Harper. I'm pretty sure if he didn't think you should've been in there he'd have removed you."

I feel like a child being scolded by my parents, but I don't fight back. Not when he's like this. I bite my tongue. After all, I was in the wrong.

"There are rules here. How many times do you have to be told before you start to understand them?" he continues. "I'm yet to look at him. I don't want to see the disappointment in his eyes. "Look at me, Harper."

I hesitate a moment longer, and the next thing I know, he's standing in front of me.

He roughly forces my chin up with his index finger. "I said, look at me." I stare into the dark depths of blackness, unable to look away. "When I ask you to do something, I expect you to do it. Do I make myself clear?" The huskiness of his voice is a soft lullaby I could listen to forever.

"Crystal." His eyes leave me, stopping at my mouth. I close my

Depths of Deceit

eyes and lick my lips in anticipation, waiting for the sparks to light my fire. The burn in my core that only he can set alight.

Only, they don't come.

I feel the hotness of his breath against my ear, spreading delicious goosebumps all over my body. "If you want to feel my lips against yours, my hands caressing your skin, or my cock in your pussy again, then you'll learn to do as you're told." He licks my cheek and releases me from his firm hold.

Only when I hear the door opening and closing again do I open my eyes and sigh in frustration, disappointed at the loss of him. I wanted him to take me there and then, to punish me for being naughty. I'm turning into a horny, wanton mess around him, and I'm not remotely ashamed of it.

I was ready for anything he was going to give out, and I would have taken it, screaming his name at the top of my lungs.

What is this man doing to me?

I lose my mind when he's near. All rational thoughts turn to ash and drift away on a gentle breeze.

The fact he's mischievous, dangerous, and a savage when it comes to sex… I'm learning to live with that. It's not like I can judge him for his way of living when I've grown up raised by a man who's no better than he is. My father doesn't have an ounce of decency about him, though. He doesn't have what Keanu has. He's never had respect from his people. He doesn't care what happens to the men that work for him. Here, at the Knox empire, it's a family. They'd die for one another, and I'd happily give my life for anyone in this building at any given time, but I wouldn't do that for my father.

This is my home for the foreseeable future and these are my people.

I've finally come to terms with that.

CHAPTER 29

KEANU

I'm fucking seething at Harper. When is she going to learn that I have rules in place for a reason? It's how I keep myself and everyone else under my roof safe. I lost my patience with her, especially when she wouldn't look at me.

She made another mistake, but she needs to learn that mistakes are what get you killed. My mistake was bridging the gap between us and touching her. The minute my hand grazed her skin, a current so furious and wild broke through me. I've never felt anything like it. Only she fuels these kinds of feelings, and no one has ever come close before her. I doubt anyone ever will again. There's no point in denying the magnitude of the connection we seem to have for one another. At this point, it seems inevitable.

I could have taken her, fucked submission into her, but I knew her body was reacting to me. She wanted that as much as I did. So instead, I took it from her, leaving her standing there, pining for more. That's her punishment for disobeying a direct order.

I'll see to her later, but right now, I need to find out what Yates has told her. I'm pacing through the halls, my sexual frustration turning into rage at one of my men, but when I breach the floor the computer room is on, Yates is running towards me. I'm instantly on alert and my anger towards him is braced for whatever he's about to tell me.

Depths of Deceit

"What is it?" I ask, getting straight to the point and following him into the communications room.

"Might be nothing, but it could also be something. Camera thirteen is out. I have no picture and I can't get it back online." I watch as he types and clicks on his keyboard.

"Have you radioed down to whoever's on that post?"

"Tried. I've had no response." He flicks his gaze up at me. "Sorry, boss. This is on me. I should have noticed it, but was distracted by——"

I hold my hand up. "Save your excuses. Whose post is it?"

He looks at the electronic rota. "Dean."

"Well, try him a-fuckin-gain," I order. I listen intently, waiting for Dean to answer his radio, but we get nothing.

"Who's the closest to him?"

"Lincoln."

"Get him to check it out."

"Already on it, boss."

Finally, someone who knows how to use their fucking radio. I throw the spare headset over my ears so I can hear what's coming through the channel. Lincoln's voice breaks the deadly silence.

"Boss, you might want to come down and see this." I can tell straight away it's not good.

"Did you find Dean?" I need to know if he's okay. That's one of my main priorities.

"Yeah, got him. He's going to have a motherfucking headache from the blow he took to the back of his head, but he's alive. But that's not the problem."

That was all I needed to hear. "I'm on my way." I remove the headset. "Get Betty and Harper and take them to Tillie's hut in the woods. It has an underground compartment beneath the wooden floorboards in the corner by the bench. Then you get back in here and find out what the fuck just happened," I rage at Yates.

We leave the room together, not wasting any time. He goes right and I go left, heading for the stairs. I race outside and down to the post where the issue is without breaking a sweat.

"What's the issue?" I take in the scene before me. Dean is sitting on a big boulder, trying to suppress the blood dripping from the back of his head. "You good?" I pull his head forward so I can get a good look at his injury. There's a nasty cut, but thankfully, it's not deep enough to need stitches.

He hisses. "I'm good. Pissed off that I was taken out from behind, though. Sorry, boss. I never saw it coming."

Sam makes an appearance. "I've swept the perimeter. Nothing out of the ordinary.

I nod. "Take Dean and get his head cleaned up." Sam helps Dean up and I watch them retreat. I swing my gaze to Lincoln. "What the fuck happened?"

"Fuck knows, but look behind the fence." He points.

There's a cigarette butt and a wooden toothpick. My men sweep the perimeter daily, and if they spot anything out of the ordinary——like this—— it gets reported, but nothing has been. "You know anyone who can get some DNA from that?" I aim my question at Lincoln as a few other men have made their way over.

I may have my hand in a lot of pots, but this technology isn't cheap to own and none of my men are qualified for this.

"As a matter of fact, I do. Whether or not she'll help is another issue entirely."

She? From his facial expression, that's a conversation for another day.

"Get straight on it. I want to know who the fuck is scouting my grounds. Get back to your posts." I bark my orders, outraged. Things are slipping around here, and I know that's down to me. I've been preoccupied with a certain someone and I need to get a handle on things before it all falls apart.

I sprint down into the woods with purpose. I locate the hidden board and yank it up in my haste to get to Harper and Betty. It opens, and the sight that greets me rocks me to the core. Betty is comforting an hysterical Harper. She's sobbing in Betty's arms and shaking.

I'm by their side instantaneously and peel Harper's arms from around Betty's neck.

"I got you. Everything's okay. You're safe, baby cakes." I rub her back reassuringly.

Depths of Deceit

"Keanu?" She peers up at me. "Oh, thank God you're alive." She wraps her arms around my neck, almost choking me.

"You were worried about me?" I'm astonished. I thought she was afraid because she was underground, closed inside and feeling trapped.

"Yes. I didn't know what was happening. I thought the worst." She looks up at me, narrowing her eyes like I've grown another head. "Why else do you think I'm a mess?"

I give Betty a discreet look to leave us. She's used to hiding out down here when there's a threat, no matter how small. When she's out of sight, I turn my attention back to Harper. "I thought it was because you were down here."

"No. It was you. I'm not ready to lose you." Her admission is new. She's never really talked about her feelings towards me, only about staying here.

"What are you trying to tell me, Harper?" The air around us shifts. Nothing and no one exists, only the two of us.

She locks her eyes with mine. "I think I'm falling in love with you, Keanu." She speaks the truth, no lip-biting. "I know my timing isn't great, but the thought of never seeing you again tore at my heart." She lifts her hands, gently holding my face in the palm of her hands. "I can't imagine my life without you in it anymore. Being here with you... this is where I belong. This is my home now."

I can feel my heart pounding in my chest. It's beating wilder than ever before and it's only for her. I remove one of her hands from my face and hold it against my chest.

"Can you feel that?" She nods, glancing at our joined hands. "That's because of you. It beats for you, and as long as it beats, I'll protect you, keep you safe, and love you just as fiercely as you love me." A single tear escapes her eye. I lean forward and kiss her cheek before it falls. "I know I don't deserve you, but that doesn't mean I can't have you, does it?" I say, finally admitting not only to her but myself that there's so much more between us than sex. There's no point denying the feelings I have for her anymore. I care deeply for Harper. I know what I'm feeling for her is love. There's no other explanation for it, and I realise that now.

"You have me, Keanu. Heart, soul, and body. It doesn't matter what you do out there, to me you will only ever be my hero, my lover, and my saviour."

"Does that mean you're okay with what I do for a living?" There's no way she can suddenly put the dark and disturbing things I do to bed. If she says yes, I know she'll be lying.

"No, it doesn't. But I know you don't set out to hurt people unless it's necessary. From what I've learnt in recent weeks, there are far worse organisations out there than selling controlled narcotics. And when you've lived most of your life detesting your father and knowing what kind of man he really is, you learn the difference between a devil and a monster."

"Oh yeah. Which one am I?"

"The devil. You do things because you have to. A monster seeks the darkness and does things because he wants to."

I can't help but smile at her analysis. "I like your way of thinking." I don't waste any more time. I claim her mouth with mine.

Trying not to fall for Harper was a losing game. No matter how hard I tried to fight my feelings, in the end, they always won.

She's the bright light in my depth of darkness.

She's the flame that lights my torch.

The embers that keep my fire burning.

The blood that runs through my veins.

The lustful pulse straining my cock.

The heaven to my hell.

And right now… I'm basking in her light as if she's my lifeline.

CHAPTER 30

HARPER

The past week has been bizarre and unconventional to say the least. Not in regards to me and Keanu, but the atmosphere around the estate. A dark cloud hung over us as if we were waiting for the impending storm to come and destroy everything in its wake.

Keanu has spent most of his time in the office or in the computer room with Yates and Lincoln, only returning to me at night when he climbs into bed in the early hours of the morning. Many times, I've asked what's going on, but he refuses to tell me and diverts my attention elsewhere, usually by making me lose my mind in him and the things he does to my body.

Betty and I have been forbidden from going anywhere near the perimeter until told otherwise, and due to the perplexed glint in Keanu's eyes, we never asked why. The only thing I do is get fresh air down at the hut once in a while, with an escort. I've been on edge, wondering what I can do to help Keanu. In the end, I decide it's better to stay out of his way so he can focus on the task at hand. At least, that was what I thought until I spotted Evan leaving the office once again.

I run down the hallway to catch up with him before he leaves. "Evan," I shout. He picks up the pace. "Evan, wait… please."

He drops his head and stops at the bottom of the stairs before facing me.

"Were you going to leave without saying goodbye?" I ask once I'm at his side. When he tilts his head back up, I suck in a shocked breath at the sight of him. He's not the Evan I once knew. He's almost unrecognisable. He has dark circles under his eyes like he hasn't slept in days. His hair is longer and doesn't seem to be styled in any way, but what's more haunting and sorrowful to see is the sober look in his eyes. He looks like he's about to give up on... everything. "Are you okay?" This man has done everything to protect me. Maybe it's time I start doing the same for him.

"I've had better days." He laughs, but it doesn't reach his eyes.

"What are you doing here?" I fear what he may say, but I ask anyway.

"I had some business with Keanu. The less you know, the better." He rubs my arm soothingly.

"I wish people would stop saying that. I'm not a china doll. I won't break by finding out what my father and Keanu are really up to. Or why you're choosing to double-cross him." I narrow my eyes as the shock on his face mocks me.

"I don't know—"

I hold my hand up. "Save it, Evan. I've pieced it together. I know you're working with Keanu to take down my father." I'm part telling the truth, the other half of me is winging it. I've seen Evan come and go a few times. Sometimes he arrives with a file in his hand and leaves empty-handed. He's obviously giving Keanu something, but in exchange for what? "What are you getting out of this deal?" I cross my arms over my chest, trying to appear more confident than I am. I could be totally wrong in my assumptions.

"Harper, this is so much bigger than you or me. It's bigger than anything I've dealt with before. I've seen the shit you're father has done, but he's crossed a line he shouldn't have and Keanu is vengeful." Someone caught his eye over my shoulder. I know instantly it's Keanu. His presence demands my attention whenever he's close. "I've already told you more than I should. If you have questions, you're asking the wrong person. I'll speak to you soon. Take care, Harper." He plants a kiss on my head and leaves. I spin around, meeting the dark black pits of Keanu's eyes,

Depths of Deceit

"You're always so inquisitive, baby cakes. Are you sure you want to enter the lion's den?" He's leaning over the banister at the top of the steps, his eyes burning holes in me.

I gulp harshly, yet with no hesitation, my mouth opens. "Yes."

"Once you enter, Harper, there's no turning back from the darkness. It will consume you and turn your heart blacker than black. You sure you're ready for that?" I know he's trying to scare me into submission, but it won't work. I've had my fair share of darkness. The only difference is now I have a voice and power over what happens to me. No one controls me anymore. I want retribution for what I've been dealt with in this life, and if my father is involved… damn right I want a piece of the action.

"You won't change my mind, Keanu. I want to help." I'm already making headway up the stairs. His black pools follow my every move. When I reach the top, I close the distance between us until I'm at his side. The place I've come to cherish, feel safe, and feel at my strongest. "If what I have running rampant in my head is anything to go by, I know I need to help you. Help to free those girls. They don't deserve to be treated like dogs."

He studies my features. Is he looking for a slip in my exterior? Any sign that I'm not fully committed?

He can stare right into the depths of me. The only things he'll find are hatred and determination.

"Right this way, but I warn you, what you'll see and hear will be hard to digest. I'm not going to sugar-coat anything because you're my…" He pauses, and my heart begins to beat faster.

"Your lover? Your partner? Your nemesis? What, Keanu? Tell me." I beg with my eyes.

"Right now, you're a fucking sharp thorn in my side." I deflate instantly. Those weren't the words I was longing for. My heart plummets, but not for long. He lifts my chin back up with his index finger. "You've come to mean a lot to me, Harper. I might not be able to give you what you want just yet, but know I'd do anything to protect what's mine, and you are mine. There's no doubt about that. Everything is just… exploding around me, and I need to be focused right now. This is hard for me. I've never had someone like you in my life. Give me time to come to terms with that."

I lick my lips, his words melting my heart, but more than anything, they're playing havoc with my core and I'm wet between my thighs. I can't control the moan that falls from my mouth.

"I bet if I slipped my hand to your pussy, you'd be soaking wet and ready for me." His hand moves from my chin to my mouth, where he rubs the pad of his finger across my bottom lip. "If only we had the time, but unfortunately, you've just entered into my world. That's your mistake for wanting to follow me."

"I'd follow you anywhere," I tell him breathlessly.

His eyes close momentarily and then he huffs loudly. "Why do I get the feeling I'm going to regret this?"

Does he mean allowing me into the fold or having me follow him wherever he goes?

It doesn't matter which to me because my mind's made up on both counts and there's nothing he can do that will stop me.

CHAPTER 31

KEANU

I'm already having second thoughts about this, but I lead Harper into the computer room regardless. The doubt is lingering at the back of my mind with every step we take. I'm in two minds whether to throw her over my shoulder, take her back to her room, and fuck some sense into her. As much as that would please me, I know Harper's persistence would only be blindsided for a short time before she'd ask to help again.

Lincoln is staring me down, shooting daggers my way when he sees Harper following me. I know what he's thinking. I've lost my damn mind, and maybe I have. I know bringing her into this could come back to bite me on the arse. Hell, it could come and bite us all on the arse. It's not just me. There's my men to think about.

I watch as she struts past me and takes a seat in the empty chair next to mine. Her confidence is shining bright, but I see the chink in her armour. It's only ninety percent confidence. The other ten percent is a mixture of fear and hope. She's scared of what she might find out but hopeful that what we tell her, she can refute. It's time to see what she's made of. I know what her tells are, so I'll be watching her closely while she gets the rundown of what's really going on.

"For Harper's benefit, start from the beginning and fill us in on what we know," I tell Lincoln, who's still eyeing me up like a crazy person. He's furious that I'm letting her in on this. He doesn't have to like it; it's my decision, my house, and what I say goes. He doesn't even know what the plan with Harper is yet. He shakes his head a little and huffs out a sigh.

"Everything?" he questions with a raise of his brow.

"Yes." I want it all out. I want to see her reactions to what she learns. "Everything from the night Tillie went missing to now."

Lincoln begins to relay everything while Harper sits there listening to it all in frozen shock. By the time Lincoln has finished speaking, Harper's sitting on the edge of her seat, gripping the arms for dear life. Her eyes glisten with unshed tears that she's trying her best to control. She doesn't want to show me a single sign of weakness. I admire that about her.

"That's everything up to the day of the security breach along the perimeter," Lincoln states, looking from me to Harper. "Which I have the results for. The DNA on the stub we found was a match for one of Benson's men."

I grit my teeth. My gut was telling me this, but now it's confirmed. War is on the horizon.

"Are you saying my father kidnapped Tillie?" She looks at me for clarification.

I nod.

"All this time, my father has deceived me. Lied to me and been doing God knows what. All the times he's left on business meetings, gone for hours. Oh no, no, no." Her hands fly to her mouth. "He's trafficking people. And your sister. Is she still alive?"

The room is silent. She's asking something no one has the answer to. I give Harper a moment to address what she's been informed of, waiting for any other reaction.

"Fucking hell. That sick, twisted, evil bastard." Those are the first words to leave her mouth, shocking not only me but Lincoln and Yates. "How certain are you that my father's involved?"

"Ninety-nine percent sure. Every bit of evidence we've gathered points to your father."

"And Evan? How's he involved? For the love of God, please tell me he's not included in your list of men to kill. He wouldn't do something

Depths of Deceit

like this." I see the horror in her eyes for a man that she no doubt values more as a father to her than her own ever was.

"You can relax. Evan is working for me now," I state, putting her mind at rest. She doesn't need to know all the facts where Evan is concerned. There's time for that.

"You mean he's spying for you?" I nod. "What if he gets caught? My father would…" She pauses, gulping loudly.

"Evan knows what's at stake, Harper. He's been around a long time, and he can look out for himself."

"That doesn't make me feel any better about it."

"Would it make you feel better knowing Evan approached me?"

That spikes her interest. "How and when?"

"The night your father sold you. Evan wasn't in on it, but he quickly came up with an idea to keep you safe long enough to work out a plan. He came to me as I was leaving and asked for a favour, which I'll admit, I was reluctant about. But he offered his services to help me tie Benson to Tillie's disappearance, along with everything else I needed to take him out for good. So I jumped at the chance."

"Foolish if you ask me."

I swing my gaze over to Lincoln, my fists clenched tight. "No one asked you, did they?" I roar, making Harper jump and Lincoln take notice.

"No, but I'm here to stop you from making stupid mistakes. Which you've done plenty of since setting eyes on her, and you're still willing to make them by involving her now."

Lincoln knows what's coming before I even make a move, but he doesn't stop me from grabbing him by the neck, hauling him out of the chair, and pinning him against the wall.

"This is my empire, my rules, and my fucking decision. If you don't like it, then you can leave, but don't ever come back," I growl in his face.

"Are you prepared to put everything on the line for her, Knox?" he manages to say through my tight hold around his neck. "Can you honestly say that you trust her?" I narrow my eyes at him. "What is she really worth to you?" I know what he's doing, and fuck if it doesn't annoy the hell out of me. "Say it, Keanu. Tell me."

171

My breathing intensifies. "Yes." I roar. "Fuck! Yes, Lincoln. I'd do just about anything to protect her because she's mine." I release his neck but can't help shoving his shoulders back against the wall one more time.

I can't bring myself to look at anyone as I admit my true feelings to the world.

"Good. That's all I needed to know," Lincoln says like nothing happened. "I might not be fully on board with Harper knowing everything, but if you trust her, then I trust your judgement." He looks behind me. "No offence, Harper."

"None taken," she says, slightly breathless.

"Now I know where you stand, we can come up with a plan that we can all agree on," Lincoln adds.

"You're a fucking sly twat, Linc," I tell him, shaking my head.

"That's one reason I'm good at what I do, but you already know that. Shall we get back to business?"

The tension in the air lessens, and I glance at Harper as I take my seat. She offers me a timid smile, knowing how hard that might have been for me. Admitting my feelings to Harper is one thing, but admitting them to everyone else is another thing entirely.

"Can I just backtrack for a second?" Harper asks, a slight arch to her brow.

"To which part?" Lincoln and I ask in unison.

"To the part where you said my name was down as the owner of the three warehouses. Why would my father put my name on them?"

She's so naive, and it has me wanting to comfort her. "Because your father was trying to be smart. No one would think to search for your name when doing a thorough search on him. Plus, if it all went south, he wouldn't be linked to the buildings, you would."

Harper gasps, holding her chest. "Oh, God. He'd have no concerns about seeing me go down for his trafficking rings, would he?"

"It won't get that far, Harper, so stop worrying," Yates tells her, gently rubbing her arm.

"Did you find anything at the locations?" she asks.

"Evan managed to get inside two of the buildings without raising any suspicion, but the places were scrubbed clean with a fine tooth

Depths of Deceit

comb. No signs of anything or anyone ever being there. We think he's pulled all his resources and now everything operates from the last warehouse. We're just struggling to find a way in and a fast exit strategy," I explain.

She nods. "That makes sense."

Yates springs into action, giving her further details on the location of the warehouse. How heavily guarded the grounds are likely to be, where Benson's men could possibly be stationed. He clicks a few buttons on the keyboard, bringing up the blueprints of the building to show the ground layout. She begins studying it, asking Yates questions about what something means. I'm surprised at how involved she's getting. I wanna say she's a natural at this stuff, but the thought soon drifts from my mind when I think about the dangers involved.

I don't miss the odd conflicting looks Lincoln is giving me, but he's wise enough not to say anything.

"Hold on. The more you're telling me about this place, the more I feel like I know it." Lincoln and I are up and out of our seats in a flash.

"How so?" Lincoln asks before my mouth moves.

"I'm not sure. But I feel like I've been there before." I spin the chair around so she's facing me and bend at the waist, getting close to her.

"Harper, I need you to think long and hard." I try my damn hardest not to come across as aggressive, but this could be a major breakthrough. It could be the piece of information we've been missing all this time.

"I'm trying." She scrubs at her forehead. I can see she's stressing out.

I entwine my fingers around hers. "Close your eyes."

"I don't see how that will he—"

I cut her off. "Just do it," I order softly. She releases a huff but does it anyway. "Take nice, relaxing breaths. In and out, nice and slow." She begins the process. "Take your time, Harper." I rub her arm gently, trying to soothe her. This is important and she needs to be calm. I'm desperate for some answers, but getting up in her face won't help. With a soft approach, I ask, "How old were you when you visited this warehouse?"

"I don't know. Maybe eleven or twelve."

"That's good. Really good. Can you remember anything distinctive about the place, how it smelt?"

"Actually, yes. Iron. It left me feeling like I had a metallic taste in my mouth. It smelt like death."

"Can you remember seeing anything?" I'm pushing here, hoping it doesn't push her over the edge, but she's doing brilliant, so I ask more questions. I'm amazed she remembers shit with being so young.

"It was an abandoned building. Nothing around for miles. I remember being in a car and thinking we were heading into the middle of nowhere. We pulled up outside and it was really dark. The only light around was coming from the headlights." I'm dying to ask who 'we' she's referencing, but she's going somewhere with it, so I don't interrupt her. "Once inside, it was no better. It was a dirty warehouse, dark and cold. Some of the windows were broken and there was graffiti lining the concrete walls. There were lots of individual rooms and more than one level to it." She pauses, and I can feel the moment she tenses. "My mother was there. I was with my mother. I recall clinging onto her hand as we wandered further inside. It was like she was looking for something or someone. I could be wrong. I think there were beds. Yes. Rows of beds in some of the rooms. That's when Father found us. He wasn't impressed at us being there. He regarded my mother and me like we were nothing. I curled into my mother's side, afraid of what was going to happen, but then my father started speaking. I zoned out for the most part, scared for myself and my mother. But the way my father was speaking made it sound like there was more to come. More beds, more room. How could I have been so naive? I just assumed he was going to use the place to help sick people." A lone tear escapes her tightly shut eyes.

I wipe her sadness away. "I know this is hard, but I need you to stay with it. What else do you remember?"

"The more my father spoke, the more tense my mother got. Which was enough to make me nervous, as my mother was always so calm. Then another man appeared from the shadows. I'd never seen him before, and at the time, I didn't think my mother had, but now I'm thinking about it and understand it more, she was shaking and struggling to stand. It was like she saw a ghost." I swing my head around and face Lincoln, wondering where the fuck she's taking us. "My mother started to retreat from my father, shouting at him and saying she wouldn't let him do this. I didn't understand what she was saying, and eventually, we were both running. I lost my bearings, but we soon found ourselves back at the entrance. In a panic, we both stumbled and hit the ground, falling on something hard. It's a good job my mother was with me because I had no clue what anything was. It was so dark. My mother threw me into the back of the car and then jumped in herself. She was driving fast and kept repeating that everything was going to be okay. I don't remember anything after that, and the next thing I know, I'm waking up in the hospital. It wasn't long after I woke up that I was told my mother died in a car crash." She opens her eyes, blinking a few times as they adjust to the light. Her desolation at reliving this childhood memory almost breaks me, but she's soon shaking it off and her vision is clear.

"You did really good, baby cakes." I don't care that I've used the nickname I have for her in front of my men. They'd be signing their own death warrant if they were to say anything.

"Yates..."

"Already on it, boss. The original blueprints look as Harper said, but they've had work done. They've added a basement or tunnel, but if I can just work my magic... got it. There's an updated version of them. Benson has made some changes. They show the tunnel leading out of the building and coming up a mile long. My guess is they use it to smuggle the girls down when it's light but need them out of sight." I guess Yates really has earned a place with me.

"Can we make it work?" I turn my attention to Lincoln.

"Possibly. We'd have to have vehicles stationed there. That's not the problem, Knox. We don't know what state she'll be in. She might not handle the noise of guns going off. Her state of mind... there's a lot to take into consideration here." I hang my head, instantly knowing he's talking about Tillie.

"I can help with that," Harper announces. "That's if you trust me enough with her. I assume it's your sister you're talking about."

"How?" I tilt my head in question.

"If you can keep them distracted long enough, it'll give me a head start with Tillie, we can exit through the tunnel and out the way of danger, so you'll all head in through the front of the building. You can follow once you've done… your thing."

The sideward smirk I'm giving her causes her to blush and has her legs squeezing tighter.

"There's still one problem," Yates says, sounding doubtful. "We still need a way to get through the front. We need another distraction before we can even think about an escape."

The cogs are turning in everyone's minds, I can see it written on their faces as I stare at them all one by one, ending with Harper. She's biting her lip nervously.

"Whatever you're thinking, you can forget it. The answer is no, Harper," I say with purpose, but she ignores my threatening tone.

"I'll do it."

CHAPTER 32

HARPER

"I'll do it," I announce without any hesitation. I don't even need to think about it and there's nothing any of them can say that will change my mind. I know the dangers involved but still, I'm determined to do it.

"Have you lost your damn mind?" Keanu bellows.

"No. For once in my life, my mind is clear. I'm doing this, Keanu, and you won't stop me." I stand my ground.

"Over my dead body. Do you honestly think I'd intentionally put you in harm's way?" He begins pacing the floor.

"I'm well aware of the consequences, Keanu. But please, let me do this."

He eyes me warily. "Why do you want to do this so badly?"

"Because…" I pause, trying to find the right words. "I feel responsible for it all."

"You can't really believe that. It was your father who took Tillie, not you."

"I lived under his roof. I should have known something wasn't right. If I had done something back then, none of this would be happening. He took Tillie and God knows how many other women or children. I can't let him ruin any more lives, Keanu. If I can help stop him from doing this, then I'll do it." His features turn hard and tortured. He's not going to let me do this, so I try a different approach. "Maybe I found myself here because it was fate that led me to you. Our paths crossed for a reason, Keanu. What if this is the reason? What if this is the only way to get your sister back and help free all the others? It's a risk worth taking, right? I share this man's DNA. I have his tainted blood running through my veins, Keanu. I've let that man, beat me black and blue, take away my freedom, tell me I will never amount to anything. He made me a shell of the person I could be and I won't let him get away with it. He needs to pay for what he's done to me and all those girls too. If it costs me my life to end this once and for all then so be it. I'm okay with that. You don't have to carry this burden alone. Let me help myself by helping you."

His gaze finds mine once again, his pupils fully dilated. "It won't cost you anything because you'll have me and my men there to protect you. Losing you under my watch would haunt me forever and my life wouldn't be worth living. I'm not prepared to find out how living without you would feel." He releases a sigh, the weight of his decision lying heavy on his chest. "If we do this, we do it my way. Is that understood, Harper?"

"Absolutely. Does that mean I'm in?" I know I sound hopeful. I bravely look at Lincoln. He's not exactly a fan of mine, but when I see him smirking at me, I know it's a turning point for us. He dips his head in a show of respect for me. It's the first time I've felt praise from him since being here. Maybe he isn't the big bad wolf I've proclaimed him to be. Keanu still hasn't answered me as he continues to contemplate the idea of me tagging along.

"She might be our only way in, Knox. I know you're still indecisive about it, but she's our best shot." Lincoln offers his advice.

"You think I don't know that?" It's rhetorical, so nobody answers.

"I can have her linked up to our comms and she'll have her own earpiece so she can communicate with you the whole time," Yates presses.

"I can do this, Keanu. You once told me that trust needs to be earned." He locks eyes with me. "Let me earn your trust; everyone's trust. I want to do this. Please, give me a chance." It's all I have left to give him. My last attempt to convince him.

Depths of Deceit

"I'm going to hell for this. Fine, you're in. But the first sign of trouble, you get out of there. No questions asked. Are we clear?"

"Thank you."

"Don't thank me yet. Now leave us. We have a lot of stuff to do. I'll come find you later." His gaze burns through me, but I welcome it. I know what he's referring to. He'll need me after everything that's just transpired, and I'm already feeling the effects of what he'll do to me and my body. Even my heart. I'm completely besotted by this man. He's lit a fire in me, and it's a flame that I never want to burn out.

"You know where to find me." I bow my head to hide my embarrassment from Lincoln and Yates and close the door behind me.

The events from earlier must have taken their toll on me, and at some point, I fell asleep with a book in my hand. When I open my eyes, the dark sky greets me through one of the windows in the hut. I came down here the moment Keanu dismissed me from the computer room.

I rub my eyes, clearing the sleep away. I expected to wake to a quiet and peaceful atmosphere, but I haven't. I scramble off the wood bench, switch the lamp off, and dive to the floor, hands covering my ears and my eyes firmly shut as I try to block out the haunting sounds around me.

It doesn't work. I want to scream, but I'm terrified that if I do, I'll give my location away.

Gunshots ring out around me and men begin shouting orders, their voices full of rage and trepidation.

I have to pinch myself, wondering if I'm still asleep and this is all a bad dream, but it's not. It's very real and I'm in the thick of it.

The Knox estate is under attack. My whole body is shaking, and a sheen of sweat coats my skin.

What should I do?

Do I run or stay here and hide?

What if Keanu needs me?

I need to get back up to the house without being spotted, but I'm frozen. My legs won't move no matter how much I try. It's like my brain can't register the signals properly.

I jump in fright when a shadow appears outside the door. I curl into a ball, waiting for the moment I'm found. I squeeze my eyes shut.

"Harper... where are you?" The soft whisper of Betty's voice calms me instantly.

"Betty, down here." I stumble over to her. The moon gives us just enough light to make out each other's shadows. "What's going on?"

"No time to explain. We need to get you to safety. Follow me." She takes my hand and leads me to the corner of the hut. She opens up the hatch we hid in before and begins climbing in. "There's another door that leads off the grounds. We need to move now." I sense the urgency in her voice, but my feet don't move when she pulls my hand again.

"Harper, we need to go now." Her voice is pleading.

"I... can't. I won't leave without Keanu. You go. I need to find him." I prise her fingers apart and release her hold of me.

"What? No. Keanu wouldn't want you to do that. He'd want you to leave with me."

I hear voices coming from the north of the woods. "I'm sorry, I can't do that. Now go, before we both get caught." I begin closing the hatch back up.

"Be careful, Harper."

"You too." I put everything back the way it was and try to gather my bravery. I know if I don't make a run for it now, it'll be too late. Taking a deep breath, I pluck up the courage I need and finally get my legs to move. I use every muscle in my thighs to power me through the trees. By the time I get to the back of the house, my legs are burning and my throat is dry and sore.

Bullets are flying in every direction. A wave of crimson coats my surroundings like a blanket of death. The stench of iron that pollutes the air is sickening, and then the dead bodies littering the grounds come into view from the outside lights and I want to vomit.

I've never seen so much bloodshed, and for what?

Who's attacking us?

The hairs on the back of my neck stand on end, making my skin tingle with awareness. This has my father written all over it. Has he

Depths of Deceit

finally come to finish the job? Is he here to kill me and Keanu? It's a big risk on his part, but then again, after everything I've learnt about him, nothing is for certain.

The thought of my father finding me fills me with dread, but more than that, it fills me with determination. There is no way I'm going back to that hell hole or shipped and sold to someone else.

I stay low and hide in the shadows where there's less chance of me being spotted. The bodies continue to drop from both sides, bullet holes and knife wounds covering every inch of them. Faces I don't recognise and the faces of Keanu's men I've seen around the estate stare lifelessly up at me.

I spot a clearing at one of the back doors. I have to take it. I glance around just to make sure no one is close and then make a dash for it. I take three strides when a body runs into me, knocking us both to the ground.

For a moment, I feel dizzy, then suddenly, I can't breathe. There's something weighing heavily across my chest and restricting my air supply. The body is unmoving, and I use all the strength in my arms to flip it over. I have to muffle my screams at the pool of blood running from underneath him. It's one of Keanu's men. I know he's dead, but I try compressing the wound in his chest anyway, tears streaming down my face. It's no use. I'm using my energy for nothing. I slump on my arse, staring at my shaking hands which are covered in the man's blood, and so are my clothes. In a panic, I rub my hands over myself just to double check it's not mine and I'm not injured.

A noise coming from behind startles me and I snap my neck around. I almost die on the spot when one of my father's men is standing a few feet away from me, a sinister smile on his face.

"Well, well, what do we have here?" He prowls towards me.

I'm looking for something or someone to help me, but I'm on my own. I drop my gaze to the fallen man beside me, and that's when I see it, hidden inside his jacket pocket.

God, I hope the safety isn't on, otherwise I will be screwed. I don't know how to turn it off. I count to three in my head, and before I can talk myself out of it, I reach for the gun at lightning speed, aim, and fire. I pull the trigger three times in quick succession. The loud bangs hurt my ears and I squeeze my eyes shut. My heart beats wildly against my rib cage, my breathing coming in short, hard pants. The deadly piece of metal still aimed high, I finally have the courage to open my eyes.

"Oh, shit. Fuck." I cover my mouth with the back of my hand, the only part that isn't covered in blood, dry heaving. I've just shot a man at point-blank range. If I wasn't so shaken up, I'd be impressed with my aim.

I don't have time to sit and dwell on how I'm feeling. It was a kill or be killed moment, and it's not like I shot an innocent. He was a horrible human being and the world will be a better place without him in it.

I finally get my legs working, continuing on my mission to find Keanu. I hope he's still alive. I breach the house. It's no better than outside. Blood splatters cover the walls and floor. Everywhere I look there are bodies. Some writhe around in excruciating pain, cursing as they try to control the loss of blood, but most have already slipped away to the afterlife, or the pits of hell, where the devil himself is waiting to greet them. I search around, praying I don't find Keanu among them.

I didn't realise I was still holding the gun until I heard glass shattering beside me and bodies flying through it. My arm is aimed ready to fire at someone. Thankfully, I hold off pulling the trigger as it's Sam and Dean. Sam is pinning someone down, delivering blow after blow to a guy with a knife, and Dean is rolling around on the broken shards of glass with another guy. I think Dean has the upper hand until the guy produces a knife and stabs Dean in the leg.

I need to help him.

He doesn't give up the fight, and it gives me long enough to think about what to do. A large piece of glass glistens up at me. If I slide across the floor just a tad, I can push the glass towards Dean and he could do some damage with it.

He's losing a lot of blood, and in turn, a lot of his strength. I need to act fast. I push off the wall and slide across the floor. My fingertips just manage to push the glass towards him. He's on his back and the big

Depths of Deceit

bloke is on top of him. He's holding the knife close to Dean's neck, and it's getting closer by the second.

"Dean! Beside you."

He's shocked to hear my voice but soon spots my intentions. He swipes the glass up and drags the sharp blade across the guy's throat. Blood coats his face, but it doesn't bother him in the slightest as he rolls the now-dead body off him. At the same time, the body of the guy Sam was fighting with hits the ground with a thud.

"Not that I'm being ungrateful, but what the fuck are you doing here, Harper?" Dean bellows.

"I… I was in the hut when all hell broke loose. Betty escaped, but I need to find Keanu," I stutter, adrenaline coursing through me.

"We need to keep moving, Dean," Sam shouts, looking around for any threats.

He rips the bottom off his shirt and begins wrapping it around the wound on his leg. "We can't leave her here. Keanu would fucking gut us." Worry mars his brows.

"Good point. What's the plan?" I watch the indecisiveness between them and roll my eyes.

"You guys need to hold the fort. You can't do that looking out for me. I have to find Keanu, and I will." I turn to leave.

Dean grabs my arm, stopping me, "Harper, if something happens to you, the boss will kill us. I'd rather take my chances guarding you. If it's my time to die, then so be it, but at least I'll go down swinging and Keanu will know that."

"I agree with Dean," Sam adds.

My heart swells at the loyalty they have for their leader, but I know I'll slow them down and they need to focus. I will not have their deaths on my hands.

The decision is taken when a small army of men breaches the room from one side. They have no choice but to fight them off.

I exchange a look with Dean. "Go, run. Stay safe, Harper."

I can't stop the tears from leaking. I've come to look upon these two men as my older, rather protective brothers. The odds seem against us, and the thought of never seeing them again weighs heavy, but my need to reunite with Keanu is stronger. "Don't die on me. That goes for both of you." I swing my gaze to Sam.

He offers me a cheeky smile. "Don't plan on it. Now go," he roars before a body slams him to the ground again.

I don't need to be told twice.

I venture further inside, trying to ignore the carnage surrounding me, but it's becoming impossible. Especially when I reach the front of the house. The main door has a pile of bodies stacked up high. Bodies belonging to my father's men. They never stood a chance against whoever was guarding it from our side. They clearly went on a rampage.

Could this be Keanu's doing?

I haven't witnessed Keanu when he's fully fired up and in defensive mode, but if this is what he's capable of, I never want to see that side of him.

I get my answer when I reach the bottom of the staircase. I jump in fright when a shadow appears on the other side of the stairs, slumped against the wall by the railings.

"Oh my God, Lincoln." I watch in horror as he slips down the wall, leaving a trail of blood behind. I spring into action and round the stairs, running to his aid. "What can I do?" I drop my gun. It hits the floor with a clatter. He's holding his right shoulder and his hand is covered in dark red liquid.

Is he bleeding out?

Is he dying?

"Don't worry about me, I'll be fin—" A bullet breezes past me and lodges itself in the wall just over Lincoln's head. My hands are shaking, my legs are ready to give up on me, and my head is spinning with pure adrenaline, but I need to stay in control if I want to help him. He's holding a gun in his right hand, but he's unable to lift it. Another shot rings out, bouncing off the railings. I reach for the gun I dropped and angle my arm over the railing, firing every single bullet in the magazine. I'm empty. I peer up ever so slowly, not wanting to get my head blown off, but I need to know if at least one of the bullets did some damage. I sigh in relief at the body lying face down that wasn't there before.

Depths of Deceit

When I direct my attention back to Lincoln, he's narrowing his eyes at me. "Why are you looking at me like that?" I ask.

"I'm wondering where the fuck you got that gun from."

"Now is not the time to be a dick, Lincoln."

"Fair point. Help me up."

I take his hand and heave him up. He's weak, and I have to use all my strength to keep him upright. I yank his good shoulder around my neck and wrap my arm around his waist. He hisses in pain and guilt fills me.

"I'm sorry. I'm sorry," I repeat over and over.

"It's all good. Head for the stairs. If I know Keanu as well as I think I do, he'll be searching the house high and low to find you." He points to the stairs, indicating for me to head that way. "I take it you came in from outside."

"Yes. I was in the woods. In Tillie's hut."

"Good. That's the last place anyone would look. It seems they stormed the house first." We begin walking up the stairs. We're in the open and neither of us is in a good position to shoot. I'm out of bullets and Lincoln can't lift his shooting hand.

"Lincoln, I know you're in pain…" I adjust his body slightly as he starts to slip from my grasp, "but you really need to get your arse moving. You weigh like a thousand pounds."

"All muscle, Harper."

"Really, Lincoln? You're choosing now to be a joker?"

"Yeah. If I'm going to die, then I'll die laughing."

I suddenly get a feeling that has become familiar to me. One I crave with every fibre of my body.

He's close. I know he is

CHAPTER 33

KEANU

I leave the tech room with a heavy heart. I tried everything I could think of to stop Harper from entering the lion's den. It's far too dangerous for her to be in there. Her father wouldn't piss on her if she was on fire. That's when I'm reminded he's the trouble she'd be running into once there. I watch as Lincoln and Yates tail off in different directions, the conversation done with for now.

My eyes flick up to the door where I know she'll be waiting for me. I resist the urge to go to her straight away. I have work that needs to be done before I lose myself in her tight body for the night, and I know if I head into her when I'm itching for a kill the way I am, I could potentially harm her, and I can't let that happen.

With my feet dragging and my shoulders slumped, I head into my office. The quicker I get this shit done, the quicker I can relax and find solace in her.

I throw myself into the cushioned office chair with a huff, the metal groaning under my weight as I pick up the files that need my attention.

Try as I might, I can't concentrate. The woman who was meant to be nothing but a mindless fuck has now become my everything.

After reading the same thing for the third time, I slam the paper down and decide to give up for the evening. I'm wound up tighter than a fucking yo-yo and I'm in need of some stress relief. My rage is still simmering in the background, but I hold it at bay. I file the papers

Depths of Deceit

and lock the important documents away for safekeeping. I'm about to head out when the office phone rings. I answer it with frustration.

"What?" I exclaim, in no mood for pleasantries for the person stopping me from getting my dick wet.

"He knows we're on to him. Get out. No time to explain. Just get out," bellows a voice down the phone.

"Evan, what the..."

"I don't have time to explain. They have kill orders, Knox. You need to..." The line goes dead and gunfire sounds out in the distance.

I'm quick to move, throwing the receiver down. I'm running up the steps two at a time. I need to get to Harper and get her to safety. Betty comes out of her room looking frightened, but she knows what to do as she passes me, heading for safety herself. I reach Harper's door in record time, barging in, but the room is empty.

"Damn it." I run over to the window to the only other place I know to find her. I push myself off the window frame and head her way. I just hope she has the good sense to stay put long enough for me to get to her, or she's used her head and hides in the secret passage she knows is under the floorboards.

I'm clutching at straws. She's fucking stubborn at times, and a part of me knows she won't leave without me. So I have to at least check the hut, even if it does lead the enemies straight to her, I need to know for sure. And if shit does go down, I'll be there to protect her.

The gunfire is getting closer with each passing second.

Lincoln is running out of my office, weapons in hand. "There you are. I was just coming for you." He looks around me confused. "Where's Harper?"

"I went up to fetch her the moment I heard the first round of bullets, but she wasn't up there. I think she's at the hut. I'm on my way there now." I reel off.

"Okay, let's go get your girl and get the fuck out of here," he mumbles.

We carefully make our way to the old service door in the basement. We make it just in time before we hear the door being kicked in, feet pounding the floorboards above us. Shots are being fired, and bodies begin to fall to the ground.

"We can't take the normal route. We'll be out in the open, too exposed," Lincoln states as something booms upstairs. My eyes scan the vast amount of ground.

"We'll take the treeline. It's a longer route, but we'll have cover. Let's hope my men can hold the fort long enough." We move in unison. We've done this dance many times before; it's second nature to us now.

My sole aim is to get to the hut, but it's making me forget that I also need to focus on not getting shot on my way there. Bullets fly past my ears from behind as we're spotted, and Lincoln is already taking potshots. I fumble as I turn back and begin to shoot as men come from behind trees, closing in on us.

Lincoln takes the first shooter down. I take out two more to our left. I lower my weapon and turn to Lincoln apologetically, ready to apologise for almost getting us killed, but he just shakes his head at me.

"Don't mention it," he grunts. His eyes flicker behind me and his gun is once again fired, but I have time to duck this time as he takes a fourth man down.

"We need to get moving," I say as we eat up the last few feet to the hut. Throwing open the door, we enter the empty room.

"Harper?" I call out, but she doesn't appear. I stamp my way to the corner where the hatch is and peer inside. "It's empty. She's not here." Lincoln frowns.

Just then, my phone rings. I grab it from my pocket in a rush and see it's Betty. "Betty. Are you okay? Are you with Harper?"

"I'm so sorry. She wouldn't leave with me. She went looking for you." I hear her cries through the phone.

"Head to the safe house, Betty. Stay safe. I'll see you soon." I end the call. "Fuck." I wrap my fist around my phone so tight I'm surprised it doesn't break.

"What's wrong? Is Betty safe?" Lincoln's worry matches my own.

"She's safe. Harper may not be. She went back looking for me." I pocket my phone and turn to Lincoln.

"Shit. We need to get back to the house." Lincoln says, and my feet pound beneath me as I stride with purpose, Lincoln right behind me. The fact she was stupid to walk into the line of fire doesn't bode well.

Depths of Deceit

If something has happened to her, I swear to God, I'll kill every person that's still alive.

Harper, where are you?

They have her, I know it. Whoever has, better get ready for a world of pain because I'm coming for her.

"Fuck, fuck, fuck!"

"Would she have made it to the house to look for you?" Lincoln asks, and the thought of her being in there with all that gunfire and bloodshed we left is disturbing. We're both running for the house. We don't bother with the treeline or staying in the shadows this time, not wanting to waste any more time than necessary.

"It's the only place she'll think to look for me," I puff out.

We make it back to the basement door in record time. The house is now eerily quiet, the gunfire now out in the woods. The door leading to the first floor from the basement won't open, but this door isn't lockable. I give it a good shove to find a body rolled over, so I push harder.

Making it through, I'm grateful that it's not one of my men on the deck, but my glee is short-lived when I see three of my own with bullet holes in more places than a kitchen sieve. There's blood everywhere. Bodies line the walls as we move through the house, weapons drawn and ready.

"Boss?" Yates whispers as we pass the tech room.

"Is everything secure?" I ask, needing to know if they have our plans for the mission to take down Benson. This attack on my estate has his name written all over it, but is he stupid enough to be here himself? I highly doubt it. He isn't brave enough to face me.

"Yes, everything is heavily encrypted and is only available with this thumb drive." He holds up a keyring with a miniature torch attached, and I frown at it. He rolls his eyes at my obvious confusion. "It's a hidden drive. No one would suspect a flashlight to be anything other than that." He pulls the head off the torch.

"Nice job," I say. "Guard it with your life. We need to find Harper. Split up. Lincoln, take the ground floor. Yates, check her floor again, and I'll check the top level." I check all the rooms on this floor, including my own, hoping she could be in there, but she isn't.

I punch the door in frustration.

Where the fuck is she?

I head deeper into the house where Betty lives and some of my men stay. It all seems quiet. Too quiet. Until the dull tones of bullets spray out from somewhere in the house, but then it's all quiet again. I move stealthily through each corridor doing my best to make no sound. I turn a corner to round back to the main stairs to find Harper doing her best to get Lincoln up them.

A shadow by the front door catches my eye. Lincoln and Harper are too busy trying to keep moving that they don't see what's lurking behind them. None of them have sensed my presence yet. I use that to my advantage, taking position. I know it's a risky shot, but it's one I need to take. I shoot, and my bullet almost takes Lincoln's ear off.

Both heads shoot my way as I rush out and make myself known.

"Jesus Christ, Knox. Could you have got any closer? You could have taken my damn ear off!"

I can't help the grin that slides across my face at his smart-arse comment, but mostly at seeing her.

I'm alarmed at the amount of blood covering her. I race towards her, "Fuck, Harper. Are you hurt?" I inspect her all over, looking for a wound but find none, then pull her into me after I help her get Lincoln back to his feet with a painful grunt. I hold her tightly as Lincoln takes the gun from her shaky hands. Her tears begin to flow and sobs leave her mouth.

"Shhh, it's okay. I'm here now. I won't let anyone hurt you again. You should have left with Betty, Harper." I'm still angry with her irrational thinking.

She pulls her head away from my chest. "I couldn't. I needed to know you were safe."

"Harper, I'm a Knox. People fear me, not the other way around. I'm capable of looking out for myself and those around me." I look down into her fear-stricken eyes. "Are you hurt?"

"No. In fact, I don't feel anything but numbness. I don't even feel guilty for killing one of my father's men in my hunt for you. I'm so relieved you're alive." There's an emptiness in her eyes now. I think she's still in shock and running on adrenaline.

Depths of Deceit

"Yeah, she saved my bacon too," Lincoln tells me with a hint of recognition.

"Did she now?" I'm impressed. "Where did you get the gun from?" I add, looking at the weapon in Lincoln's hand.

"I picked it up from an already dead body on my way back into the building. It was him or me and instinct took over, and well... I just pointed, aimed, and shot three bullets into his chest. I was shocked at first but strangely proud of myself at the same time." I see the pride in her stance.

"As much as I'm loving this little reunion, we need to locate Yates and get the hell out of here," Lincoln says, handing the gun back to Harper's now steady hand again.

Yates appears at the top of the stairs that lead to the top floor. "I hear it's time to get out of here. He winks at Harper and moves past us to make sure the way is clear. I don't have time to rip him a new one for his obvious sign of affection, as platonic as it may be.

"Wait, what about Sam and Dean? A large group attacked them and... and..." Her grip on my shirt tightens immensely.

"Don't worry about them. They know the drill," Lincoln says.

I breathe a sigh of relief. "Thank God."

He grabs a set of keys from beside the front door.

"What are you doing? We aren't taking a car." I forget that he's still new around here and doesn't know about the escape hatch. Lincoln tells him where we need to go and we all make our way there, keeping our wits about us, eventually making it to the hut in the woods.

I order them to put the call out for my men to fall back and get to the safe house. Yates is the first to grab his radio, giving the code for what they have to do and where to meet, in case anyone is listening in to our comms.

"Lincoln. Call the cleaners. Get them to do a full sweep of the grounds. Move all the bodies and burn everything."

Harper gasps in my arms. "That's your home. My home." A single tear falls, and I wipe it away gently.

"It's just bricks and mortar, baby cakes. I have other estates. I just chose this one because it was my father's. It needs to be this way. It's the only way of getting rid of the evidence. Come on, we need to go."

We're not out of the woods yet, but at least I've found Harper and she's safe. I don't know what the damage from tonight is, or how many of my men have fallen, but I'll get my answers when we reach the safe house, and their deaths will be avenged. Their blood is on my hands and the only thing that will make their deaths easier to take is killing the people behind it all.

Geoffrey Benson… I'm coming for you.

CHAPTER 34

HARPER

Knox hasn't let go of my hand since we reunited. It's like he's afraid to let go in case I disappear. The secret hiding place I thought was just a room under the floorboards also leads out into an underground tunnel. The tunnel is long and brings us out to a clearing deeper into the woods.

Keanu lets go of me long enough to walk over to a massive bush. He starts pulling branches away with the help of Yates to reveal a black vehicle that'll take us to a safe house. I leave them to it, walking over to Lincoln to tend to his wound that won't stop bleeding.

I rip a strip of material off the bottom of my T-shirt, like I saw Dean do before. "This may hurt a little."

He nods, and the muscle in his jaw tenses as he prepares himself for the pain. I wrap the shredded clothing over his shoulder and try to tourniquet it the best I can. He grunts his disapproval as the pain proves too much for him.

Knox appears at my side and looks at my handiwork with a smile until he sees where the material came from and he growls at my flesh on show for his men to see. I place my hands on my hips and pop one out in annoyance.

"Would you rather me let him bleed out just so my belly button isn't on display, huh?" I tap my foot, waiting for him to see reason.

"I would rather no other man, friend or foe, ever see what's under those clothes. Only me, baby cakes."

He steps up to me and threads his arms around my waist pulling me in for a rough kiss. I wind my own arms around his neck. Lincoln knows when he's not wanted and goes to get in the car. I giggle at the thought of him being embarrassed.

"Something we said?" I ask, and Knox pulls me tighter to him.

"I couldn't care less. If I want to be sentimental and ruin my hard reputation for you, then I will. I could have lost you."

The moment is spoiled when Yates yells that we we're all set. We climb into the back of the car where Knox slides me across the seat, puts his arm around my shoulders, and holds me close while he goes through what needs to happen next, including making a call to Dr Wells to come and sort out Lincoln's wound, and potentially more wounded men when or if they arrive.

Soon enough, we reach the safe house, which is better than I was expecting. I'm quickly ushered inside and out of sight from the eyes on the street. I feel safer already.

Over the next hour, more and more of Knox's men turn up in different states of medical distress. Thankfully, Dr Wells arrived around the same time as us. I help the doctor the best I can by fetching bowls of hot water, clean cloths, and bandages that were stored in a pantry. After watching him work on the men who need him most, he instructs me to help the others. He has me cleaning up wounds and patching up scratches while he's retrieving bullets from various limbs and body parts.

"You're a natural, my dear." I smile with pride at his praise. It helps calm my nerves and stops the shaking in my hands. "Clean open cuts and sew them up, but only if you're sure there are no bullet fragments or dirt left inside. Once done, take one of these pre-filled needles and jab it into their thigh. It's just a strong antibiotic to make sure they don't suffer from infections. Most of them I've already numbed up so you're good to go." He must see the scared look on my face because he reaches out his hand and places it comfortingly on my shoulder. "You can do this. I've shown you how and I'm the best." He winks as he hands me some stuff. "You can start with Lincoln. I just took the bullet

Depths of Deceit

out of him. He needs cleaning up and stitching." And just like that, he walks away, leaving me to help patch up these men.

Terrified and full of apprehension, I make my way over to Lincoln with a smile, masking my internal fear.

"Hey. The doctor sent me over to patch you up. He showed me how. You good with that?" I ask.

He adjusts slightly but agrees. I start to prepare all the items I need to work on him, but I get the strangest feeling I'm being watched. Shrugging it off as it's probably just Dr Wells keeping an eye on his protégé, I keep my focus on Lincoln's care.

"You know, I haven't had a chance to thank you for saving my arse back there, and here you are again, patching me up like some sort of modern-day Florence Nightingale," he scoffs but then whines in pain from the movement.

"No need to thank me. I'm sure you would've done the same for me." His gaze is fixed on what's going on out the window instead of looking at me or what I'm doing.

"If you had said that last week, I might've had to think about it, but after today and what you've done… you've more than earned my respect. Not just mine, theirs too." He nods his head at the men surrounding the room before he finally looks me square in the eye. "I'm sorry I doubted you. Your loyalty has been shown today and Knox has noticed it too. Granted, he saw it before I did, but he sees you." I snort out a little nervous laughter. "It's true. He hasn't let you out of his sight since he found us on the stairs. You're just as much his as he is yours."

I look around me and Keanu is staring holes into me with an intense fire burning in his eyes. If we were alone, I would jump his bones. I smile and turn back to Lincoln.

"I've fallen hard for him, Lincoln, and it scares the shit out of me. I can't imagine my life without him now. What if he doesn't want the same things I do?" I ask.

"Did you not just hear what I said? You've nothing to worry about. He doesn't have an adorable nickname for any other girl. He doesn't go all soft and gooey in front of his men unless you're around. You have tamed the mafia king, Harper. He might act like a caveman with you, but that's only because he cares. For the first time in his life, he has something real to fight for. Something worth dying for. You heard him admit his feelings for you. He loves you, Harper." He hisses as I stitch up the last little piece of skin, making me jump as I mull over what he just said.

"Shit, sorry. The numbing must be wearing off." I cover the stitching with a sterile wound dressing and help him to put his shirt back on.

"Thank you, Harper," Lincoln says before walking away, cradling his hurt shoulder and going to stand by Knox's side.

"Gather round." Knox's voice booms around the building. Everybody moves quickly; some with heavy groans of pain as they rush to their boss's command. I move to the edge of the room and prepare for whatever Knox does in this type of situation. "It's been a rough night. We've lost men, but that won't stop us from seeking revenge for them. They may have fallen, but not without a fight, and we will not stand by and let their deaths mean nothing. Trouble's brewing and war is just around the corner. Get some rest because tomorrow is a big day. We'll hit that warehouse and end this once and for all. Full briefing in the morning." His eyes meet mine as he dismisses his men. He looks stressed out, and who can blame him after the night we've had?

He prowls towards me like a predator sneaking up on his prey. From the lustful glint in his eyes, I know he needs a release and that's exactly what I'll be for him.

He needs me, as I need him.

CHAPTER 35

KEANU

I leave Harper sleeping in the bedroom. She was thoroughly exhausted when I'd finished having my wicked way with her.

She followed me up the stairs wordlessly, no questions asked, and when I closed the door behind me, cutting out all the sound from downstairs, she stripped bare without me even telling her what I needed. I ravaged her body more times than I can count and eventually, at three o'clock this morning, she passed out and was sound asleep.

I, on the other hand, can't sleep. I'm too wired and I have a lot of work that needs sorting before I can even think of relaxing. I'll relax when Benson is dead and his empire is burnt to the ground, and in a matter of hours, it will be.

I head down the stairs to my men. Half of them are trying to sleep, but the pain they're in is a constant reminder of what they have endured, and there's more to come. The other half are already busy getting ready for war. Lincoln must have set them up with jobs in my absence.

Everywhere I look, my men lay bandaged up in some way. It's enough to have the rage simmering beneath the surface to rise to a new high. Benson had men come into my fucking home, my estate, and shredded it piece by piece, taking some of my most loyal men in the devastating quake. I won't let that slide. It's never been in my nature to back down from a fight, no matter the odds. And currently, the odds are stacked against us.

I straighten my back, stretching out my aching muscles; which is nothing compared to what my men are having to deal with. I walk further into the room, my presence alone stamping my authority. I may have lost a lot tonight, but I've not lost who I am or what my bloodline stands for.

You can knock down my castle, paint the sky red, and strip away my armour, but you won't ever defeat me. The only thing you'll accomplish is pissing me off and having your looming death lingering over your head, always wondering when it'll come, because it will, and when you least expect it. I'm going to kill Benson and anyone else who stands in my way.

I never heard her approach, too busy turning into the devil I am. "Keanu?" Her angelic voice filters through my thoughts, casting a beacon of light over my darkness. "Are you okay?" She's at my side in seconds. "Only your eyes turned black and you looked like—"

I cup her chin between my forefinger and thumb, tilting her head up. I know what she was going to say; I don't need her to confirm how much of a monster I am. I never want to hear those words slip from her lips. "I'm fine, just thinking." Leaning forward, I kiss her mouth tenderly. "I have work to do." I release her from my hold reluctantly and focus on what I need to do. She's never seen this side of me, but I can't let that distract me. There's too much at stake.

I cross the room and find Lincoln and Yates with Sam and Dean in the kitchen, who look to be in a deep conversation and don't see me appear. My men are busy preparing, cleaning the weapons, gathering more weapons, bullets, and bulletproof vests from the room in the basement that holds a backup storage of everything we may need at a time like this. This place has always been my secret stash house and it's finally come to use. That's why I'm the best at what I do. This was my idea, one my father thought we'd never need. I guess I was right.

Yates eventually looks up and stops me. "Boss." He straightens his back, the other three following suit.

"Give me numbers, Yates," I say, getting straight to it.

Depths of Deceit

"We've lost twenty-two men. That leaves us with sixteen, including these guys," he points to Lincoln, Dean, and Sam, "And you, boss."

"And the injured?"

"The doc and Harper have patched them up the best they can. It's not ideal but they're all prepared to fight regardless," Lincoln says.

I have to agree with him. It's not ideal, but I know my men. They'll fight for me until their very last breath. "How's the shoulder?" I nod at Lincoln.

"It's been better. It won't stop me from doing my job, though." I sense a touch of distaste coming from him.

"I don't doubt you." I don't have time to feed his ego, so I turn my attention to Dean. "And you, how's your leg?"

"No ligament damage. Hurts like a motherfucker, but the doc has given me some strong painkillers. It'll numb the pain long enough to get the job done."

I nod. "We hit the warehouse at zero four hundred."

"Wait, what?" I spin around and face Harper, who's lingering in the doorway. "That's less than twenty-four hours from now. Is that not too soon?" She sounds panicked.

"We'll have the element of surprise. They won't be expecting it so soon after attacking us." I see a daunted look in her eyes. "It's now or never, baby cakes." She's still not assured, but that's all I can give her. I turn my attention back to my men. "Do we have everything here we need?"

"Yes," Lincoln answers. "We're just getting the bags ready to load into the vehicles when it's go time."

"How many cars do we have?"

"Three, but two of them are Range Rovers, so we have enough space," Dean informs me.

"Good. I want my men rested, ready for war this time tomorrow. Dean, get some rest." I know not a single one of them has gotten a wink of sleep since arriving here, and I need my best men on top form. The rest of them will get rest after we've finished up tonight. "That's an order. Lincoln, Yates, Sam, and I will do a quick sweep of the grounds and make sure there are no surprises waiting for us. After that, we'll begin with the plan."

I get a head nod and a round of 'Boss' before they disperse.

"I don't like this, Keanu," Harper says, coming to stand by my side and leaning against the table.

"I'm not asking you to, but you need to get on board with it fast." She looks at me like I've just slapped her. "I'm sorry, but I need to be blunt with you, unless you want me to lie and tell you not to worry about it." I arch my brow. "You wanted in. This is what being in looks like. You having second thoughts?"

She crosses her arms over her chest. "Absolutely not."

"Good. As much as I hate the plan where you're involved, it's the only good one we've got. Without you, fuck knows when we'll get another chance like this."

"I won't mess this up for you, Keanu. We'll get your sister back." She smiles at me, but it doesn't reach her eyes.

"I know you won't." I pull her towards me and wrap her up in my embrace, kissing her head. "Are you sore?" I whisper closely to her ear.

"No, I'm fine. I wasn't harmed." I adjust my hold on her so she can look at me. "Oh, you mean... No, I'm not." I feel the moment she squeezes her legs together.

"I want you back upstairs and naked in two minutes." She's gone from my embrace quicker than a speeding bullet. I can't stop the cheesy-ass chuckle that squeezes past my lips. I lock up and make my way up the stairs where I find a fully naked Harper gliding out of the en-suite like a beautiful angel. What's left of my black heart skips a beat as I take in the perfection before me.

Her long legs eat up the distance to the bed as she seductively climbs upon it and gracefully lies on top of the covers.

My dick takes notice and is now standing at full attention again. Grabbing my shirt at the back of my neck, I rip it off over my head before I strip out of my jeans and underwear. I stand before her as naked as the day I was born with nothing but my raging hard-on between us.

There's a twinkle in her eye. I don't know where it came from but it wasn't there before. I can't stop looking at her as I realise that if some-

Depths of Deceit

thing should happen to either one of us tomorrow, this could be our last time together.

"What are you waiting for?" she says in her, 'come get me' voice. I try to shake the deep thought out of my head as I take position between her creamy white thighs. Her sweet heady scent from her glistening pussy invades my every sense. My hands want to touch her, my nose wants to lean down closer and breathe her in deeply, my eyes want to feast on her sinful body for the rest of my days, and my dick wants to take full advantage of her widely spread legs to punish her pussy.

I crush my lips to hers in hungry need and line myself up with her wetness. Her hands delicately slide over my hips around to my back as she pulls me towards her gently until I'm fully seated inside her.

I had intended to try and fuck some sense into her, but the slow, sensual way I just entered her has me wanting new things with her for tonight's activities.

"You know it's you, right? It's only ever going to be you from now on. There's no one else for me, Harper. My woman now and forever. Do you understand what I'm saying to you?"

Her chest rises and falls with a hitch as she takes on board the meaning behind my words.

"Yes, I do. And I feel the same," she says, accepting my words for what they are. A declaration I thought I would never make. The L word is a curse in this life and until I know nothing will ever come between us, this will have to do.

I pull my hips back and slowly push forward, making her feel me inch by agonising inch but tormenting myself at the same time because her soft, velvet walls hug my cock perfectly. My eyes roll into the back of my skull and my limbs shake as the intimacy takes hold of me. I'm not a soft and gentle type in the bedroom, but tonight, I want to memorise every feel, sound, and sight. I want to take her slowly and tenderly. I want to bare my soul to her and have her feel the same.

I delicately push back into her over and over and she whispers my name, allowing it to carry on the breeze through the open window and out to the sleepy dead of night.

This, right here with her, feels right. It's perfect. She's perfect.

She pushes back, meeting me halfway. She wants to be my equal in everything. I see it in everything she's doing.

I find my rhythm as I take her with the respect she deserves. I worship her body from top to toe. Slipping the tip of her nipple into my mouth, I gently suck on it, making her gasp, and her body arches off the bed, pushing her breast firmly into my face. My free hand is roaming everywhere, over the soft skin of her neck, down the side of the fleshy mound that is her other breast. The dip leading to her hip is like velvet to my fingertips as I reach her thigh, gripping it firmly. Her moans of pleasure hit my ears like a bird's song, the most beautiful sound that I want to hear for the rest of my life.

Letting her nipple go with a pop, I shift to the other, making sure to give it the same attention. I slide my hand under her arse and hoist her level with my thrusts. The angle creates new mewls to leave her lips. Her breathing takes on a new tempo that matches the pace of our skin slapping together. I can feel her tightening around me and know she's close to her orgasm.

My name falls from her lips over and over as I continue to work her body, taking her to heights she's never been to before. Her dainty fingers let go of their grip on the white sheet beneath her as she holds onto my biceps instead. Her nails embed into the fleshy muscle of my arms, leaving half-moons in their place as she moves onto my back. I welcome the pain as she digs them into the middle of my back and claws her way across each shoulder blade and up to my shoulders.

I feel her pleasure begin to take over her, and my name gets louder and louder as I up the pace when I feel my own orgasm stir. My balls tighten, but I have to get her there first.

I crash my lips onto hers and swallow her pleas. The last thing I want is for my men to hear how she sounds when she comes. That sound is reserved for me alone.

I drive into her a couple more times before she detonates in a spectacular explosion, and I can't hold off any longer. I thrust and hold myself deep inside of her still convulsing pussy, my seed coating her inner walls.

"Shit. I've never come so hard in my life, baby cakes," I tell her as she pants erratically while staring deep into my eyes.

Depths of Deceit

"Me either. Let's do that again." She laughs, pulls my head down closer to hers, and kisses me deeply. I'm ready to say yes to whatever she asks for, but she needs rest, ready for tomorrow. Pulling out of her, I find the sheet at the bottom of the bed and cover up her lower half, still allowing me to perv at her tits while she sleeps.

"Get some sleep, baby cakes. We have a long day ahead of us tomorrow."

She closes her eyes, and she's out like a light. I wrap her up in the safety of my arms where she falls into the peaceful abyss of what I hope to be sweet dreams.

I creep off the bed and dress as quietly as possible. I reach the door but pause, taking one last look at the sleeping beauty. I hate the thought of leaving her here, but I need to get this recon mission done. Only when the mission is complete will I find out what really happened to Tillie and know for sure if she's dead or alive. Harper will be safe from her father, and I will finally be able to put the last seventeen months behind me and start looking at the future.

CHAPTER 36

HARPER

I'm sitting in the back of an SUV with Knox and Lincoln as they go over what they want me to do one last time. I'm so scared. If this goes wrong, it'll be all my fault, and I don't want to let Knox down.

I stare at the most recent photo of Tillie, studying it to memory.

"Harper, did you hear me?" Knox asks, nudging me out of my spiralling thoughts.

"Create the diversion, giving you the opportunity to get in. When you have everything under control, I start the hunt for Tillie in the rooms. Once located, we get out. Oh, and you're all on comms should I need you." I repeat the things I need to do over and over in my head.

Knox huffs. "I don't think this is a good idea. You're distracted, and that shit gets you killed." He hates that he caved and agreed to let me do this. If he could find another way, he would take it, but he knows I'm his best chance at clearing the entrance undetected so they can get in there and take control of the building, giving me time to find Tillie. God, I really hope she's here.

There's also the chance my father may be here. He's obviously making rash decisions. First the auction and Keanu copping wind of it, selling me off which backfired and the raid on Keanu's estate. He's running out of options, but that could work in our favour. He's rattled and his guard may have slipped.

Depths of Deceit

The thought of seeing him again after everything makes me shudder with sickness, but my presence here could cause him to lose it altogether.

Either way, I'm getting the guards away from the front of the building and we're ending this once and for all.

"Forget it, I'm going in." Before he can say another word, I'm out of the car and rounding the corner to the warehouse. Knox is cursing all kinds of hell in my ear until Lincoln calms him down.

My heart is pounding wildly against my chest, my hands are shaking something stupid, and the closer I get to the building, the weaker my knees become. I take a deep, calming breath in through my nose and out through my mouth. I try not to choke on the stench of cigarette smoke I inhaled as I get closer.

I reach the metal gate and spot two men guarding the front entrance. The gate is locked up tight, which is what we expected.

I thank my lucky stars that the men don't look familiar and will have no clue who I am. It's a good start. I'm dressed in everyday clothes, trying my best to look like I've taken a wrong turn somewhere and found myself out here in the middle of nowhere. I remember the story Lincoln told me about them finding girls who have no family or friends. Someone who wouldn't be missed.

A twig snapping under my boots gains their attention and has me sucking in a breath.

"Remember what we spoke about, Harper, and you'll be fine," Lincoln says through the comms in my ear.

The guards have their guns aimed high and pointed in my direction.

"Can we help you?" one of them asks, giving me an unpleasant glare.

"I hope so. I think I'm lost. I must have taken a wrong turn and this place is the first sign of life I've seen for hours. I've been walking around trying to backtrack to the road I was on." I act as innocent as I can.

"Are you alone?" the other man asks.

"Yes. My phone battery has also died so I can't call for help; not that I have anyone to call." I give them my best puppy eyes. "Can you help me get back to the main road?"

I watch as they regard me, looking me up and down. It makes me feel uncomfortable. My skin burns, scotched from their stares, and I feel dirty and cheap.

Keanu's voice filters through, *"Relax, Harper. I can see your shoulders tensing from here."*

"I'm trying, Keanu," I whisper.

"What was that?" the taller of the men asks.

My heartbeat picks up. I'm screwing this up. I think fast. "I said I'm trying... I'm trying to get home. I have a cat. His name is Keanu. I named him after Keanu Reeves. I loved him in *Speed*. Have you seen it?" I know I'm chatting utter rubbish, but I think I managed to dig my way out of it.

Lincoln laughs. *"Nice save, Harper. Now you need them to open the gate and lead them away for us to get access."*

"Where were you heading when you got lost?" the taller man asks. He's the guy who is more nervous about my presence.

"Home. I met some friends for drinks on the opposite side of town. I got a taxi there, but I've lost my purse, so I had no option but to walk it. It started to get dark, and everything looks different in the dark, doesn't it?" I laugh awkwardly. "That's when I must have taken that wrong turn. What feels like hours later, I'm starving, cold, and lost. Then I saw the little spotlights over here and headed in this direction. Then I found you two." I smile.

"I don't believe you. You don't seem scared by the fact you're all alone or that we're pointing guns at you." He narrows his eyes.

"I just thought you were soldiers for the army and you're guarding something top secret. Am I wrong?"

"Nah, I'm not buying it. Something about you seems off."

I place my hands on the steel gates. "Please. I just need help finding my way——"

"Beat it, sunshine. You're not supposed to be here," the quieter of the two says.

My plan is failing, and the chances of getting in there and finding Tillie are getting slimmer.

Depths of Deceit

"Harper, get out of there before they get more suspicious," Keanu says.

It's now or never, Harper. That's what Keanu had said to me when I had doubts about it happening too soon. I need to do something... and fast.

"Did you not hear what I just said, lady?" He gets closer to the gate, a mean look in his eyes.

"Okay, let's cut the shit. Do you have any idea who I am?" That gets their attention, along with everyone else in my ear.

It's Keanu I hear first. *"Harper, whatever you're thinking, you'd better fucking stop and walk away. That's an order."*

Then Lincoln. *"We'll find another way. Retreat, Harper."*

I ignore the voices and concentrate on the two men standing in front of me.

"And who might that be?" The taller one glares again.

"Harper fucking Benson." Saying my name out loud after everything I've learnt about my father tastes like acid and burns like hell.

"Excuse me?"

"Harper, don't do this," Keanu pleads.

"How do you think my father will react when he finds out you had his daughter standing close enough to touch, yet you did nothing about it?" I trick them into believing my scheme.

They turn and face one another. "If we let her go and she's telling the truth, Benson would kill us," the smaller of the two says.

"But what if she's playing us to let her in?"

"I have no intentions of getting inside." I lift my hand and start playing with my nails.

"Then what are your intentions?" they ask in unison.

"I want to see my father. Is he here?"

"Well played, Harper." Lincoln speaks. *"Get them to give you his whereabouts."*

"He's not here. He had... other business to attend to." I get the feeling neither of them knows the true whereabouts of my father, but I play along.

"Well, isn't that unfortunate? I guess I'll be on my way then." I turn and begin walking away, offering a sarcastic wave to them.

Keanu is the next to speak. *"Harper what are you doing? We could have done with more information."* I roll my eyes. *"I saw that."*

"Just wait, will you? My father's around here somewhere. I know these two idiots won't just let me walk away," I whisper.

Like I knew they would, they unlock the gate. "I'm afraid you're not going anywhere, Miss Benson," one of them shouts after me.

I pick up the pace. "Is that so?" I laugh. "You'll have to catch me first, boys."

"What's your plan now, Harper?" Keanu's not happy.

"The gates are open! I'll keep them away long enough for you and your men to enter," I say louder as I'm starting to pace into a slow run.

"Get her!"

"It's now or never, Keanu. You told me that. Now, go. Do what you do best."

"For fuck's sake, Harper. Please don't do this."

CHAPTER 37

KEANU

I bang my hand against the headrest in front of me, Sam's body flying forward from the impact. "She's going to get herself killed, or worse... returned to her father," I say through gritted teeth. I want to run after her and kill those motherfuckers. I don't have enough men to send one to go after her. This wasn't part of the fucking plan.

"I know what you're thinking, Knox. She may have gone against your orders, but the gate is open and unmanned. This is your chance. She's given you that. Don't waste it," Lincoln says, always the voice of reason. "If I know Harper, she'll get back to you no matter what it takes. She'll always come back to you."

I'm super pissed at Harper for diverting from the plan, but now isn't the time to dwell on that. I know she'll make it back to me. I won't give her the choice not to. She's given me something no one has in the last seventeen months. She's given me a chance to find my sister and stop this trafficking ring once and for all. I owe her so much for seeing it through.

I eventually give the order and it's all systems go.

My men have geared up, injured or not. They followed me here without a single doubt in their minds. Loyal to a fault. They respect me as much as I respect them and we will get this job done.

I send half of my men in, instructing them to take the back route around the warehouse and only enter when I give the order. Once they're in position, the rest of us breach the gates, guns aimed high and ready to take down anyone who crosses paths with us.

The devil inside me has come out to play, and he's not taking any prisoners. It's shoot to kill time. No foreplay, no torture. Just a bullet to the head or heart. I'm not fussy.

The thought of Harper being hurt or captured is rattling around in the back of my head, but I need to have faith that she'll come back to me.

Focus, Keanu.

Lincoln gives me a wary look, but I nod sternly, letting him know I'm good.

"Breaching the entrance now. Hang back until I make the order," I say through the comms at my men guarding the rear of the building, hoping Harper is still listening in on the new plan. *"If anyone tries to escape, kill them. Watch out for innocents,"* I add. "Remember, no girl or woman is to be harmed, and keep an eye out for the prize," I tell the guys with me as we stealthily prise the door open without alerting anyone about the company they're about to have.

The front of the building is pitch black and no one is in sight.

I flick my fingers to the left, giving Sam and Dean the go-ahead, and head to the right with Lincoln and Yates watching my rear.

The smell of vinegar and ammonia is potent and burns my nose. Then a hint of floral and fruit takes over. I know straight away what the odour is.

Heroin.

A huge amount of it by the stench.

I flick my head behind me as Yates and Lincoln get a whiff of it.

"This is either a heroin production factory or Benson is drugging the girls so they're completely out of it," I tell them.

I soon get my answer when we come to a row of doors, and behind each one are a dozen dirty beds, the occupants just as filthy, lying with needles in their arms. They are completely zoned out of reality. It must be feeding time here.

Depths of Deceit

We enter each room, flipping the girls over one by one, looking for Tillie. The youngest one is around seven or eight years old.

My blood boils at the thought of what she's been through and how long she's been here.

But that's about to change.

Yates attaches small devices in hidden places, ready to detonate when the time's right.

"You see anything?" I speak to the comms, waiting for Sam or Dean to answer.

"Half-naked comatose girls. No sign of Tillie or Benson," Dean informs me.

"Head up a level, your side. We'll meet you there."

"Yes, boss," Sam and Dean reply in unison.

Taking the stairs, we arrive on the second floor. There are just as many rooms as there are girls. But no Tillie.

Where are Benson's men?

Something doesn't seem right. The hairs on the back of my neck stand tall, and there's a sharp, stabbing pain in my chest. I hold my fist up, halting my men. *"Hold your position."* The comms are all making a noise.

"Boss?" I can't make out who spoke as everyone speaks at once.

"Something's off," I inform them. No one says anything, waiting for my orders. *"Harper, you still with us?"* There's radio silence. *"Harper, do you copy?"* Still nothing.

"Fuck," I whisper, but the roar behind my words is enough for Lincoln to stare wide-eyed at me.

"You don't think those fuckers from before have her, do you?" He asks what I'm already thinking.

"At this point, I don't know what I'm thinking." I try Harper again. *"Baby cakes, I need you to say something... anything."* I'm aware my men will hear everything I'm saying, but I'm passed caring. *"Come back to me, Harper. That's an order."* There's more silence, and an eerie quiet falls over us.

My head drops, and the darkness I was holding on to, saving for the massacre of men, sizzles to the surface.

Something has happened to Harper. I feel it heavy in my chest, constricting my air supply.

I'm about to give the order for my men to go in all guns blazing but hold out when a static noise blasts my ear.

"I'm sorry, Harper can't speak right now. One of my men is balls deep inside her." A sadistic laugh erupts.

My anger hits a new height, one I've never reached before. I've never allowed myself to as I knew I'd never come back from it. The black hole would eat me up and swallow me entirely.

"I swear to fucking God, if you or your men touch her, I'll make you wish you were never born."

"It's a little too late for that, Keanu. And by the sounds of it, she's enjoying the feel of a real man." Another sinister laugh follows, bouncing off the walls with an echo.

He's close by.

"I'll fucking kill you, Benson." The ominous tone in my voice scares me. I've never had something worth losing before now. I've already lost my parents and Tillie, there was no one else.

Until Harper.

I'm used to my men coming and going, comes hand and in hand with the job when you join a mafia organisation. They knew what was at stake when they forged a liaison with me.

She never asked for this life, and she certainly never asked for a father like the one she has. She never asked to meet me either. I never gave her a choice. She's here because of me and I'll die here today as long as she makes it out of here alive, safe, and never has to worry about looking over her shoulder again.

"Let's cut the dramatics, shall we? I have another surprise for you. I know you're not a fan of them, but this one I'm sure you'll appreciate." There's an edge of triumph in his voice and I don't like it. He thinks he's winning this war, but I'm about to be victorious and wear the king's crown for good.

"I'm coming for you, Benson. There's no escape for you. And when I do, I'll fucking gut you like the pussy you really are, and every man that follows you!" I remove the com from my ear with frustration. There's no point keeping it, he'll be listening anyway.

Depths of Deceit

"Yates, send a text to everyone. We're heading to the battlefield," I order, my voice dripping with venom.

So much rage.

Rage I'm saving for a worthless piece of shit.

CHAPTER 38

HARPER

The two guards catch up to me, and I find myself blocked into a corner on the grounds with nowhere to run. My lungs are burning, my legs are shaking from the pounding they took from running, and my nerves are shot.

I don't know what I was thinking. I just wanted this plan to be successful for Keanu and my only focus was making sure Keanu and his men had the best chance of getting into the building and ending this fucked-up mess. I diverted from the plan and that's on me. I'll deal with the aftermath of my poor decision-making when we're all home and safe.

"There's nowhere for you to run," one of them says.

"Fuck you." I shock myself with the conviction in my voice. I won't go down without a fight, that's for damn sure.

Keanu needs me and so does Tillie. I told him I'd get her to safety if we found her. I'm waiting for the moment they say the word *go*, and I'll be there, searching for her. Oh, God. I hope I haven't jeopardised that with my irrational thinking on my feet.

They edge closer to me, caging me tighter.

The next thing I know, pain slices across my cheek, and my knees and palms hit the gravel with a hard thud. Once the shock wears off and I grasp what happened, my hand instinctively goes to cup my cheek as the sting intensifies.

Depths of Deceit

I'm still seeing stars when I feel an unpleasant tightness around my arms. I'm hauled to my feet and dragged back the way we came. When I see the gates at the front of the building fast approaching, I start to panic. I fumble around my ear for the comms piece, but it's no longer there. It must have fallen out when they backhanded me.

I'm screwed. I fucked up. I have no way to stay in contact with Keanu to learn the new plan. No way to know if he's found Tillie. I'm completely in the dark and on my own.

Has he tried to make contact?

Will he know I'm in trouble?

My mind is working overtime, and I missed what turns we took or where I am in the building. I'm suddenly filled with dread and uneasy apprehension. An ice-cold chill runs the length of my spine and I immediately know why.

"The backstabbing bitch returns." I hear my father's voice as he appears from the shadows, a smug grin on his face. I watch as one of the men hands something over to him. My father's grin turns sour like he's eaten a piece of rotten fruit. " Did the feel of his dick inside you turn you against me?" He speaks with such displeasure. He's never been this crude towards me. Keanu has clearly rattled my father's cage.

Good. I can't wait to see the man before me crumble to the ground as Keanu takes it all from him. He deserves everything he gets and so much more. A simple bullet to the head would be too easy for him. I know he's my father by blood, but I've never been his daughter and he's never treated me as such. I tried so hard to make him love me, but I've no love left in my bones for him. The day he sold me was the last crack in my armour. As far as I'm concerned, my father is dead, already in the pits of hell, burning for eternity.

"You always were a disgrace. I knew I was right about you." he spits, getting closer.

"You know nothing about me. You never took an interest in my life. It was always about you." My voice starts out in a whisper but gets louder.

"I know more than you think, Harper. You think I'm unaware that you've been spreading your legs for that man? The same man who's always been an enemy of mine. Not that it matters, because I hold the key to bringing that man down once and for all, and you have a front-row seat to the action." The look on my father's face is enough to break me.

"What... what do you mean by that?" I stutter.

"You'll see soon enough." It's then I notice what's in my father's hand. He brings it to his ear. I watch and listen intently, never taking my eyes off him. His evil grin grows.

"I'm sorry, Harper can't speak right now." I gasp at the lie coming from my father's mouth. But he's not done there. *"One of my men is balls deep inside her."* My mouth hangs open, but the crude laugh behind me has me slamming it shut and fear licks my skin at the thought of my father's words coming true.

I instantly know who he's speaking to and my heart beats faster.

"It's a little too late for that, Keanu. And by the sounds of it, she's enjoying the feel of a real man."

"He's ly—" My words are muted by a man clamping his hand over my mouth, the other around my throat, restricting my air supply. I claw at his fingers in a desperate fight to breathe. It's no use. I'm just making his hold on me tighter.

The rest of the conversation is mumbled as my ears have started to ring. I faintly hear my father laughing before his voice turns serious and he mentions something about a surprise. What that surprise is, I have no idea, but it can't be anything good.

My father barks orders at the few men surrounding him and the room is a flurry of noise and whispered words.

I'm suddenly hauled up on my feet by my hair, the roots burning. My hand instinctively reaches for the one doing the pulling, but there's no let-up and I have no choice but to go with them. I'm only released when I'm forced to stand in front of my father. His beady eyes seek out my tear-streaked ones.

"Why don't I tell you a little story while we wait for lover boy to come up with a plan to rescue his pathetic little whore." His bitter words don't affect me anymore. I learned long ago to ignore them, but I get the feeling that what he's about to tell me is going to wreck me. "I'll jump straight in as we're pushed for time." He smirks, not caring

Depths of Deceit

that Keanu and his team are making their way up. "There was a woman and small child who stumbled in on something they shouldn't have. Here in this very building. They saw and heard something they shouldn't have, and that meant consequences for them. More so the woman as she should have known better, and to bring the child along, that was her second mistake. The child was too young to understand what was going on, but still... they needed to be dealt with accordingly. They somehow escaped and made it out of the warehouse, after the mother threatened to expose the whole operation, and as you can imagine, that only angered the man more. They didn't make it very far after fleeing, and she unfortunately had a car accident. The mother died instantly, but somehow, the child survived, but not unscathed. The child suffered with short-term memory loss from a blow to the head, and it turns out the child doesn't remember anything leading up to the event or how they ended up in the hospital." He smirks again, but it's filled with something more. I just don't know what.

Everything rushes at me at once. The memories Keanu managed to get out of me. The woman and child he's referring to are me and my mother, and the man... was him.

Fresh tears begin to fall at the lies I've been fed all my life.

Tears for my mother, as I mourn her death all over again.

"Mother didn't die because of an accidental car crash, did she? You had her run off the road." My voice breaks at the truth that comes back to me in a flashback of unwanted nightmares. "You knew I was in the car that night. You tried to kill us both. Why, you sick murdering bastard?"

"Feisty. And to answer your question, yes, I fucking did. That bitch followed me here, saw what I was doing, and threatened to tell the police about my whole operation. I couldn't let that happen, not when I still had so much to accomplish. Your mother shouldn't have brought you along, but the pathetic bitch never left you behind, ever. But I guess you could say my luck had come in. Two birds, one stone and all that. You would have been nothing but collateral damage." He bares his teeth at me.

"You really are sick. Firstly, for trying to kill off your family, and secondly, for thinking trafficking underage children and women to be an accomplishment." I'm horrified that I have this man's blood running through my veins. "Did you ever love her?" It's a pointless question, but I ask it anyway.

"Love is a strong word, Harper. She had one job to do and she couldn't even do that. I needed an heir and she gave me... you." He sneers down at me. "A weak, pathetic bitch, who spreads her legs for the enemy." His anger towards me heightens, and I receive another crack across my face that sends me sideways and I bang my head against the concrete floor. My vision becomes blurry and my headache has intensified.

"There's movement on the stairwell," I hear someone say behind me.

"Bring her in," my father orders.

Bring who in?

I try with all my might to clear my vision and my question gets answered when a young girl is dragged into the room and thrown to the ground, only stopping when she reaches my side. She's completely out of it and doesn't have a clue what is going on. I have a sick feeling in the pit of my stomach. I reach out and gently swipe her matted hair from her face, and through my foggy vision, I see a double of Keanu, only younger and with delicate features. I gasp in shock.

It's Tillie.

"What have you done to her?" I rage. The horror of this small, fragile girl is too much to take.

"Rein it in, Harper. The fun is about to start."

My father's sinister face will forever haunt me.

Then... all hell breaks loose. Guns are raised and the noise of movement echoes off the walls around me.

"Ah, Keanu Knox. You took your time. Welcome to the party!" My father lifts his arm like he's the god of darkness.

Through the pain, I find Keanu, and when our eyes meet, I see nothing of the man I once knew. The man who's just entered the room is a monster. His eyes are pitch black and he looks murderous.

My devil has come to play.

CHAPTER 39

KEANU

My men know the plan. We get Harper safe and away from her father's hands, and then we obliterate everyone else in the room, find Tillie, and finish the mission. I don't intend to fail. This ends tonight. Benson's shady business deals will die along with him.

We breach the top level, aware of our surroundings as Benson knows we're here. The element of surprise is gone, but it's nothing we can't handle.

My Glock is cocked and aimed in front of me, ready to take out anyone who crosses my path. I enter the concrete room, Lincoln, Yates, Sam, and Dean flanking me and spreading out. Seconds later, the other part of my team arrives. Their guns are aimed at Benson's men, but mine are set on one person.

Geoffrey Benson.

I'm saving all the bullets in my magazine just for him.

I glance at his feet, acutely aware that Harper is there and injured. All the rage I feel for Benson comes rushing to the surface and I see pure darkness. The devil I know I am is making an appearance. I never wanted Harper to see this side of me. The real me, but I need to let the darkness consume me to get her out of her safety.

She's huddled up to someone, and I almost crumble to my knees when I see who it is. I've finally laid eyes on my little sister after seventeen long, hard months of her absence. I'm delighted to see she's alive, but she's hardly moving.

"Mr. Knox. As you can see, we started without you." He greets me like it's a normal fucking day. He's a psychopath.

"What the fuck have you done to her?" I roar, my words booming off the walls, emphasising every syllable.

"Why is everyone so worried about her when you should be worrying about yourself? Anyway, she looks far worse than she is."

Is he fucking serious?

"You've lost your mind if you think you'll get away with this, Benson." I'm furious beyond comprehension. The fact he's hurt the only two women I will ever love means he's got a death wish. "You're a dead man walking."

"We all die at some point, Knox."

"I don't plan on dying tonight, but your time is up." I aim my words, strong and true.

"You'll die tonight. In more ways than one, but first, you have a choice to make." He gives his man a firm head nod. Harper and Tillie are forced to stand. Neither of them is in good shape, but Tillie seems much worse. I know she's dosed up with drugs. Harper has a nasty cut on her head, and blood is dripping down the side of her face.

I've never been in shackles before, no one's ever gotten close enough, but I can feel the ones around my heart tightening beyond apprehension.

I know Benson's intentions. I would have done the same to my enemies if the roles were reversed.

"You've shown me your weakness, Knox. Not one, but two."

"I have more strengths than weaknesses, Benson. That's what you should be more concerned about." I smirk.

"I was going to sell your dear sister on, I mean that was the whole point of grabbing her in the first place, to make a huge profit from the snatch, but then I thought to myself... People would pay a hell of a lot of money for some alone time with the famous Tillie Knox. She's a fighter, and that turns them on all the more. The money was rolling in until you started sniffing around like a damn dog."

"You fucking bastard. I'll kill you." I take a step towards him,

Depths of Deceit

freezing when his men grab the girls harshly, and my instant reaction is to shoot both fuckers in the head, but I can't. I won't put Harper or Tillie in any more danger than they are already in. I can't take my eyes off Harper or my little sister as they stand there helplessly.

Benson's quick movement has me snapping my head back to him. He reaches behind his back and pulls out two guns. One is aimed at the back of Tillie's head and the other at Harper's.

"Time to choose, Keanu." The sick fucker has the nerve to smirk. He's enjoying seeing my mask fall.

I hang my head and let my shoulders drop. He's got me. He knows I'll never choose between them. "If you kill them, you'll end up with bullets in your body from every gun my men have aimed at you. Are you willing to die tonight too, Benson?" It's the only play I've got left.

"I haven't shown all my cards yet, Knox. Do you think I'm new to this game?" He chuckles.

It's then I feel a gun aimed at the back of my head. My men move, but it's too late.

"Glad you could join us, Evan. You took your time," Benson says, looking behind me.

"My apologies. I got caught up with some... Business." Evan's voice hits my ears.

Have I been played?

Was this Evan's plan all along?

I've never been doubled-crossed, and it's a feeling I vow never to let happen again.

I spot Lincoln shifting his weight on his feet. I look up and he's giving a 'what the fuck' look. I give him a discreet shake of my head, which he understands.

"Now that I have your attention, you have a big decision to make. Who are you going to choose, Keanu? Your darling little sister who's been missing and fucked in every hole by more men than you imagine." I glance at each of his men in turn, imagining their corpses with lifeless eyes. Because that's all they will be after tonight. "Or will it be your whore, who really is good for nothing?"

I glare at him. "I'm going to enjoy watching you bleed, Benson."

He pushes his guns further into the backs of their heads. Harper lets out a frightening whimper, and my sister still hasn't got a clue what's going on.

"Tick tock, Knox." Benson's voice is starting to grate on my last nerve.

I need a new tactic if I want to save them both. I need Benson rattled. "Who's the brains behind this operation, because it sure as shit isn't you."

"What makes you think that?" He narrows his eyes.

"There's no way you've pulled all this off by yourself. You don't have the brains or the manpower for it. You've been making mistakes recently, but before that, everything was going smoothly for you. You've had help. Who is it?" I aim for the jugular. "You're a pawn in your own game, Benson. Sooner or later, you'll be of no use. You'll start to lose the loyalty of your men… if you haven't already, then you'll lose whatever cash you have left in buying loyalty elsewhere, but by then, it'll be too late. The shithole you've built will start to crumble, and you'll die along with your pathetic empire. You're nothing, Benson. Never have been, never will be." His eyes and neck twitch. It's faint, but I see it. I've hit a nerve, which means I'm on to something.

"If anyone's empire is falling, then it'll be yours, Knox, not mine. Look around you…." He points his guns to the area around us. "You're the one with a gun pointed at your head."

I don't have time to think of the consequences. My feet are moving before my brain can register. It may be the only chance I have. Benson is distracted, and Harper and Tillie have a little breathing room from Benson.

I roar out Lincoln's name as I sprint towards Harper. He knew my intentions before I even started moving, and he's already zoning in on Tillie.

Bullets are flying everywhere, ricocheting off the walls and piercing the glass windows. Broken shards fall like a sharp waterfall.

Harper's body hits my chest hard as we collide. My gun is aimed at Benson's disbelieving face.

I use my body as a shield for Harper, Lincoln doing the same with Tillie.

Half of Benson's men are dead, the other half don't know where or

Depths of Deceit

who to aim their guns at. Evan included. I'm still unsure whose side he's on, but the fact he didn't blow my head off in my pursuit of saving the two girls is a good sign for now.

"You're outnumbered and outgunned, Benson," I mock. "It's game over for you. Tell your men to stand down, or they will die."

"Fuck you, Knox." He aims his gun right at me. Harper lets out an almighty scream. I hold my hand up, signalling for my men to stand down. Benson dies by my hands only and not before I've made him suffer. A bullet would be too kind for someone like him, and he deserves untold pain for what he's done. "I may be outnumbered, but that doesn't mean you can't die."

Everything happens in slow motion. I hear the mechanism of a gun click. A bullet flies past my head, and Harper's scream of panic drills through my skull. I bask in her beauty. If this is the last time I'll see her, I want to remember every little thing I've come to love about her and wait for the pain to hit me, but it doesn't come. What does is Benson's impeccable groaning. The gun drops from his grasp, and he's holding his shoulder as blood leaks through his fingers.

"You traitorous fool." Benson's words are laced with agony, disappointment, and betrayal.

I swing my head in the direction from which the bullet was fired, just as Evan begins lowering his weapon. I stare at him, bewildered.

He shrugs. "You told your men to stand down, not me. Plus, I've only wounded him. I knew you'd want to finish the job yourself."

"For a second there, I thought you had double-crossed me," I say, relieved.

"Were you doubting me, Knox?" Evan smirks.

"Kind of." The corners of my lips lift, but only slightly.

"I knew you were up to something," Benson grits out in-between panting like the dirty dog he is. "Ever since my wife...."

"Don't you dare speak about her," Evan roars, catching us all off guard. "You murdered her in cold blood and tried to do the same to my daughter." He tenses, noting his mistake.

Everyone in the room is stunned into silence.

"What did you say?" Harper's timid voice is no more than a whisper.

"I'm sorry, Harper. I wanted to tell you, but I couldn't do that until I knew you were safe and Benson was out of the picture. If he found out, he would have killed you. He already tried once. It was my fault you were there that night. I told your mother to meet me and arrange someplace safe for you both to stay. I wasn't going to risk your lives again. I was doing what I thought was right to keep you safe." Evan's shoulders drop like the weight of the world has just left him.

"When... how long have you known?" Harper is struggling to form words.

"Since the day your mother had the accident. She told me her plans of following Benson. I told her it was too risky and that she shouldn't, but she wanted proof, and one way or another, she was going to get it. She couldn't leave you at the estate, so she took you with her. She never thought Benson would be so ruthless. She made me promise never to tell you until it was absolutely necessary and only when you were free from him." His death glare finds Benson. "It wasn't until Keanu came on the scene that I finally had the help I needed to take him down for good. I couldn't do it on my own, not without risking getting caught or killed, and I couldn't bear thinking of where that would have left you."

"All this time... I never knew. How deep do the lies and deceit go?" Silent tears stream down her face.

"I'm so sorry. Please, forgive me," Evan pleads.

"I... I don't know what to—"

"How sweet! Daddy's come to save his daughter." The man I believed to have been her father laughs, but it's not filled with any joy. "Have you finished with your little reunion? Why waste your time on her? She's just like her mother. Just another whore."

"Did you know?" Evan aims at Benson.

"No. If I had then you wouldn't be standing there looking down at me like you're better than me. And you of all people. I thought she had better taste."

Harper's voice turns icy. "You're the lowest of the low. You used and abused me, just like all the girls you took prisoner. You took away their lives and freedom. Well, not anymore." Before I can get a grip of

Depths of Deceit

Harper's arm, she's somehow got past me and is heading straight for Benson.

"Harper," I call out, but it's like she doesn't hear me.

In one swift movement, she bends down and picks the gun up that was lying an inch or two from Benson's slumped body. With shaky hands, she lifts it and points it down at him.

"Put the gun down before you hurt yourself, sweetheart," Benson says coldly.

"You don't get to tell me what to do anymore." She holds the gun with two hands, trying to steady her nerves.

I flick a look at Lincoln. He's passed my sister over to Yates and my other man. They all have guns pointing at someone who isn't our ally, just in case this turns sideways.

I try coaxing her to drop the gun. "Baby cakes, you don't have to do this. I'll take care of it. You don't want to do something you can't come back from." I take a couple of steps closer.

"He needs to pay for all the hurt he's caused me and every other girl he's violated. Tillie included. Look at what he's done to her, Keanu." I glance back at my sister, who's too weak to even stand on her own.

"I can see that, but you don't need to do this. Trust me when I say he'll pay for it." The closer I get, the less she shakes. It's like she's seeking comfort from me. "Just not by your hand. You're the light in my darkness, Harper, remember." I'm at her side now, and I know she sees me in the corner of her eye.

"You don't understand. I need to do this. I need to be sure he's dead." Her tears freefall. I'd be surprised if she can still see clearly.

"You don't have the balls. You're a useless bitch. Exactly like your moth—"

The gun goes off rapidly, even after the chamber is empty. She's still pulling the trigger with no let-up.

"You dirty, manipulating fucker!" she screams.

I take the gun from her hand, bring her in close, and turn her around so she can't see the damage she's done to him.

"It's okay, baby. He can't hurt you anymore."

She buries her head into my chest and lets out a wail. Her cries bounce around the room.

"Yates, take Harper and Tillie to the safe house. Dean and Sam will go with you." They nod and spring into action. Harper is coming down from an adrenaline rush and she's becoming weaker by the second. I lift her chin and take in the angry-looking red marks on her face and head. They really did a number on her. "Yates is going to take you and my sister back to the safe house. I won't be long." Her eyes find mine. She wants to put up a fight, but she doesn't have the energy for it. "I need you to be there for Tillie. Can you do that for me?"

Her eyes widen. "Oh, God, Tillie. Is she okay? She was completely out of it when she was brought in." She angles her head around my body and seeks out my sister. I smile fondly. My sister's going to need someone to help her through this and I'm glad it's someone like Harper.

"Go. I won't be long." I kiss the good side of her head and pass her over to Dean's waiting hands. She takes one last look at the man who caused her nothing but heartache and misery, shuddering from head to toe.

I don't know if she'll ever get over what's happened here tonight, especially the part where she filled Geoffrey with bullet holes.

Has the darkness of my world collided with her light?

Will she let this consume the goodness inside her entirely?

CHAPTER 40

HARPER

I killed a man. Not just any man, but one I thought was my biological father. Knowing he isn't makes me feel slightly better about the situation.

Fucking hell, what am I turning into?

I'm becoming a monster just like him. I guess the apple doesn't fall too far from the tree, whether we're blood or not. I knew Geoffrey was trying to get under my skin when he goaded me into pulling that trigger.

Everything he ever said to me, called me, every pounding of fist and palm I took because I wasn't doing as I was told. I *always* did as I was told. I was never good enough for him. To him, I was nothing but an embarrassment. Then I remembered all the girls he kept here and what misery they've been through. It all became too much, and every hatred, loathing, distasteful emotion I ever felt for him came to the surface, and before I knew it, I was pulling the trigger, unable to stop. It was like my body had been taken over by an evil side that was lurking deep inside of me, and she wasn't letting up. I knew he was dead, yet I couldn't stop. It was only when I felt Keanu's presence that I relented. He removed the deadly weapon from my grasp and wrapped me up in his arms, and I let everything pour out. I'm relieved that a man capable of the things he was is dead, and I'm thankful that no one I've come to care deeply about was harmed in all this.

Should I be disgusted with myself for what I've done?

Because I'm not.

What kind of person does that make me?

I'll never be the same person after what's transpired here. Doubt for the person I once was creeps in, and then it turns to fear when I think about going to prison for it.

How the hell do I explain to the police what I've done?

Will Keanu come and visit me?

Will he look at me differently?

My nightmare is only just beginning. I'm going to lose everything and everyone I care about because of what I've done.

I start to voice my concerns to Keanu, but he shuts me down and tells me it's okay, that it's over now. He'll meet me when he's finished up here.

Whatever that means.

When he spoke to me, asking me to look after Tillie for a while, his expression gave me nothing, and I didn't have time to gauge his reaction as I was ushered out of the building and into a car with Yates, Dean, and Sam.

Tillie is wrapped up in a blanket by Yates as she's practically skin and bones and shaking like a leaf. He whispers something into her ear and her eyes open wider. It's the first sign of communication from her.

I try not to think about what Keanu and Lincoln are doing. Or Evan, for that matter.

Evan... my real father.

I'm still trying to wrap my head around it all, but there are other things I can do to take my mind off my fucked-up upbringing. Right now, there's a girl who needs more support than me. She's got a hard road ahead of her, and Keanu asked me to be there to help her through that transition. That's where I'll focus what little energy I have.

The vehicle starts moving, and it's filled with strained silence. I'm used to silence, but not from the people around me.

Are they disgusted with what I've done?

"You did what you had to, Harper." Yates speaks quietly from the seat next to me.

Depths of Deceit

"He was a downright disturbing man and the world will be much brighter without him in it," Dean adds from the driver's seat.

I smile, but it's weak. I know they're trying to make me feel better, but I'm not at the stage where it's sunk in yet, and the only person I seek comfort and reassurance from is still at that warehouse. His opinion of me is what matters most. I need to see him and hear him tell me that it's all going to be okay and that his feelings and promises to me are still the same.

As for Evan, I have a lot of questions I need answering. I don't know when the right time for that may be as there's just too much going on, but more importantly, I'm not sure if I'm ready to venture down that road yet. He lied to me and has since I was twelve years old. That's not something I can easily forget.

Maybe, one day, I'll get there.

It's been three weeks since I pulled that damn trigger and killed Geoffrey Benson. I'm slowly coming around to the fact that I was the one who ended his miserable life, but the fact he won't be able to hurt Tillie or any other girl or woman again makes me feel less remorseful.

Keanu had a team set up the new estate, as the old one is a burnt-down wreck. I have to hand it to his interior decorators, they got the place up and running quickly. Yates has set up all the security systems and has a new computer room twice the size of the old one. I think that was Keanu's way of saying thank you. This estate is twice the size of his father's and has three floors, a grand staircase running up the right side of the house as you walk into the foyer, and a glass window from floor to ceiling so you can see the grounds surrounding the place. Speaking of the grounds, they are just as spectacular here as they were at the old place, and Keanu even had a new hut built at the side of the grounds, this one is closer to the house. There's a lake that runs down one side of the estate, ending in a pond. Betty has a new veggie patch, and now she has a couple of chicken coops too.

I didn't think it would feel like home, but it does.

I still wake up in the night, screaming and covered in sweat as the moment I shot Benson comes back to haunt me. Maybe it's his way of constantly reminding me of what I did, but Keanu is always there when I wake. He wraps me up so tight in his arms that it's like he's soaking up all of the darkness and letting it seep into his pores, taking my burden and making it his own.

I have so much respect and love for that man. He says he's the devil, but to me, he'll only ever be my saviour.

I know he's struggling to see me like this, not knowing what to do. I don't want to burden him with my problems when he's finding it hard between helping Tillie and getting order back to normal.

Tillie's a broken shell of the person she once was, so Lincoln tells me. We've become closer since the time I fixed up his shoulder, and I've found myself opening up to him more than I do to Keanu. Talking to Lincoln helps. He gives it to me straight and doesn't care how I take it, and oddly, I need that.

Tillie was shut off in her new room as she went through her withdrawal from the drugs she was force-fed. From her begging, screaming, and animalistic frustration, it mustn't have been a pretty sight. Keanu kept reassuring me that everything would be okay. They did everything by the book to get her clean. She was a little disorientated when she came to the new house, not fully understanding why she wasn't home, but Keanu thought it best not to tell her what went down just yet. Once she was clean, it took her a couple of days before she started roaming around. I'd tried each day to talk to her, but she was having none of it. She hadn't even gone down to the hut that was built for us. I hadn't gone in myself yet, afraid it would tip her over the edge. Keanu has gone out of his way to make sure she has similar places she can go to here as she did when she was at home. The last thing I want is for her to think I'm stepping on her toes. Just me being here is a massive difference for her. Before she was taken, it was her, Keanu, and their father. I'd like us to get along, but she's not opening up to anyone at the moment, and I'm not going to push her.

I woke this morning with a newfound determination to put Benson behind me. I can't take back what I did, nor can I change how it went down. I need to move forward if I want any sort of normality.

I never asked Keanu what happened when I left and I don't intend to either. The police haven't come knocking for me, so I'll take that as a sign that Benson's body and that if his men will never be found and all traces of us ever being in the warehouse have been wiped clean.

I'm so deep into my thoughts when I walk into the kitchen that I almost don't see Tillie sitting at the far end of the table. Betty's busy at the stove making breakfast, so she doesn't see me enter, but Tillie does. Her eyes zone in on me. I pause, debating whether to turn around and give her some space while she's out of her room. I'm looking backwards and forwards from Tillie and Betty, wondering what the hell I should do.

"You can sit down." It's the first time she's spoken to me since we found her. Her voice is raspy and quiet.

"You sure? If you want to be alone, I can come back later."

"It seems this place is just as much yours as it is mine. If not more," she whispers the last part, but I hear it.

I don't have an answer for her and I'm getting a hint of resentment from her. I don't know if it's because the man who held her captive for so long was linked to me, or if it's because I'm in Keanu's life.

"Morning, Harper. Would you like some breakfast? I'm making Tillie's favourite. Homemade blueberry pancakes." Betty beams at me.

"That sounds amazing. Thank you." I half smile, not knowing if I'm doing right or wrong. It may only be a few words, but this is the most interaction I've had with Tillie. Yates seems to be the only one she's spent time with. I'm guessing Keanu has him on Tillie duty. He's clearly doing something right with her.

"How are you feeling this morning? Did you sleep okay?" I ask, trying to get her to speak to me.

"Why do you care?"

Okay, then. Definitely not on good terms with me.

"Tillie, have I done something to upset you?" The tension in the room is killing me, but I can't let it fester any longer.

"I don't even know you, Harper," she snarls.

"True, but I'd like to change that. You mean a lot to Keanu and I'd like us to get along." I offer her a small but meaningful smile.

"I bet you would."

Keanu chooses that moment to make an appearance. "Morning, my three favourite ladies." He plants a kiss on my head and sits down in the chair next to me.

Tillie stands abruptly. "Betty, I'm sorry, but I've suddenly lost my appetite." She breezes past us.

"Tillie. Don't be rude. Sit back down," Keanu orders.

She spins around, narrows her eyes at me, and flips Keanu a sarcastic smirk, "No, thank you."

He must catch on to the atmosphere in the room. "Sit the fuck down, now," he roars, making Tillie and me jump at the same time.

Tillie studies her brother's face before sitting again, and Betty makes a discreet exit.

"I know you're struggling, Tillie. What happened to you... Fuck, I can't begin to imagine..."

"Then don't," Tillie says, cutting him off.

"I'm really trying here, Tillie. But nothing anyone says is getting through to you. Especially, Harper. Why the animosity towards her?"

"Keanu, it's fine. Honestly, just leave her alo—"

He cuts me off, raising his hand. "It's not fine at all. She needs to accept that you're part of my life now." He stares at Tillie. "I'm waiting for you to start talking."

"Seriously, you don't see what's wrong here? You're sleeping with the enemy. Her father stole my life from me." I inwardly cringe at her words. "Her father did unspeakable things to me, and so did his men. She shares his DNA, Keanu." Although her words are only half-truths, they cut me deep, and I see she's struggling to hold back her tears. I almost crumble to the floor from witnessing her pain.

"You don't know all the facts, Tillie. You were so out of it when we found you, you could hardly stand and your eyes were so far in the back of your fucking skull you didn't hear a single word of what was said that night. Benson is a sick fucker, and Harper isn't oblivious. In fact..."

"Keanu, please. She doesn't need this right now. She's been through so much. It won't change what happened," I say, not wanting to bring up the past and reopen wounds that still haven't fully healed.

He pauses to rein in his temper. "Harper may not have gone through what you did, but she's got her own demons where Geoffrey

Depths of Deceit

Benson is concerned. She had to put up with harsh beatings from the man she thought was her father and was meant to keep her safe. He took his frustrations out on her, then he fucking sold her at a trafficking ring party, and if I hadn't intervened, she would have suffered the same fate as you. The night you were found, it was only with her help that we could get to you. She made that happen, and in doing so, she learnt the truth of how her mother died, of how she was meant to have died along with her. Then she shot the guy because she couldn't let a man like him live after seeing what he was doing. And to top it all off, she found out who her real father is and she's still trying to wrap her head around all that and dealing with shit from you." He places his head in the palm of his hands whilst I try to control my emotions.

"I... I'm sorry. I didn't... I didn't know." The tears she was holding back leak from her eyes, and now I can't hold back my own.

"It's okay, honestly. The last thing you want to hear is my bad memories when you have so many of your own to deal with. I didn't want you thinking it was all about me."

Keanu lifts his head. "Do you see now? She's just as traumatised as you, only for different reasons. I'm sorry I was harsh with you, Tillie, but nothing else was getting through to you. You walk around this place with dark clouds behind your eyes and I was getting worried that nothing would bring you back to me. I want my little sister back."

"I'm so sorry." Her tears really begin to pour out and I can't stand not giving her some comfort. "All I see is a black tunnel, and I'm looking for a way out, but I can't escape the darkness."

I rush over to her and hold her so close to my chest that I feel her bones digging into me. But I don't let up. I want to help her like Keanu helped me. I cling to her, taking all her darkness and bearing it as my own. I take her pain and make it my pain. I'll lessen the hurt and shame I know she's feeling and help her through that tunnel into the light once again.

"Don't let what happened to you define the rest of your life, Tillie. He'll be laughing in his grave, thinking he's won. You survived. We survived when so many others didn't. Rise up again, but this time be stronger, be braver. You can get through this. You have people around you who truly care for you and we're not going anywhere." I speak from my heart, meaning every word.

We can help each other. We share something that no one else in this estate can understand.

We'll rise again and we'll do it together.

"You're right. I'm sorry for the way I've been acting around you. I was just angry. Whenever I looked at you, all I could see was him. Then I got here and it was all new to me. Everything I once knew is gone, and I just... I felt like life had moved on without me. You were here with my brother. I guess I felt pushed out. I apologise to you, and also you, Keanu."

"Apology accepted. Now, if you'll excuse me. There's a man named Yates I need to have a chat with." I cringe again, but for a whole other reason Tillie is unaware of.

"Go easy on him. Whatever he's doing, it's working," I shout as he heads for the door.

"Yeah, I'm aware, but I'm not making any promises." I chuckle, highly amused at his over-protectiveness towards his little sister and extremely turned on by him too.

"What was that all about?" Tillie asks.

"You don't want to know. But my advice is don't get involved." I laugh wholeheartedly. I haven't felt this happy or free in a long time.

If this is my new life, then I'm grateful for it, and I'm not about to waste another second drowning in self-pity.

From today onwards, I'm living my life how I want and with who I want, and that's all because of the dangerously handsome man who protects me without even trying.

I might be the light in his darkness, which he keeps reminding me of, but he's my reason for breathing.

CHAPTER 41

KEANU

Since Benson's death, everything seems to have calmed down, more so on the business side of things. Personal stuff is up in the air and I'm trying to give Tillie and Harper some breathing space after what they've endured, but I miss my sister, even if she has changed. I have Yates keeping an eye on Tillie as I don't want her going anywhere on her own. I've seen the way he looks at her, but… he's the only one who seems to get her to open up, and he's slowly bringing some of the old Tillie back.

I'm also in dire need of my fix of Harper. I miss the feel of her wrapped around my dick. I miss feeling her lips on mine and having her breathless and wanting more. I've become addicted to her presence and I want to make it permanent. So, whilst Harper is busy getting to know Tillie, I use the time to set a plan in motion and go out to get what I need.

The item in my pocket is burning a hole, knocking against my leg in a constant reminder of what I'm about to do.

"Where's Harper?" I ask Lincoln.

"She said she was heading to the hut to read as Tillie was tired and went to lie down in her room."

With a stern nod, I turn and head to the new cabin she goes to frequently to relax now that Tillie has given her blessing to use it. It was built for both of them, each having their own sides, and I'm glad it's finally being used.

Every step I take is full of purpose and determination. The next few minutes will either make or break me and change the course of my entire life, but it's a risk I'm willing to take. Where Harper is concerned, I'm willing to risk everything.

I reach the door and silently watch her reading. She's staring at the book with such intensity that I'm worried the book is going to suck her into the pages.

I lean against the framework, placing my hands in my pockets. She must sense my presence because her eyes swing in my direction. She smiles and places the open book down so she doesn't lose where she is.

"Hey, is everything okay?" she asks.

"Why wouldn't it be?" I start playing around with the box in my pocket.

"Because you're as tense as I just was reading that chapter. I was holding my breath." She chuckles.

I laugh softly. "That good, huh?"

"I'm getting to the good bit. Let's just say the alpha is winning." She smiles sweetly at me.

Will this alpha standing in front of her be winning?

"Why so serious? Something has happened, hasn't it? Oh, God. Is it Tillie?"

"And you say I'm tense." I smirk, remove my hands, and sit down on the soft couch next to her.

"You still haven't answered me, Keanu. What's going on?" Worry lines her brow.

"Everything is fine. I promise."

Her hands fly to her chest. "Oh, thank God."

I take her chin in one of my hands, lifting her face. I gently run my finger across her jaw and over her lips.

"Are you happy here, Harper?" I need to know where her head's at before I do this.

"Of course I am. I've never been happier. Even after everything we've been through… I feel like I finally belong somewhere and that's here… with you." She blushes slightly. "That's if you still want me here." Now she's just as nervous as me.

"I want you to be happy, whether that's here with me or not." I'm hoping it's the former.

"It doesn't matter where I am, as long as it's with you."

"Even knowing what I do for a living?" I need to be certain she'll have me in whatever form I am. I'm a mafia boss and run some shady shit. With that comes the price of constant potential danger.

"I know what you do for a living, Keanu. It doesn't scare me. You don't scare me."

I kiss her, slowly and softly, letting the kiss linger while I dig around for the box. When I pull away, she's breathless. Just the way I like it.

"Marry me." I flip the black velvet box open and reveal the princess-cut white gold diamond ring.

The goods from the steel safe at the old estate were recovered when the blazing fire went out. Lincoln went to retrieve them himself. I was going to give her my mother's ring, but I thought of Tillie and knew my mother would want her to have it. It just felt like the right thing to do, and one day, when the time is right, I'll make sure Tillie has it.

Harper gasps, her hands flying over her mouth in shock. "Keanu… oh my… it's gorgeous."

She hasn't answered me and I'm starting to second-guess everything. "Loving me comes at a cost, Harper. I won't sugarcoat it. I live a dangerous life. To some people, I'm the devil, but with you, it's different. I'm much more than that. You only ever see the good in me. I've never allowed myself to feel or love as it was a risk I never wanted to take, but I'll risk everything I have for you. You're the light in my life. I need you to keep me grounded and not let the darkness that surrounds me daily take over me completely. I know I'm not perfect and I'll never claim to be. I can't promise I won't smother you with my over-protectiveness, but what I can promise is that I'd die to protect you and I'll spend every day we're together loving you until my lungs give out. I love you, Harper. Will you do me the honour of becoming my queen?" I hold my breath and hope with everything I am she accepts me and all my faults.

Her eyes fill with tears. "Yes… yes, I'll marry you." Unaware of her reaction and flying high on ecstasy, she catches me off guard when she flings her arms around my neck and jumps on my lap. I wasn't prepared. I fall forward and we end up on the floor.

I bring her body closer to mine. "You've just made this devil very happy." I run my palm up the length of her side, finishing at her chin. I gently rub the side of her face with my thumb.

"But you're my devil. I can't wait to become Mrs. Knox. I love you, Keanu."

"I love you more, baby cakes." I crash my lips down on hers. She opens her mouth, granting me full excess, knowing it'll lead to hot sex.

I'll never stop loving this woman, and if I die tomorrow, I'll die a happy man.

THE END

EPILOGUE

TILLIE

I know I said at the beginning that this was my brother's story.

Keanu may have once thought the only thing he was good at was keeping the Knox name running and keeping the empire strong, but he soon learnt there's more to life than just that. He's found his true calling in loving Harper, and I'm over the moon for him. I know we had our differences, but Harper makes my brother happy and there's nothing more concrete than getting ready to say, 'I do' in front of a hundred people. They've set a date and the wedding preparations are in full swing.

But enough about 'happy ever after', that's not in the cards for me. Not anymore.

I don't know if I'll ever be ready to tell anyone about the horrors I endured while in the hands of my family's greatest rival.

For almost two years, I had to abide by Geoffrey's rules and anyone he put me in front of. If I didn't, I was punished.

I learnt that the hard way.

I'm a fucking Knox. It's in our blood to keep fighting. Just like I knew my brother would have done. I knew he and my father wouldn't stop their search to find me. No matter the cost or what I went through, I had faith I'd one day be rescued and see them both again. I never expected to hear the news about my father's death, though, and finding it out from my captors was the worst torture of all. Benson and his men knew I wasn't just a stranger who found herself in a terrible situation. He knew from the moment he saw me that I was Tillie Knox, and he made me pay tremendously for that. There was no special treatment for me there. I wasn't a princess like they all made me out to be.

A princess…

I never thought of myself as one, but in comparison to how I was treated at the hands of those men, I guess you could say I was.

No matter how many times people tell me to be strong, and that everything's going to be okay, my life is never going to be the same again.

Benson may be dead along with all his men, and he can no longer hurt me, but they don't know the full truth. They don't know that it's only the beginning, nor do they know what I've suffered. What I've lost and may never get back again.

They'll never understand.

Would you?

No matter how hard it is to hear, would you listen, never judge, and hold my hand?

My name is Tillie Knox and my story is a hard one to read, but maybe one day, when I'm strong enough, I might just let you hear it.

If I'm ready to tell my side of the story, would you listen?

About the Author

K J Ellis was born in Staffordshire, Stoke-On-Trent in the UK. She's thirty-one years old and lives with her partner of sixteen years, Adam, their six year old son, Logan and two year old daughter Niamh.
She's a bubbly, out-going person who's always up for a laugh.
She is an avid reader and loves a good MC or Mafia book.
Besides the love for her family, she has an obscenely and pretty unhealthy addiction to Nike trainers—so much so, she has a wardrobe just for shoes. She asks you not to judge her.
(Doesn't help matters that she works in a shoe shop.)
She entered the book world around seven years ago as a reader, then had a hand in swag making and blogging for authors before having the courage to write a book herself.
Seeing the love that the book community has to offer only pushed her more, prompting her to finally release her debut book, Isaak, in the world for you all to read.

Coming Soon

Standalone
No Matter The Weather

CLUB 21
Sapphire's Saviour (Book 2)
Crystal's story (Book 3)

7 Deadly Sins Series
Envy

Other Books By KJ

COUNTERPUNCH SERIES

Isaak ~ Book 1

Mr And Mrs Brookes

Novella ~ Book 1.5

Owen ~ Book 2

Saxon ~ Book 3

Jason ~ Book 4

Stargazing Series (Book 11)

Worth Lying For

Club21

Phoenix's Purpose ~ Book 1

N.L.W Anthology

Oh Santa

A Dandelion Anthology

Love Ever after

A Books On The Beach Charity Anthology

Hope

Social Links

Author group link
https://www.facebook.com/groups/299056614378189/

Amazon link
https://www.amazon.co.uk/K-J-Ellis/e/B08LDR91XY/ref=dp_byline_cont_pop_book_3

Author page link
https://www.facebook.com/KJ-Ellis-Author-104813721422926/

Goodreads page
https://www.goodreads.com/author/show/7989746.K_J_Ellis

Instagram page
https://www.instagram.com/kjellisauthor/

Tiktok
https://www.tiktok.com/@k.j..ellis.author?_t=8h5i1Fdm7iC&_r=1

Bookbub

Printed in Great Britain
by Amazon